A BALANCING KIND OF LOVE

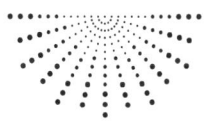

JOANNA CATES

My wonderful husband Dean and children, Tom, Amelia, Imogen and Eleanor – My World.

KIRSTY

The taxi driver slammed on his brakes, and I jolted forward in my seat. We waited for a car with blinking indicators to pull away from the kerbside. When the driver manoeuvred his taxi into the space, I noticed stationary cars crammed full of passengers with suitcases, all eager to jet off on their adventure.

I stepped out of the vehicle and waited for the driver to hand over my luggage. The man groaned and struggled to lift each suitcase from the boot of the car, and he muttered something under his breath about a kitchen sink.

With a smile, I handed over a crumpled £5 note. The old me would have scolded the driver for being such a moaner. After all, he was the one who wouldn't let me help him.

I liked to believe this was an improved version of myself, patient and not hot-headed and quick to jump down somebody's throat. The driver didn't know I'd planned a six-month sabbatical away from work, not a holiday. Hence the amount of luggage. To be fair, my cases *were* bloody heavy, and I struggled to lift them.

Sweaty and breathing heavily, I grabbed hold of a shiny luggage trolley and dumped my cases on top, then made my way into the building.

Sounds of crying babies and the squeaky conveyor belt filled the air with noise. Then a group of beer-drinking lads drowned these out, shouting and wolf-whistling at a group of women. They all wore pink t-shirts and tight-fitting shorts and made their way towards departures.

I laughed when one woman raised her top and flashed her ample bosom at the young men. The bride-to-be slapped her friend on the arm before waving at the back of their departing heads. The conveyor belt sped off into the distance.

Of all my friends, I would have been the one to flash my generous assets at passing strangers, especially when on holiday, but that was the old me. I planned to leave that side of my life behind because I didn't want to be that sort of person anymore.

Kirsty Young, aged forty, and finally ready to grow up.

It didn't take long for me to drop off my suitcases and make my way to customs. My hand luggage passed through the x-ray machine. The two security guards whispered to each other and re-routed my bag to the inspection area.

Dread filled the pit of my stomach whilst the security guard unzipped my bag and trawled through my belongings. He placed each item to one side before unveiling the contents of a silky black pouch.

'Before you say anything, it's a crystal dildo and not a dangerous weapon. Before you look any further, I have another vibrator in my case as well as some love eggs. As far as I'm aware, it's not illegal to pack them in my hand luggage.'

'Don't worry, love, it's not illegal. My wife has quite the collection at home and takes hers on holiday. I'll have to tell her about the crystal thingy, though. We pulled your bag to one side because it contains a bottle of liquid foundation, that's all. Have an enjoyable holiday.'

Flames of embarrassment spread over my cheeks, and I grabbed my bag and made a hasty retreat towards the departure lounge.

My mobile phone pinged, and I fumbled around until my

hand touched the cool metal casing. I'd missed several calls and text messages from Henrietta, my best friend. As soon as I found somewhere to sit, preferably with a large glass of wine in my hand, I'd have to phone her back.

With a groan, I remembered I had to exchange currency. I always left things to the last minute and had forgotten to order some to get delivered in time.

After I made my way over to the Exchange Unit, I coughed loudly to get the attention of a sleepy cashier, too busy scrolling through his phone to notice he had a customer.

The guy glanced up and spluttered. 'Are you interested in taking out one of our currency cards? You'll get a better exchange rate today. It will only take five minutes to fill out the form, and I have to run a few security checks.'

On the verge of saying 'no', I heard a loud tut and sigh from behind. Speechless, I turned around and stared into the piercing brown eyes of an extremely handsome but cross man. He looked familiar, but I couldn't place him.

The cashier blushed. 'I'm sorry, sir. Please accept my apologies for the wait. I promise this won't take long.'

'Well, hurry up. My flight leaves soon, and I need to exchange my money,' the rude stranger said.

I glared at the bloke, then re-directed my gaze to the cashier. 'Don't apologise. You're only doing your job, and he'll have to wait his turn.'

I bit my tongue after the guy gave another loud 'tut' and had to fight the urge to give this oaf a piece of my mind. Half-inclined to take my time with the application, I resisted because I wanted to make sure I gave myself enough time to visit duty-free and the bar before I caught my flight.

The cashier handed me my euros, and I took my time putting them safely away in my purse before I left. With a scowl at the stranger, I whispered under my breath, 'Don't miss your flight.' Then I made my way to the bar, ordered a large glass of white wine, sat at a table tucked in a corner, and checked the messages on my phone.

A new message flashed up on the screen, and I jumped. My boss's wife Isabel had sent it. Over the years, we'd become good friends, and as I worked for a male-dominant company, we often gravitated towards each other at social functions. She confided in me about the state of her marriage. My boss was a male-chauvinistic pig, albeit a generous employer. Several years ago, he made a pass at me but I turned him down and kept my job. A rumour went around the office that he was in a relationship with his secretary, although I didn't want to believe it, as Zoe was such a friendly person. Isabel wanted to leave him but needed the support of her family, so she'd hired my friend Paul, who ran a private detective agency to get proof of the rat's infidelity. My reply to Henri and Isabel would have to wait until I got to Ibiza because it was time to board my flight. I gulped my wine and stood to collect my belongings. A prickling sensation tickled my neck, and I sensed somebody staring at me. A glance towards the bar showed me the rude man from the currency exchange, and he averted his eyes when I returned the stare. Hopefully, he wouldn't be on the same flight as me. The barman topped up the man's glass of wine. Our gazes met again, and this time, I averted my eyes first, but not before he touched his forehead in a mock salute. Where did I know him from?

THE FLIGHT WAS UNEVENTFUL, and I sat next to a delightful couple on their way back to Ibiza, where they lived throughout the summer months. They regaled me with stories about their lives and recommended several clubs and bars to visit. I didn't have the heart to tell them I hadn't packed my clubbing shoes and planned to sit by the pool and recharge my batteries, not go out raving. Instead, I typed their details into my phone and promised to look out for them if I ended up on a night out with friends.

Before long, the plane shook as the wheels connected with the ground, and I took in a deep breath of air. A nervous flyer, I didn't realise until then I'd held my breath and dug my fingernails into my palms, covered in perspiration. I let out a nervous sigh and waited for the plane to come to a standstill.

It didn't take long to go through passport control, and I collected my suitcases from baggage reclaim. When I walked through the arrivals lounge, I caught sight of my friends Emma and Dominic, who stood between a hand-painted banner with my name scrawled all over it. The grand gesture was typical of this gorgeous couple. We'd been friends since school. They'd settled in Ibiza twenty years ago and now ran a successful holiday-let business, and I'd spent many a long weekend visiting them over the years.

Dominic grabbed hold of me in a big bear hug, and my feet lifted off the ground.

Emma slapped Dom on the back. 'Put her down. You'll suffocate her.'

She gave me a big hug and instructed Dom to put the cases in the car.

Emotions overwhelmed me, and I burst into tears. 'I've missed you so much.'

Emma's stricken face stared back at me. 'Whatever's the matter?'

'Oh, don't mind me. I'm tired and emotional and overwhelmed at seeing you both. I'm sure I'll be okay once I've had a good night's sleep.'

Emma gave me another hug. 'Come on. Let's get back to the house, and you can tell me what's wrong. I've never known you to cry, so something's upset you.'

Dom stood waiting for us by the car and took a look at my tear-stained face.

'What's wrong, gorgeous girl? Who's upset you? Give me their number and I'll sort them out.'

Emma shook her head. 'Let's get home and we can have a

glass of wine and a good old catch up. I'm sure Kirsty will talk to us when she feels ready.'

The journey back to the villa took twenty minutes, and before I knew it, we'd parked in front of the electronic gates, which opened slowly.

Their two dogs, Hunter and Buddy, came bounding out to greet us, and Dom ordered them to stop after they jumped up and down around my legs. It was lovely for them to recognise me, as I had known them since they were puppies. Dom rescued them after someone had dumped them behind a waste cart. They were two of the friendliest dogs I'd ever known.

Dom took my cases into the guest room, and Emma poured us a generous glass of crisp white wine.

She nodded towards the back door. 'Let's sit outside, under the stars, as it's quite stuffy indoors.'

'I'm going to take the dogs out for a walk and leave you girls to catch up,' Dom said.

The moonlight reflected off the dark-blue pool water, and insects chirped around us.

I sank into a sumptuous garden chair and let out a deep sigh. Patiently, Emma waited for me to talk.

Fresh tears streamed down my face. 'I shouldn't burden you with my troubles as soon as I've got here,' I said.

Emma handed me a crumpled tissue from her jacket pocket. 'Listen, I'm always here for you, and you need to tell me what's wrong. This isn't like you, and I'm worried.'

I sniffed and blew my nose. 'Where do I start? I'm not happy with my life, and it feels so empty. I hate the person I've turned into and if I don't sort myself out, I'll explode.'

'What's different? What changed?' Emma asked.

I shrugged. 'You know me, the life and soul of the party. I don't want to be that anymore. I want to meet somebody and fall in love. Perhaps even have a baby... oh, I shouldn't have said that.'

Emma smiled and patted my hand. 'Don't be silly. Babies

aren't a taboo subject for us. Dom and I accepted a long time ago that we'll never be parents. You know what I went through every time I miscarried, so we stopped trying. Anyway, I've got three babies to look after with Dom and the dogs.' Emma giggled.

'I've left it too late to even think about having a child, but it doesn't help that I've never wanted a serious relationship. You know me, I love sex but have always had a bit of a phobia about commitment. My life feels so shallow now, and I'm at a loss about what to do.'

'Well, you're in the right place to sort yourself out, and we'll do everything we can to help. How long have you felt like this?'

My eyes closed, and I sighed. 'I've felt out of sorts since I turned forty. And though I've been in a casual relationship with the same bloke for a few months, we're using each other as a convenience. The sex is great, but that's all. It's not going anywhere, so I've called it a day. It upset him at first, but then he agreed he couldn't see us ever having a proper relationship. Do you think I've waited too long to have a baby?'

Emma chewed on her bottom lip and glanced at her hands. 'Not at all. You'd make a fantastic mum. I'd assumed your career was your baby. Look, my advice is, if you meet the right person then things could happen naturally, but don't go looking for love … it will find you.'

I held my head in my hands. 'I've heard that so many times. Why haven't I ever met anybody who wants to commit to a proper relationship? I get plenty of male attention, but am I not marriage material?'

'Of course you are. I've known you for a long time, and you've always been so hard on yourself. I know the image you portray isn't the real you. Yes, you're confident and there's no denying you're bloody gorgeous. And you're kind and funny and caring, but along the way, I think you stopped loving yourself and settled for what's on offer in a *relationship*. This sabbatical will give you a chance to examine your life and learn how to love yourself again.'

After a thunderous splash, cold water cascaded over us. We

shrieked and laughed. Dom resurfaced and swam over to the poolside with a grin.

'Why don't you two come on in? The water's lovely and cool, and it's great to swim under the stars.'

When Dom spun around and swam off, his firm white buttocks bobbed up and down in the water.

'I haven't unpacked my bikini,' I said.

Dom rested his arms on the ledge of the pool. 'Don't worry. Swim in your birthday suit. I won't look.' He winked.

Emma chuckled. 'Yeah, right, you'll peep through your fingers at the first chance you get. We'll give it a miss. Kirsty feels exhausted, so we'll have another glass of wine before bed.'

I said, 'Perhaps tomorrow. I'll be in a better mood by then.'

ALL NIGHT, I tossed and turned, struggling to get comfortable and acclimate to the heat. Usually, it took me a couple of nights to get used to a strange bed. I woke early, feeling bedraggled, and made my way to the kitchen. The excited dogs greeted me and ran to the back door, where they waited for me to let them outside.

The powerful aroma of coffee engulfed my senses, and I poured myself a cup and took it out to the patio.

I jumped after Emma called out, 'Good morning, lovely lady. How did you sleep?'

'Oh, blimey. I didn't see you there. What are you up to?'

Emma stubbed her cigarette into an ashtray and took a sip of her coffee. 'Yoga and meditation. Most mornings, I get up at sunrise and meditate. It puts me in the right frame of mind for the day. You're welcome to join me. I didn't mention it last night because I thought you'd benefit from a lie-in.'

'Perhaps tomorrow. I'll go for a swim now. The pool looks amazing.'

I finished my coffee, shrugged off my dressing gown, and made my way over to the infinity pool. The spectacular views overlooked the town and ocean. Behind the wired fence, plump, juicy lemons dangled from branches, ripe and ready to be plucked and turned into mouth-watering limoncello. Dom started this as a hobby, and it had grown into a reputable business.

Emma walked towards the house and shouted over her shoulder, 'Watch out. It might be a tad cold. The heating hasn't been working for a couple of days. The pool man's coming out tomorrow to fix it.'

I plunged into the cold water and let out a gasp whilst my body got used to the temperature. She wasn't joking. Determination washed over me, and the tension left my body with each stroke I took. I needed to pull myself together and sort out my life with some important decisions to make, which I knew would not be a quick fix.

2

MAX

The airport seemed quiet for the time of day, and I felt grateful I didn't have to avoid getting tripped up by excited kids and their Trunki suitcases. But I was still in a rush and a foul mood. My secretary had forgotten to order me euros, and then I got held up at the Exchange Unit whilst the woman in front signed up for a deal that would give her a minute discount from a rubbish exchange rate. I tutted, and she turned around and glared at me. If looks could kill …

Momentarily, her beauty stunned me, and she looked familiar. Finished with her transaction, she sauntered past me, and the smell of her perfume invaded my senses. 'Don't miss your flight,' she whispered.

I stuffed the euros into my wallet and walked towards the bar. Normally, I'd wait for my flight in the VIP lounge but had seen the woman make her way over to the bar, and I felt curious to find out where I knew her from.

I ordered a glass of wine and studied the food menu. Much to my frustration, I spent too much time in airports. My family owned a chain of hotels throughout Europe called *Brightside Hotels*, named after my late father, Gregory Bright. After he passed away two years ago, I took over the role of CEO. Now I spent my time travelling from one hotel to the next. We'd built up and maintained a five-star reputation, but it was hard work and I never seemed to get any time to myself, and as for relationships … I don't know how my mother coped over the years. She raised my brother and me single-handed whilst my father jetted off to work. Father worshipped the ground she walked on, and it broke my mother's heart when the love of her life died of a heart attack at only 65 years of age.

I didn't want to go down the same path as my father and tried to maintain a healthy lifestyle by taking advantage of the hotel gyms. Airport food wasn't the best choice, but at least I didn't have to cook for myself.

I would love to have met somebody who adored me the way my parents did one another, but I didn't have time to date. No saint, I've had the odd one-night stand with women I met through work, although never a member of staff.

Time had flown by so quickly, and now in my forties, frustration bubbled at the surface, unhappy with how I lived my life. I wanted to find a balance that allowed me to meet somebody and settle down. I wanted to fall in love.

THERE SHE WAS, that woman. I sat quietly and sipped my drink whilst I studied her beauty; until she caught me staring at her. Then I recalled where I'd seen her before.

The previous year, we spent Christmas in Kent at our hotel in South Talling, rather than the usual family tradition of Cyprus. My brother Anthony got quite miffed, as it meant we had to drag him away from his playboy lifestyle and spend time in a cold and blustery country. The hotel was busy, booked up with work functions, and I recollected the woman had her arms draped around a man who looked ten years her junior. I don't know why, but I felt a pang of jealousy as I took in the sight of this stunning woman being entertained by a young Adonis with a smug look on his face. She wore a silver sequined dress that flattered her curves, and she had a cracking pair of legs. It wasn't her fault, but I resented how she made me feel. Why would she notice a tired, miserable man in his forties when she had a much younger man in tow? However, I cheered up when she rebuffed the advances of my brother. It put his nose out of joint when he offered to buy her a drink and she turned him down.

Today, she wore jeans and a jacket, and her face glowed with her natural beauty. She looked stunning and had an air of elegance about her I found extremely attractive. She shifted her gaze to the monitors above her head and stood. My boarding gate was still to be announced, which told me she wouldn't be on my flight to Cyprus. I watched her depart and sighed wistfully. If only I could have met someone like her.

The server topped up my wine glass, and I picked up my phone to study a text message from my mother. My brother's behaviour in Cyprus concerned her, and she wanted me to come out and talk to him. We'd both inherited generous sums of money when my father died, and Anthony took this as an opportunity to walk away from his managerial role at our hotel in Ibiza. At this rate, he would squander all his money, and my mother worried she would have to bail him out. Even though she wouldn't hesitate to do so because he was her favourite and could do no wrong in her eyes. Until now.

My mother longed for a grandchild and presumed Anthony would meet somebody and start a family, even though I was two years older than him, and she never questioned my single status. After all, who would run the family business if I got distracted by a wife and family?

I glanced up at the monitor; time for me to catch my flight and sort out the mess my brother was making of his life.

3

KIRSTY

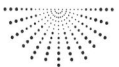

The sun beat down on my pale skin as I wriggled my toes and stretched my arms above my head. The tension would not leave my body, even though I'd relaxed by the pool for the past two hours whilst Dom and Emma worked in the office—a quaint outbuilding, adorned in vivid purple bougainvillaea, and tucked around the back of their garden. It felt as though I had the place to myself, and the only sound came from the growl of my stomach.

Whilst I walked into the kitchen to explore the contents of the fridge, my phone pinged with a text from Isabel. She wanted me to call her as soon as possible. Normally, she wouldn't disturb me on holiday, so I abandoned the idea of lunch, poured myself a cold beer, and dialled her number.

She answered on the first ring. 'Hi, how are you? I'm so sorry to disturb your holiday, but I need a friend to talk to, and you're the only person who understands what I'm going through. My pig of a husband came home last night reeking of perfume and had the audacity to tell me I'm imagining things when I confronted him. He called me delusional, jealous, and paranoid.' She took a breath. 'I wish I could pack my bags and leave.'

I walked outside and sat in the shade. 'What're the latest

developments with Paul? Has he found any evidence of Richard's infidelities?' I asked.

'He's been gathering evidence but doesn't want to raise my hopes until he has concrete proof, but it's any day now.'

'Look, if you need to escape for a while, why don't you ask your mum to have the kids for a few days and come out to Ibiza? Emma and Dom would love to meet you, and they have plenty of spare rooms.'

I pulled the phone away from my ear when Isabel screamed.

'Really? They wouldn't mind? That sounds fantastic. Mum's always offering to take the kids overnight, and they have an inset day at school on Monday. Do you think it's too short a notice for me to come out this Sunday?'

Isabel's enthusiasm was infectious, and we cut the call short so she could talk to her mum and book a flight.

As I approached the office, I heard Dom's raised voice but couldn't make out the Spanish conversation. He slammed the phone, then threw a screwed-up piece of paper into the waste bin and hammered his fists onto the desk before he noticed me.

'Sorry about that. I just heard that some drug-crazed party people have trashed our villa over the other side of the island. The police have arrested them, and now we're in danger of losing our letting licence for allowing drugs to be used on our premises. Not that we had a clue. We rented the house out to a group of young ladies on a girl's holiday. The site manager assured me they'd been on their best behaviour and couldn't understand why things escalated so badly. Emma and I need to drive over there and sort things out,' Dom said.

Emma sighed. 'The girl's parents are happy for us to leave them stewing in a police cell overnight to teach them a lesson, but I want to get them out of there as soon as possible. We both know how frightening it is to be locked up in a Spanish jail, don't we?'

I rolled my eyes. 'It taught me a lesson. I never smoked a joint in public again nor flashed my boobs off to a police officer.'

'It didn't help things when I flashed my knickers at them, too.'

Emma giggled. 'Will you look after the dogs for a couple of nights whilst Dom and I sort things out?'

'Of course. Actually, I came to ask you if my friend Isabel could come and stay for a couple of nights from Sunday. She wants to leave her husband and has hired Paul's Detective Agency to catch him in the act, as he's a cheating son of a bleep. I said you wouldn't mind if she stays here for a couple of nights so she can recharge her batteries. Paul's found a strong lead, and the shit is about to hit the fan.'

Emma said, 'We don't mind at all. You're doing us a big favour by looking after the house, and it will be good to meet her. Oh, I nearly forgot, can you make sure the pool man fixes the heating today?'

Dom walked towards the door and turned around. 'Keep your hands to yourself and don't get any ideas. Lucas is good at his job, and I wouldn't want you to scare him off because you're such a flirt.'

Playfully, I punched him on the arm. 'Don't be so cheeky. Haven't you listened to me? I'm a changed woman and have put all that behaviour behind me.'

Emma winked. 'When you see him, you may change your mind.'

THE DOGS WHIMPERED and twitched in their sleep, curled up next to each other in a basket hidden under the shade of a tree, protected from the midday sun.

I still couldn't relax and get comfortable. This heat was too much, so I unclasped my bikini top and was just about to take off my briefs when the gate hinges creaked.

The pool man ... his face broke out into a big, toothy grin and he stopped and stared at my naked bosom. My sarong lay draped over the back of the sun lounger on the other side of the pool, so I had no choice but to cover my modesty with my arms and walk in a dignified fashion to recover it.

What was Emma thinking? Why would I try to flirt with this little old man who must be at least seventy years old? I know I can be a bit of a floozy, but really.

'Buenos días, señora. I fix the pool,' he said.

'Gracias. Would you like a drink?' I said. The gate swung open again and stalled his reply.

Oh, my goodness—now it was my turn to grin, lost for words —*this must be the pool man.*

My cheeks flushed when we made eye contact. 'Good day, madam. My name is Lucas, and I am here to fix the pool heating. This is my grandpapa, Pablo.'

With my mouth agape, I pointed towards the pool. 'There it is.'

What an idiot. He knew where the pool was, but I couldn't concentrate when my body was on fire with butterflies doing a flamingo dance in my belly.

I picked up a magazine from the table and fanned myself. 'Can I get you both a drink? It's extremely hot,' I said.

Lucas looked up, then down, and then our gazes met again. 'Thank you, madam. We would love a glass of ice-cold water.'

'Please call me Kirsty.' I giggled and retrieved my bikini top from the back of the chair. Then I made my way into the kitchen. It all made sense, now, why Dom told me to leave the pool man alone. I hadn't even been without sex for a week, as my former lover and I had a rather energetic farewell. But, boy, one glance at the pool man, and I felt horny as anything.

I glanced in the mirror, horrified to see a bright-red sweaty face staring back at me. *I can't go back outside looking like this.* Embarrassed, I dashed to my bedroom, spritzed my face with cooling rose water, and applied a liberal layer of lip gloss. All done, I fetched the drinks.

The ice clinked in the glasses as I sashayed my way over to Lucas and grandpapa.

'Here you are. This should cool you down. You must be boiling in this heat?' I said.

'We get used to it, but I'll take my grandpapa home soon. I need to buy a new pump for the pool and will come back this afternoon. Will this be okay with you?'

'A-absolutely,' I said. 'I've got nothing else on.'

Lucas grinned. 'Sounds good. I'll come back as soon as possible.'

My insides melted when he held my gaze for a few seconds.

'Control yourself and stop flirting with the pool-man,' I muttered to his retreating back.

As soon as the gate slammed shut, I ran to my bedroom and stripped off for a shower. Freezing water cascaded over my body, and I stood still for a few minutes before I covered my body in cool, soapy suds. Lucas was gorgeous, and the physical attraction between us undeniable. But how could I ever change if I planned to flirt with him the minute he came back? Fingers crossed that grandpapa Pablo would chaperone the next visit.

No such luck. Each time a car door slammed, I reapplied my lip gloss, held my breath, and draped my body over the sun lounger. Around 3 pm, the gate swung open, and I peered over the top of my sunglasses. Lucas stood there, dressed in a crisp white t-shirt and denim cut-off shorts that clung to his bronzed and muscular thighs. White teeth glinted in the sunshine when he greeted me.

'No grandpapa Pablo?' I asked.

'No, he gets exhausted in this heat so has stayed home for a siesta. I don't always take him to work with me, but he enjoys it.'

'Does he live with you?'

Lucas's eyes glazed over. 'Yes, I lived with him for several years when I was fifteen. Now it is my turn to look after grandpapa as my nana passed away last year.'

'Ah, that's sad. How long were they married?'

'Fifty years. They were childhood sweethearts and ran away from home when they were fifteen to get married.'

It always amazed me when I heard of marriages that had lasted so long. Would I ever meet somebody I could grow old with?

'I'd better let you get on. Would you like a drink?' I asked.

'I'd love a glass of cold water, please. I'm so hot.'

I licked my lips. 'Indeed, you are,' I said.

Lucas averted his eyes, and a blush spread over his cheeks.

I MUST HAVE READ the same line in my Kindle three times before I gave up. Whenever Lucas came out of the pool room, my breath hitched, and warmth spread throughout my lower regions.

After a while, a loud throbbing noise filled the air. The pool motor had kicked in.

Lucas shouted, 'I've fixed the pump, so I'll clean the pool and go on my way.'

My mouth gaped when he pulled his t-shirt over his head and revealed a muscular torso with a six-pack. Oh my.

ALL TOO SOON, the sunshine bounced off sparkling water, and Lucas tidied away the equipment.

My heart beat faster when Lucas approached.

'That sure was thirsty work. I don't suppose you have a bottle of beer in the fridge? Dom usually keeps the fridge well-stocked, and we always sit down and put the world to rights when I finish. Will he be back soon?'

'No, they had a problem with a villa and went to sort it out. I'm house-sitting because they won't be back for a couple of nights. Sit down, and I'll grab us both a beer if you don't mind my company.'

'It will be my pleasure. I can't wait to get to know you better.'

It was no good … the sexual attraction between us grew

intense, and my head felt dizzy whilst I grabbed two bottles of ice-cold beer.

When I bent to reach the lower shelves of the fridge, I glanced over my shoulder. It was clear how much of an effect I had over Lucas.

In one swift action, he took hold of the beer bottles and knocked off the caps. I sat there mesmerised whilst he glugged down the contents of one bottle.

He wiped his mouth with the back of his hand. 'I needed that,' he said. 'Now tell me more about yourself. Are you married?'

'No, single. What about you?'

He shook his head. 'I was engaged to be married, but she left me when my grandpapa came to live with me. I have been on my own ever since.'

'It sounds like you're better off without her. It's her loss.'

'I can't believe you are single. You are stunning,' Lucas said.

I fluttered my eyelashes and held his gaze. 'You flatter me, but I bet you say this to all the women you meet.' I sighed. 'Would you like another beer?'

'I wish I could stay for longer, but I need to get back to cook grandpapa's dinner. Perhaps I can come back later?'

I was just about to take Lucas up on his offer when reality hit me like a bucket of ice-cold water.

'Sorry, I have plans for tonight.' I sighed again.

He bid his farewells, and I could have ripped Lucas's clothes off there and then when I saw the disappointment reflected in his big, soulful eyes.

How will I ever change if I caved in to temptation?

4

MAX

*W*hen I made my way through reception, I caught sight of my mother and brother seated around the patio bar, deep in conversation with hotel guests. Music and laughter filled the air whilst the smell of tobacco smoke overpowered the fragrant blooms on display.

Too tired to inform my mother of my arrival, I greeted the night-time receptionist with a polite nod and headed to the presidential suite. It was time to order room service after a long, hot shower.

Around midnight, raucous laughter startled me from my slumber and papers that rested on my lap fluttered to the floor. I should have gone straight to bed and not attempted to read the hotel's financial reports.

For the rest of the night, I tossed and turned, and images of the woman from the airport filled my dreams, so in the morning, I felt exhausted.

❦

'GOOD MORNING, Mother. It's so nice to see you up and about this early. You looked like you were having fun last night.'

Mother raised an eyebrow and frowned. 'Last night? When did you arrive? Why didn't you come over and say hello?'

I shrugged. 'I felt tired and had some paperwork to read, so I went straight to my room. Anyway, I'm here. Would you like to join me for breakfast?'

'That would be lovely. We have a lot to catch up on. Shall I phone Anthony to see if he wants to join us?'

That's all I needed; an early morning confrontation with my brother.

'Don't disturb him. I'm sure I'll meet up with him at some point today. Anyway, I want to spend time with you and hear all about your antics.'

We made our way to the restaurant. Staff scurried about and greeted me with a curt nod, and my mother with a warm, friendly smile, as sleepy guests made their way to breakfast.

Although never my intention, I intimidated my staff.

Within moments of taking a seat, coffee and water appeared on the table. I made a mental note to compliment the staff on its efficient and professional service at the employee meeting planned later that day. Perhaps this would help them realise I wasn't such a tyrant?

Mother stirred two spoons of sugar into her coffee and smiled. I looked at my watch and glanced towards the door.

'Whilst we're on our own, I'll get straight to the point. Yesterday, I had a meeting with the accountants, who confirmed your fears. Anthony will run out of funds if he carries on with the way he fritters his money away. He's built up a significant overdraft on his director's loan account because he still has full control over the company credit card. We need to address this, so I'll arrange a meeting for the three of us but wanted to forewarn you.'

Mother shook her head. 'I'm sure this is a misunderstanding and exaggeration on the accountant's behalf. Anthony is a young man, who grieves the loss of his father, and we should allow him to live his life as he chooses.'

At her words, I bit my lip. Mother seemed to forget that I'd lost my father, too. I had no choice but to take over control of the business and push all my emotions to one side. My father and I had been best friends, and I missed him so much. With a deep breath, I said, 'On another note, you sent me a text because you worry about Anthony's behaviour. It has also been reported back to me that his drunken antics and the way he conducts himself around our female guests is unacceptable.

'He behaved quite rudely to one of our guests when she turned down his advances. Unfortunately, the young lady is friends with the daughter of one of our family friends, and they told me all about it. We both know Anthony needs telling such behaviour is unacceptable, and as he won't listen to me, I'd like you to talk to him.'

A look of horror washed over Mother's face, and I got ready to relent and say I'd talk to him but then persevered. 'He won't want to upset you, and you can explain his antics will ruin the family's reputation if he carries on. We should give him a managerial position at one of our other hotels. He's forty-two years old and needs to stop with his playboy lifestyle and share the family responsibility. After all, he lives off the profits.'

Mother took a compact mirror out of her handbag and studied her reflection. With a sigh, she snapped it shut. 'I don't feel comfortable enough to broach the subject with Anthony, but perhaps I might remind him it's about time he settles down and finds a wife. I would love one of my children to make me a grandmother, and you're too busy to settle down.'

This comment was so unfair, and I bit my tongue yet again. Little did my mother realise I longed to meet somebody I could marry and have children with. Anyway, my mother may already have a grandchild that we didn't know about, as Anthony was such a rake. I shook off the remark.

'Enough said. Let's not talk about Anthony anymore. What have you been up to since I last saw you?'

'I keep myself busy. Once a week, I meet up with a group of expats and we organise meals at different restaurants. Sometimes we plan to go for walks, which never happens, as it's too hot or they're hungover. Most of them are lovely, but there are a few who irritate me. There are a couple of outrageous flirts who try to get me to go out on a date, but they don't understand I'm a widow, not a single lady. I miss your father and cannot see myself with another man.'

I reached across the table and patted her hand. 'It's been two years, Mother. Father passed away at such a young age, and I know he would be the first one to encourage you to meet someone else. You're elegant, attractive, and kind, and only sixty-eight. I don't think you should be on your own for the rest of your life. You have my blessing if you choose to find yourself a new partner.

Mother shuddered. 'I'm too old for all that nonsense now. It would horrify your brother at the thought of another man taking your father's place. Anyway, I'm not on my own. I have the support of friends and plan to take up aqua aerobics here at the hotel. It looks straightforward, and I need to exercise. That will keep me busy.'

My brother would only worry that his inheritance may fall into the hands of another man, I mused.

'You must be careful with such energetic exercise with your hip, and from what I've seen of the aqua classes, there's a lot of jumping about. The doctor mentioned you may end up with a hip replacement if you don't look after yourself.'

'Oh, poppycock, you do fuss. I've read that aqua aerobics is suitable for a woman of my age. Is it too early for a margarita?'

I glanced at the hands on the *Breitling* watch I inherited from my father. It was just before 11 o'clock.

'Sorry to leave you, Mother, but I have a meeting with the wine rep now, so I'll see you at three. Hopefully, Anthony will remember to turn up.'

She blew me a kiss. 'Don't worry. I'll remind him. We've made lunch arrangements. See you later.'

As I walked away, I made eye contact with a gentleman who

sat at an adjacent table. He looked up from his newspaper and grinned. 'Good morning to you, Mr Bright. I hope your mother is well?'

Mr Williams was one of our regulars. His wife died eighteen months ago, and the last time I saw him, he was full of grief and looked frail. Today, he seemed different, a picture of health and perhaps even younger.

'Good morning to you, sir. Thank you, my mother is well. Why don't you go over and say hello? She's sitting behind the pillar, and I'm sure she'll welcome the company.'

With a mischievous grin, I headed to reception. *Too old for all that nonsense* ... not if I had anything to do with it.

Elena, the wine rep, stood to greet me and we gave each other a hug. Several years ago, I had a brief fling with her, but it didn't lead anywhere, although she wanted it to. Even though we got on so well, and the chemistry was amazing, I wasn't ready to commit to a relationship. But, on a positive note, I introduced her to her husband Roberto, who owns several wineries and vineyards throughout Europe and supplies our hotels with fine wines. I'd known him for several years, and we'd become good friends. As soon as he met Elena, his bachelor days were over and it didn't take long for the two of them to fall in love and marry. I acted as their best man.

'How are things with Roberto and the children?' I asked.

'The kids are growing up fast and keep me on my toes. I come to work for a break. As for Roberto ...'

'What's he done now?'

'Gone and bought himself a new toy. A helicopter.'

My eyes widened. 'Oh, wow, lucky man.'

Elena frowned. 'Yes, I suppose so, but he's always making up excuses to go off and fly in the damn thing. Although, he wouldn't bring me here today in it. He said he would catch up with you in a few weeks and take you out for the day.'

I beamed. 'That sounds fantastic. You know what us boys are

like with our toys. I feel a little envious. Tell him, we'll put a date in the diary because I'll be back in Cyprus in a few weeks.'

'That sounds like a plan. Are you ready to sample our new wines, or would you like to go for a coffee, and I could leave you with a few bottles?'

'I need to keep a clear head for a meeting with my brother later, so coffee would be the sensible choice. You always get me drunk and try to seduce me into buying more wine.'

Playfully, Elena slapped me on the hand and laughed. 'Don't let Roberto hear you say that. You know how jealous he gets. I'm just relieved he seems to have forgotten we had a fling all those years ago.'

'Oh, he remembers, all right, and warns me to behave myself around you at every opportunity.' I let out a deep sigh and paused for thought.

'What's wrong, honey?' Elena asked.

'Don't mind me. I wish I had what you and Roberto have. Though I'm ready to settle down, the family business takes up most of my time and I won't ever get the chance. It's a shame we haven't just met because I've reached that stage of my life where I want to commit to a relationship. I'm to blame for that.'

Before I knew it, tight arms wrapped themselves around my body, and I closed my eyes and inhaled sensuous perfume.

'Don't be so hard on yourself. We were never right for each other, although the sex was amazing. You're one of my best friends and I love you. We both do. You're like a brother to Roberto. Now you need to find time for yourself and deserve to find love. Would you like me to fix you up on a date with one of my girlfriends?'

My lips brushed the top of her head. 'If only it were so easy. Sod it. The meeting can wait until tomorrow. Let's forget about coffee and sample your wine instead. That's if you're free? Roberto will have to pick you up in his new toy, and I can get one of my staff to drive your car home.'

'That sounds wonderful. I'm more than happy to bunk off for

the afternoon, but don't get me drunk and have your wicked way with me. Although if Roberto won't pick me up, you can book me a room here.' Elena giggled and brushed her fingers across my chest.

I took hold of her hand and kissed it. 'I promise to be a gentleman and stay on my best behaviour, and I shall even treat you to dinner.'

The tension left my body as we made our way to the bar. I couldn't remember the last time I felt this relaxed. Things had to change in my life.

5

KIRSTY

*S*unlight peeked through the shutters, and Buddy and Hunter scraped at my bedroom door, eager to be let outside to chase the birds. I groaned and let out a yawn. Every time I lifted my head off the pillow it throbbed. I shouldn't have drunk so much wine last night, and it didn't put out the flames of desire Lucas had ignited in me.

All night, I tossed and turned through vivid dreams of Lucas. I woke with an urge to satisfy myself and reached into my bedside cabinet for my crystal wand, which I slipped from its velvet padded sheath. The dogs would have to wait.

I brushed the cold tip of the rose quartz across my thighs and over my stomach before I rested it against my bud and gasped when my body reacted to the touch. Aroused, I rubbed the wand up and down my clit and the sensations intensified, then I plunged the cold shaft deep inside me, again and again. On the brink of an orgasm, it wasn't enough, so with my other hand, I reached down and pressed against my sensitive area. I thrust the wand faster and faster inside me and stopped when the energy from the crystal connected with mine. The heat from the crystal collided with a powerful and intense orgasm, and I continued to move my fingers around my bud. Euphoria and contentment swamped my emotions, and I let out a cry. Satiated, I slipped the wand out of my pool of moisture and let out a contented sigh, all thoughts of Lucas pushed to the back of my mind.

Once I'd calmed, I jumped out of bed and went to the kitchen to let out the two excited bundles of fur. In their excitement, they'd kicked over the water bowl. When I bent to mop up the puddle, I swayed after a wave of dizziness overcame me.

When was the last time I ate a decent meal? Before my friends left, Emma had made sure the fridge was stocked, so I studied the contents. At the sight of ripe, succulent tomatoes and fresh avocados, my stomach growled. Decision made—scrambled eggs for breakfast.

I must take the pool cover off and water the potted plants after I've eaten, I thought after I saw the note clipped to the fridge.

The dogs joined me outside and sat around my feet whilst they waited for me to feed them scraps of food.

'Not today, boys. I could eat a horse, and you've just polished off your breakfast. Lay in your baskets.'

When they skulked off with their tails between their legs, I chuckled.

Two cups of strong coffee satisfied my thirst, and my thumping head subsided. The morning sun bounced off the pool cover, so I padded over and unwound the tarp.

I shrieked, *'What's happened to the pool?'* The water had gone green, which couldn't be good. *I suppose I'd better phone Lucas and see what he says.* The dogs ignored me.

That morning, I'd planned to swim several lengths, but that wasn't an option now unless I wanted to end up looking like a swamp monster.

I dialled Lucas's number, which I found pinned to the corkboard in the kitchen, and he answered on the first ring.

'Morning, Lucas. I need your help. The pool water has gone green.'

He teased, 'Green? Are you sure you're not making up an excuse to see me again?'

'No, and my friend is coming to stay tomorrow, and she won't want to swim in a swamp.' I giggled.

'Don't worry. I'll come over this morning to sort you out.'

What about the pool? I grinned. 'See you soon. I'll be ready for you.'

As soon as the call ended, I ran to my bathroom and turned on the shower and jumped beneath the spray before the water had warmed. A few moments later, I tugged the labels off my new leopard-print bikini and dressed. The fabric just about covered my ample bosom, and the briefs left nothing to the imagination. *Oh, well, a girl has to look her best for a gorgeous man, even though I won't have sex with him.*

The gate swung open, and I rearranged my position on the sun lounger to appear relaxed, but with my best assets on display. Disappointment sank to the pit of my stomach when a toothless grin greeted me.

'Good morning, Pablo. How are you today?' I shouted.

Pablo nodded and touched the tip of his baseball cap. 'Good morning, good morning. How are you?' he said.

Moments later, Lucas walked through the gate and waved. For a second, his eyes fixated on my cleavage, and when he glanced upwards, our eyes locked.

'Good morning, Kirsty. You look beautiful today. Don't worry about the water. It's just a chemical imbalance because of the temperature change after I fitted the new pump. I'll add something to balance things out and will come back after lunch to check it's all right. We're on our way to another job, and I'll come back once I drop grandpapa home. Will you be here?'

'Yes. Would you like to join me for lunch if you have time? It sounds as if you'll be too busy to eat.'

The dogs made for good company, but I could do with adult conversation, and Isabel's flight wouldn't arrive until tomorrow night.

'That would be lovely, thank you. And I shall bring a bottle of wine.'

'I look forward to it. See you later,' I said.

What have I done? I'm not the greatest of chefs and have just invited temptation to lunch. I'd better put on a chastity belt if I want to stick to my resolutions. Or, perhaps, one last fling before I find Mr Right won't hurt? Will it?

❧

RAYS BEAMED down from a cloudless sky, and beads of perspiration formed on my sun-kissed body. I longed to jump into the depths of the cool water, now a vivid blue mirror-image of the sky.

The prepared salad and bottles of rosé wine chilled in the fridge. The steaks thawed under a net, ready to get cooked on the barbeque when Lucas arrived.

As the sun hung at its highest point, somebody tapped on the gate, and Lucas strolled in. He wore a crisp white shirt and tight denim shorts, which complemented his muscular thighs. When he walked closer, the smell of his aftershave enveloped my senses, and butterflies danced in my belly after he leant towards me, and his soft lips brushed against my face.

'These are for you.' He handed me a bunch of bright, colourful flowers.

'Thank you.' I blushed. 'Let me put them in a vase of water, and I'll pour us wine. Are you okay with rosé?'

Lucas took the bottle out of my hand. 'Sounds good, but I'll pour the wine whilst you put the flowers in water. I know where Emma keeps the glasses.'

He strolled over to the outdoor fridge and bent over to put another bottle of wine in the cool interior. Hypnotised with the vision of his pert ass, I licked my lips and groaned.

Get a grip, girl. He's only just got here.

'I hope you like steak and salad?' I shouted from the kitchen window.

'Let me help. Shall I heat the coals on the barbeque?' Lucas said.

'Oh, I didn't realise it had to be heated. I assumed it would be gas. I must confess, I'm a rubbish chef, so perhaps you'd better cook the steak. Although, I've prepared a salad, which is a speciality of mine.'

Lucas laughed. 'I'll cook the meat, and you can top up the drinks. I took the afternoon off work and rode a taxi here, so I'm at your disposal for the rest of the day.'

I gulped. With any luck, the steak and salad weren't the only things on the menu.

The meat sizzled when the juices bounced onto the flames, and I sighed in contentment and sipped my wine whilst Lucas took control of the barbeque.

'Phew, this is hot work. I'd better take my shirt off before I make it wet,' he said.

A bit like my lady garden … control yourself, Kirsty.

'Let's eat in the shade. It's scorching out here,' Lucas said.

'I can't wait to jump in the pool to cool down if it's safe?' I said.

Lucas sipped his wine then gazed into my eyes. A slow smile spread across his face, and he cast his eyes towards the floor. 'I have a confession. I didn't need to come back to check the chemicals because I knew the treatment would work in a couple of hours. I just wanted an excuse to see you again.'

A blush spread over my face, and I ran my fingers through my hair and stuck out my chest. 'I'm flattered you should be interested in someone like me. I must be at least ten years older than you?'

He stroked my arm with firm fingers. 'Age is just a number. From the moment I saw you, I wanted to find out more about you, and we can't deny the attraction.'

'No, but I'm working through some issues, and I don't think one-night stands are what I need.' I stuck out my bottom lip.

He raised his hand to my face and brushed the hair from my

forehead. 'I'm not asking for that—I enjoy your company—that's enough for me.'

Disbelief washed over me. 'Is it really? We'll see. Let's eat something before I get drunk and allow you to have your wicked way with me.' I giggled.

Lucas laughed. 'That's my plan.'

He cooked the steak to perfection, and my salad just about survived the heat. After lunch and several more glasses of wine, we sat on the sun loungers. Lucas stood and unbuttoned his shorts.

I gasped when the denim hit the ground and he stood in front of me with his hands on his hips.

The tight Lycra swimming trunks clung to his skin. His bulge met my eye level when he grabbed my hand to pull me to my feet.

'Come on … let's go for a swim to cool down. I may spend every day fixing pools, but I rarely get the chance to swim in one,' he said.

I let out a shriek when cold water splashed over my stomach and Lucas's head resurfaced.

'Come on in. It's so good,' Lucas shouted.

'Make room. Here I come.' I dove into the pool.

Whilst I swam to the surface, water filled my nostrils, and I coughed and spluttered and tears streamed down my face.

Why is it women on TV always manage to look sexy when they come to the surface?

Lucas swam over and slapped me on the back. 'Cough it up. You must swim in the water, not drink it.' He laughed. 'Although, I could give you the kiss of life if that helps?'

'I'm okay. Come on. I'll race you, and the winner decides the prize at the end.'

I wasn't a strong swimmer—there was no way I would win—but I wanted Lucas to come up with the prize, and I could hazard a guess at what it would be.

'On your marks, get set, go.'

Lucas's determination to win was clear, as his strong and agile body cut through the water like a torpedo.

I made it halfway across the pool and laughed as Lucas waved his arms about in victory.

'I get to decide the prize,' he cheered.

My prediction proved correct when he swam back towards me. 'A kiss for the winner,' he said and pulled me into his arms.

How can a girl resist such charm?

'One small peck on the lips is all you get.' I tilted my lips towards his. Lucas cupped my face in his hands and, gently, placed his lips on mine. Though I didn't want the kiss to end, we broke apart, and Lucas gazed into my eyes. 'Please, can we have another race so I can do that again?' He fluttered his eyelashes.

'You need to save your energy for what I have planned for you.' I grabbed his face, and our lips collided in a passionate embrace.

Our tongues explored each other's mouths, and I ran my hands up and down Lucas's taut body. He picked me up in his muscular arms, and I wrapped my legs around his waist. His excitement pressed against me.

I cast aside my bikini top, and Lucas took hold of my breasts and sucked and bit my erect nipples. His powerful arms lifted me out of the water onto the edge of the pool, where he tore off my briefs. My legs parted, and my head jerked backwards when Lucas circled my sensitive centre with his tongue. My heart beat faster and faster whilst he licked and sucked my swollen bud, and after a while, I surrendered at the point of no return when a powerful orgasm erupted throughout my body.

As quick as a panther, Lucas jumped out of the pool and pulled a condom out of his shorts. Whilst he ran back over to me, he ripped off the foil and folded the sheath over his rock-hard manhood. 'Come back into the water with me.' His words came out at a near growl.

Without hesitation, I jumped into the pool and climbed onto his massive shaft. The water slapped against our bodies whilst we rocked back and forth, again and again. With one last thrust, Lucas opened his eyes and groaned. His body shuddered in an explosive orgasm.

'I'm so sorry. That was too soon,' he said.

'Don't apologise. You made me come already,' I said as my breath hitched. 'Anyway, I hope you're not in any rush to leave me?'

'No, but I must phone my neighbour to see how my grand-papa is. She agreed to keep an eye on him and give him his dinner.'

I wrapped my sarong around my waist. 'I'll pour us a glass of wine whilst you make your call. All that *swimming* was thirsty work.'

A look of alarm spread over Lucas's face whilst he listened to the voice on the phone. He threw his mobile onto the sun lounger and ran around and picked up his belongings.

'I must go back home. Grandpapa collapsed on the kitchen floor. She said he is okay but they've phoned for a doctor just in case.'

'That's not good. Can I do anything to help?'

'No, don't worry—he's as tough as old boots—I'll ring for a taxi and will call you when I get a moment. Thank you for such a lovely afternoon and sorry I've got to rush off.'

'I understand, and thank you for a great time, too. I hope your grandpapa is all right.'

Within moments, the taxi arrived, and he'd gone. I sat and stared into space and touched my face whilst I traced the memory of a kiss.

My brief holiday romance was over.

6

MAX

Last night brought just the pick-me-up I needed. As always, Elena made for delightful company, and we spent the afternoon and early evening in the hotel restaurant, where we consumed several bottles of wine. Roberto had made plans to take out some important clients in his helicopter and visit a restaurant on the other side of the island, so he couldn't collect Elena. He agreed it was a good idea for her to stay the night in the hotel and drive home in the morning. We finished the evening seated around the outside firepit under the watchful gaze of the planet Mars.

A moment of hesitation stretched whilst I stood outside Elena's hotel room to bid her goodnight. The attraction between us still existed, but this was one boundary I would never cross. We agreed to meet for breakfast, and I went back to my empty, lonely room.

❦

'THAT WAS the best night's sleep I've had in ages,' Elena said when she joined me at the breakfast table. She looked bright-eyed and fresh as always, whereas I felt jaded and hungover. My staff bustled around our table and gave each other furtive glances.

'I think we've given the employees something to gossip about,' I whispered.

'Let them gossip. You're entitled to a private life. I find it highly amusing how many *dagger* glances I get from the waitresses. Your future wife could be right here in this hotel, and you wouldn't know it. Why don't you date any of your staff?'

I shrugged and stared into my coffee cup. 'How will I ever know if they're interested in me or my money? I want to meet somebody away from the hotel business who likes me rather than my family's wealth. Yesterday taught me I could take time off and enjoy myself, and I plan to do it more often and live a *balanced* life. Then I might meet someone.'

'Check you out, Mr Zen. Next thing, you'll tell me you're taking up yoga.' Elena grinned.

'Don't mock me.' I laughed. 'The yoga instructor who runs classes here has an excellent reputation, and I could do with help to limber up. Back to reality, though. I have to face my brother this morning at our meeting. I just wish he'd grow up, take some responsibility, and help run the family business. Talk of the devil.'

My mother and Anthony crossed the restaurant.

'I'll love you and leave you and will go home to relieve the nanny. She had to sleep over last night to look after the children. Roberto stayed in a hotel with his clients. Typical man—the one night I stay out, he has to do the same.'

'Well, next time, both of you will have to visit and be my guests at the hotel. That's if Roberto brings along his helicopter. Thank you again for last night and drive home safely.'

Elena pulled me into her arms, and we stood together for a moment. She kissed my cheek and wiped away the traces of her lipstick with her fingers.

'You will meet Miss Right one day, and she will be one lucky lady. Don't work too hard, and I plan to check out your yoga poses next time I visit. You never know, it might inspire Roberto to take up classes too, as he can't even bend over to tie up his shoelaces. Love you lots and see you soon. Thank you for yesterday ... just what the doctor ordered.'

As soon as Elena strolled out of sight, Anthony stood by my side and smirked. 'You sly old fox. What will your best friend say about his wife spending the night with her ex-lover?'

My mother tapped him on the arm with her handbag. 'Stop teasing your brother and casting aspersions on his reputation. He's an honourable and faithful man, just like your father.'

We made our way to my office and sat around the boardroom table.

'Shall I phone for some wine or a G&T, Mother?' Anthony said.

I frowned. 'Not yet. We all need to keep a clear head.'

'That sounds ominous. What have I done now?' Anthony rolled his eyes.

I took a deep breath and took some paperwork out of a folder. 'I met up with the accountants a few days ago, and they feel concerned with your overdrawn director's loan account. The bar and restaurant bill you run up each time you stay at one of our hotels is astronomical. This playboy lifestyle has got to stop. Mother and I think the time has come for you to return to work. The manager in Portugal has resigned, and you can take his place.'

Anthony's face flushed red, and he opened his mouth to reply.

I put up my hand. 'Before you say anything, the hotel staff is efficient, so you won't have to work long hours. Think of all the time you could spend on the golf course. We'll pay you a decent salary on top of the dividends you receive. I don't expect you have much left of your trust fund father left you, do you? I shall leave you twenty-four hours to give me an answer. Now, Mother has something she'd like to add.'

Mother averted her gaze and then looked back at Anthony. 'Oh, that's enough for one day. Let's get a glass of wine before lunch,' she said.

'Thanks a lot, Mother,' I muttered under my breath.

'What's that, dear? I didn't quite hear you.'

'Don't worry. I'll meet up with you tonight because I have lots of paperwork to catch up with.'

'That's your own fault,' Anthony said. 'You shouldn't have bunked off work yesterday.'

Grrr, he made me so mad. As for my mother, it didn't surprise me she didn't mention Anthony's unacceptable behaviour around our female guests. Well, if he wouldn't buck up his ideas, things around here would have to change. *They forget I have the majority shareholding in the company.* The accountant had emailed over Anthony's latest credit-card spend, and it totalled more than the monthly mortgage on my house. It had to stop. I picked up the phone and dialled a number. If I cancelled Anthony's credit card, then he couldn't spend any money on it.

I supposed it only right to tell Anthony what I'd done, so I sent him a text and hoped my mother had taken her credit card out with her.

In a foul mood after spending time in the company of my family, I wanted to put as much distance between us as possible. My plan was to catch up with work and fly back to the UK in the morning. If all went well, I aimed to take the weekend off and catch up with a few friends at my local pub. That's if they hadn't forgotten I existed.

7

KIRSTY

*T*he orange sun appeared over the horizon while I sat outside, deep in thought and exhausted from interrupted sleep. My journal and pen remained untouched on the table in front of me.

Last night's storm had left an earthy scent in the air. When the thunder roared and lightning lit up the sky, the dogs had whimpered in fear and scratched on my door, so I gave in and let them sleep on my bed. However, I think I needed the company as much as they.

Lucas hadn't been in touch, and I didn't want to contact him, even to find out how his grandpapa was. The interlude was nice while it lasted, though nothing more than a one-night stand, again.

Though I'd brought my journal outside to allow the words that filled my mind to pour onto the empty pages, I didn't have the energy to face what I knew already.

I'd only been in Ibiza for a few days and had caved in to my carnal lust with the first handsome stranger to cross my path. *Do I have an addiction to sex?* I took a sip of my hot coffee and picked up my pen.

Dear Journal,

I've done it again. Another one-night-stand notched up on my belt, and all that's left behind is a sense of remorse. Why do I do it to myself? I thought I wanted to change and meet somebody with whom I could plan a future. Yes, the sex was great, and Lucas is gorgeous, but where's my self-respect? Why do I repeat this self-destructive pattern again and again? I thought I'd come to terms with my past even though I struggled with self-esteem when young. After all, I was the fat girl in the class, who had a face covered in pimples and wore hand-me-down clothes my sister had grown out of. I stayed invisible to boys until I gave a hand-job to a guy on the football team. Rumours spread that I was easy and free with my favours. Boys overlooked my spotty face and fat thighs, and I relished in the attention ... any attention was better than nothing. My friends tried to warn me I'd get a name for myself, but I didn't care. For the first time, I felt powerful and in control. By the time I went to college, my spots and puppy fat had disappeared, and I developed an hourglass-figure and big boobs. Men craved my attention, and I had the pick of the bunch, but nobody ever wanted to date me. After I left college and got a job, I'd lost count of the number of one-night-stands I had. Why should I keep a record? I was young and healthy and always practised safe sex, and it didn't hurt anyone. Or so I thought.

I wish I could go back in time and tell myself that self-respect was far more important than the attention thrust upon me by boys who didn't want to get to know the real me. Boys who didn't want a relationship, just an inexperienced fumble down a dark alley.

*I **can** change. I'll learn to love myself and meet the person I deserve in my life.*

MY PHONE PINGED and several text messages came through at once. The storm must have interfered with my signal because Emma sent a message late last night.

We plan to leave first thing in the morning and should get back just after lunch. Put the wine in the fridge. I could really do with a few glasses.

MY MELANCHOLIC MOOD lifted when I read the next text.

I am so sorry I haven't been in touch sooner. My grandpapa broke his hip, and I spent the night with him in hospital. I won't get the chance to see you before you leave, as I need to be always with him. Yesterday was incredibly special, and I only wish I could have spent more time with you. I hope, one day, our paths cross, but it will be my poor luck that you've met a fortunate man who's swept you off your feet. At least I will have the memories of our time together. You are special and deserve the best in life. Much love, Lucas xxx.

I SENT a brief reply and wished his grandpapa a speedy recovery.

The last message had come from Isabel, who'd packed and got ready to leave for the airport, even though her flight wouldn't leave for several hours. Dom had agreed to pick her up from the airport, so this gave Emma and me a good chance to catch up before Isabel's arrival.

The electric gates crashed together, and I burst into tears. When my friend reached me, I wailed, 'I've only gone and done it again, Emma.'

'What on Earth's happened? Tell me everything.' Emma topped up my glass of wine and took hold of my hands.

'I had sex with Lucas.'

Emma's eyes opened wide. 'You what? Lucas the *pool man*? How'd that happen?'

'Well, the pool turned green after he fixed the pump, and he came back to check on it, so I invited him to stay for lunch. We drank a lot of wine and ended up in the pool to cool down. I didn't plan to sleep with him, but …'

'He's bloody gorgeous, Kirsty. If I wasn't married to Dom, I would have tried to shag him years ago. Was it good? Has he got a big dick? Ah, he's such a lovely bloke and so good to his grand-papa. You lucky cow—don't beat yourself up. You're both single and nobody's hurt—it's just a holiday fling.'

I hiccupped. 'I know, but I promised myself I'd stop with the one-night-stands. He sent me a sweet text this morning. His grandad broke his hip, so he has to look after him.'

'Well, you could borrow my nurse's outfit if you like and help look after the patient?'

I laughed and paused my reply when the sound of the gate opening grated across the ground.

We stood to greet the arrivals, and Emma pulled me into a tight hug.

'Don't worry. Everything will sort itself out. You'll meet Mr Right one day. If not, you could easily come back and visit us, and I'll set you up on a date with Lucas. I'll even offer to sit with grandpapa Pablo.'

I gave her a sad smile. 'I know, I just feel upset with myself and will get over it. Lucas is a kind man, and it's a shame he's not looking for a relationship because I would have liked to get to know him more. Oh, well. For the record, he has a very nice penis.'

'Did somebody say penis?' I spun around as Dom scooped Emma into his arms.

'Put me down and stop eavesdropping on our conversation. This is girls talk and not for your ears. Where's Isabel?' Emma said.

'She's just popped to the loo—too many vodkas on the plane— what a lovely lady.' Dom sighed.

I said, 'Yes, she is and doesn't deserve to be married to such a waste of space. This weekend will do her the world of good. Thank you so much for letting her stay.'

'It's our pleasure. Dom is in his element, surrounded by all these women.' Emma patted his upper arm.

Dom grinned. 'Too right. Do you want me to dress up as a naked butler for the weekend?'

Isabel walked towards us, arms laden with wine and chocolate. 'Oh, dear. I may come over all unnecessary if I see a naked bottom.'

She wore a delicate pink *Ted Baker* maxi dress, and a pair of *Gucci* sunglasses rested on top of her immaculate blond head of hair. She oozed style, elegance, and grace. When we first met, she intimidated me, but as soon as I got to know her, I discovered how down-to-earth she was, with no airs or graces and an amazing friend who would do anything for you.

'I don't think we'll need a naked butler, Dom, but I should imagine our guests feel quite hungry. Do you want to start the barbeque?' Emma said.

'Would you like a glass of wine? Silly question. Come and take a seat and I'll let you and Emma get to know each other whilst I help Dom with the barbeque,' I said.

'Isabel, do you eat steak?' Dom called out.

'Yes, please, medium-rare. And a sausage if you have any spare. I love a bit of sausage.'

Dom spat out a mouthful of beer whilst Isabel, oblivious to her unintentional double entendre, turned her attention back to Emma.

'Behave yourself, Dom. Isabel's not smutty like Emma and I. Although, when you get to know her …'

'Don't worry. I'll be on my best behaviour. I still can't believe her husband is cheating on her. He must need his head testing. What a bastard,' Dom said.

SALAD BOWLS and succulent steaks were served up and Dom passed a plate of sausages to Isabel.

'Thank you. They look plump and juicy,' she said.

Dom went to reply but grunted after Emma gave him a sly kick under the table.

My stomach growled whilst I forked a piece of steak onto my plate. 'This looks good. I'm famished.'

Dom glanced at me and winked. 'It must be all that exercise you had yesterday.'

I threw a screwed-up napkin towards Emma. 'I told you not to tell Dom that I slept with Lucas. Thanks a bunch.'

'Don't blame Emma. Lucas phoned me earlier to tell me about his grandad and said you cooked him lunch—that's all—he didn't kiss and tell. Not like you.' He sniggered.

'Who's Lucas? Is this a holiday romance, Kirsty?' Isabel asked.

'No, nothing like that, just a brief encounter in the pool,' I said, trying hard not to blush.

'With the pool man.' Dom sniggered again.

'Really? Tell me more.' Isabel sat up straighter.

'There's nothing to tell. I invited Lucas around for lunch, and we had sex. His grandpapa had an accident and broke his hip, so Lucas had to rush off. He has to look after him, so we won't be able to meet up again before I leave.'

'Good for you. I envy your freedom—you can bonk who you like,' Isabel said.

'Come on, Dom, let's clear up the kitchen whilst the girls catch up.' Emma rose and gathered plates.

The sound of the kitchen door shutting broke our silence.

'To be honest, Bel, I've been beating myself up about sleeping with Lucas. That's a story for another night, though. How did Richard react when you told him you were coming to Ibiza?'

'I don't know. I didn't tell him. The children are staying with my mother, and I left his dinner in the fridge with a note pinned to the door. I don't suppose he's seen it because he stays late at work every night and comes home reeking of perfume. He must think I'm so gullible. Paul feels confident he's days away from proving Richard's infidelity, and then I can leave the cheating so and so.'

I shook my head. 'I don't know how you've put up with it for so long. He's a good boss, but such a womaniser. You deserve so much more, and if I can do anything to help …'

'Let's not talk about it tonight. Wine and good company are all I need right now. Tell me your plans. Where are you jetting off to next?' Isabel said.

'I'm undecided. It's a toss-up between Portugal and Cyprus, then I may make my way to Australia to stay with an old school friend.'

'My parents are friendly with a family who owns hotels throughout Europe. Would you like me to contact Max to see if I can get you a good deal? His mother spends most of her time at their hotel in Cyprus—it's rather plush—five star. Richard and I went there for our anniversary one year before the children were born. We had the firm's Christmas party at their hotel in South Talling last year, didn't we? I think you met the brother, Anthony —bit of a flirt—extremely handsome, though.'

'I vaguely remember a drunk bloke who made a pass at me. Have you got a photo of him?' I asked.

'Yes, we're friends on Facebook, although I haven't been on social media for a while. I can't be bothered with all that stuff. I prefer to keep in contact with my friends via telephone or email. Let me have a look.'

I smiled. Isabel could be so old-fashioned. Originally, Isabel had plans to take over the family business when her father retired but put her career on hold when she met Richard and had children.

She handed me her phone. 'Here's Anthony with his mother. Do you recognise him?'

'No, although it's not a surprise because I had quite a lot to drink that night.'

'Let me have a look at their website to see if they have any more photos.' Isabel retrieved her phone. We studied the screen together.

Brightside Hotels. The hotels seemed exquisite and out of my price range. The one in Cyprus looked incredible, with tastefully decorated rooms and a swimming pool that overlooked the ocean. I scrolled through the images and stopped when one caught my eye.

'Who's this?'

I recognised the man: *That rude and obnoxious guy from the airport.*

Isabel said, 'Ah, that's Max. He took over as CEO after his father passed away. I've known him for years. He went to school with my brother and was so friendly. Though he's changed and I pity him—he seems sad and not the person I used to know. Max has turned into a workaholic whilst his brother spends most of his time partying. Anthony is such a cad.' She shook her head. 'My father had to make a discreet call to Max after Anthony upset one of my niece's friends. The idiot made a pass at her whilst she was on holiday and behaved quite rudely when she turned down his advances.'

Rudeness must run in the family.

'If you like the look of Cyprus, I can email Max to get you a good deal and put you in touch with Margot, his mother. She'll take you under her wing, but make sure she doesn't lead you astray, because she's quite the party girl herself. Margot may try to fix you up with one of her sons.'

Not a chance. One son a miserable, obnoxious bloke, and the other a playboy lech.

However, the hotel in Cyprus did look amazing, and it would be good to meet up with Margot, who sounded fun. Hopefully, Max would be at one of their other hotels whilst I visited.

Isabel yawned and stretched her arms over her head. 'How rude of me. Please, accept my apologies. The children woke me up early and I'm ready for an early night.'

'Me too. The storm kept me awake last night, and Emma and

Dom would appreciate an early night too, as they had an early start this morning. Let's call it a day and we can have a lovely time tomorrow. I'll see if Dom would give us a tour of the island.'

We hugged goodnight and went to our rooms. I picked up my kindle from the bedside cabinet and settled down to read, but within minutes, the device dropped from my hands and I fell into a deep, dream-free sleep.

8

MAX

A torrent of abuse followed me all the way back to England after I'd cancelled Anthony's company credit card. Even my mother tried to persuade me to reconsider—two against one, as always. If my father were alive, he would have backed my decision a hundred percent because he never tolerated shirkers or free-loaders. In our youth, we had to earn our pocket money, so I couldn't comprehend why Anthony thought he could get something for nothing now. I know he had his trust fund to fall back on … if he had anything left.

I sent him a terse message.

If you want to spend the company's money, then you'll have to earn it. The job offer in Portugal still stands, and you have until the end of the day to decide. Subject closed.

THE SUN REACHED its highest point, and a cool breeze blew away the cobwebs whilst I waited for a taxi. Often, my PA would collect me from the airport, but Rachel had taken a day off, as I hadn't planned to leave Cyprus so soon. The return journey to South Talling took just under an hour, so I sank back in the seat and rested my eyes. Before I knew it, the taxi driver stopped outside the hotel and roused me from my slumber.

Brightside, South Talling—the first hotel my family owned, and my favourite. Here, as a young boy, I'd spent many glorious weekends. My father used to take me to work to get me out from under my mother's feet, and we shared lunch in his office whilst he regaled me with stories about how he learnt all about the business from his father when he was a young lad. Bert, the doorman, greeted me with a smile that reached the corners of his wise, kind old eyes. I'd known him forever and always made sure we had a drink together whenever I came home.

'Got time for a drink, Bert? I could do with a cuppa and a catch up before I get buried under a pile of paperwork.'

'Always time for you, Max. Let me get the new lad to take my place on the door, and I'll meet you in the conservatory.'

Once we'd taken our seats, a server brought a selection of afternoon-tea sandwiches, delicious dainty cakes, and two cups filled to the brim with hot coffee.

I studied the feast. 'Tuck in. I can't eat these all on my own— must watch my figure.'

'Or you'll get a belly like mine.' Bert laughed and patted his waistcoat, which hid a generous paunch.

'If I had a wife who could cook like Mabel, then my belly would look like yours.' I chuckled.

'Well, it's about time you settled down and found yourself a wife. I can't wait to meet the next generation of Bright's before I pop my clogs. I promised your father I'd help teach his grandchild the ropes, the same way I did with you. "Learn from the bottom up" is what he'd say. Can't you get one of those dating app thingies and find yourself a wife?'

I shook my head. 'You're not going anywhere soon. Although I intend to find a partner once I can take time off from the business.'

'That's good to hear. You work too hard and deserve a break.

Best you get that brother of yours to pull his weight. How's your mother? Such a fine-looking lady. If only your father hadn't met her first.'

'Don't you let your wife hear you say that. She'll have your guts for garters.' I chuckled. Bert was a charmer and an incorrigible flirt, and like a second father to me. He should have retired several years ago, but insisted he stay on at the hotel, and I never objected. Next to Mabel, this hotel was his life. They had no children, and he treated me like a son.

My phoned pinged—a message from Anthony. *Here we go again.*

After careful consideration, I've decided to take up your job offer and will start next week. In the meantime, please can you reinstate my company credit card so I can clear my hotel bill?

I typed a quick reply:

That's good to hear. Don't worry about the hotel bill. I'll ask HR to deduct it from your first pay packet. The card will be re-instated as and when you prove you're trustworthy. I'll have Rachel book you a plane ticket, and I'll fly to Portugal next week to make sure everything's in order. Thanks, Anthony—excellent decision.

ONE PROBLEM SOLVED. I said goodbye to Bert and headed for the office. A high stack of paperwork and post-it-note messages covered my desk. I pushed them to one side and fired up my computer to check my emails.

With Rachel not at work, I had to scroll through numerous messages to make sure I hadn't missed anything important. One message stood out for me, from Isabel Cartwright. The name seemed familiar. The penny dropped. She was the little sister of my best friend from school who'd married a prize bully—Richard Cartwright. It took me by surprise that Isabel married him. Maybe he'd changed since school. I don't suppose the marriage went down well with her brother Tim. I scrolled through my list of contacts until I found Tim Bantham. It would be good to catch up. We hadn't seen one another for over ten years, so I sent him a text.

He replied straight away.

As luck would have it, I'm at my parents' house for a few days. Are you free to go out for a beer tonight? Be good to see you.

WITHOUT HESITATION, I agreed to meet him in the pub along the road.

🐾

THE SMELL of smoke and beer greeted me when I entered the pub. The smell was reminiscent of my university days with Tim. We'd been best friends throughout our school years, and this had continued through university until he met his wife. Our friendship drifted apart, but we kept in touch on and off for several years, albeit by social media and text messaging.

Tim sat at a table with two pints of beer in front of him, and he stood to greet me with a handshake.

'Maxwell Bright, good to see you, old chap. You haven't changed one bit.'

'Neither have you,' I said, although Tim's face appeared sunken and drawn with dark shadows under his eyes. 'How's Georgia and the kids?'

He closed his eyes and sighed. 'Bit of a sore subject. She left me and went home to her parents.'

His downcast gaze suggested this was a recent development.

'Oh blimey, sorry about that. I thought the two of you were inseparable. Do you want to talk about it?'

'Not really. I've come out to cheer myself up and take my mind off things. Tell me what you've been up to since I saw you last.'

I picked up my pint glass and sipped the beer. The froth tickled my top lip.

'Work, work, and more work. Since Father died, the business has taken over my life. The hotels are doing well, but I need more help with managing everything. Do you fancy a change in career? I could do with someone like you on my team.'

Tim grinned, and his eyes lit up. 'Does the job come with accommodation? We've put the house on the market, and I don't think my parents want me to overstay my welcome.'

'We can sort that out, no problem. Come to my office tomorrow and we'll discuss things if you're serious. Though you've never managed a hotel before, you have the right leadership skills. The job comes with lots of perks, and you get to travel. It will be like old times when we used to work for Dad on the weekends. Only, this time, I won't expect you to serve food or change sheets. You'd be my deputy manager.'

We clinked our glasses. 'Now it's my turn to get the beers in,' I said.

When I returned with the drinks, I placed the two pints of frothy beer on the table and said, 'You'll never guess what? Your brother-in-law just walked in. He's deep in conversation with some woman at the bar. Has he changed much since school, or is he still a bully? I was so surprised when I heard he married your sister.'

Tim grimaced. 'No, still a bully, and a two-timing cheat. The only good thing to come from their marriage is two brilliant kids. Say nothing, but Bel plans to leave him as soon as she gets proof he's unfaithful.'

'Well, the proof's sitting over there. He's practically got his hand up her skirt—what a bastard. I've never liked him. How can he cheat on your sister?' I sipped my beer. 'Oh, she emailed me about a friend of hers. Asked if her mate could stay at the hotel in Cyprus. Family rate, of course. Kirsty Young—do you know her?'

Tim picked up his phone and studied the screen. 'Yes, she works for the family business. What a looker. Bloody gorgeous. Isabel is with her in Ibiza— they've gone on one of those girl's weekends away. All the rage, apparently.' He sighed. 'I wish Georgia had gone away with her friends more often. Anything to make her happier. Look, here's a photo of Bel and Kirsty. They keep popping up on my Instagram. It looks like they're having a whale of a time.'

I glanced at the image, and my breath hitched. What a small world. The screen showed the woman from the airport. Now I could put a name to the face. It seemed our paths might cross again. I had to agree with Tim—she *was* bloody gorgeous.

'Come on. Drink up,' I said. 'Let's get away from here before Dastardly Dick spots us. Do you fancy a few drinks at the Base? I'll even buy you a cocktail with an umbrella if you say yes.'

Tim nodded and grinned. 'Sounds good. You can be my wingman now I'm young, free, and single.'

I laughed. 'I'm not sure about young, but of course I'll be your wingman. It will be like the good old days before you met Georgia.'

'Don't remind me. I never got a look in with women with you around. All they wanted was to talk to me to get closer to you. I was always your wingman.' Tim laughed.

'You had your fair share of female attention before Georgia came along. Now look at us, both single.'

'I dread the thought of starting all over again. Still, it's early days, so let's have some fun. Although, I mustn't drink much because I've got to meet my new boss tomorrow.'

❦

THIS WAS the first time I'd been to the Base for a long time, and it had changed. The shelves, lit by subtle red lighting behind the bar, hung full to the brim with a variety of spirits and bottled beer. Music blared from speakers, but not so loud that you couldn't hear each other talk. Though still early for a Monday night, men and women mingled on the dance floor.

Dutch courage took hold of Tim, and he grabbed my arm.

'Come on. Let's show these people how to dance.'

'No way, mate. It'll take a few more drinks to get me up there.'

About to protest, Tim shut his mouth when a petite brunette jiggled her way over to him and beckoned him onto the dance floor. After a few songs, they draped their arms around each other and gazed into one another's eyes as if they were the only two people in the room.

'Looks like you've been blown out, mate.' The barman spoke with a soft Irish accent. 'Come and take the weight off your feet, and I'll get you a drink. Name's Jack.'

A petite lady joined me at the bar and held out her hand. 'And I'm Annie, Jack's girlfriend. I could do with the company as he's rushed off his feet as usual whilst I'm left talking to myself.'

'That would be great, thanks.' I glanced over at the dance floor, and Annie turned her head to follow my gaze.

'Is the one snogging that girl your mate?' Annie asked.

I nodded. 'Well, it looks like my wingman's services are no longer needed. I'm Max, by the way.'

Annie seemed familiar, and then I remembered she was the woman in the pub with Richard.

'Weren't you at the Rose & Crown tonight?' I asked.

'Yes, unfortunately. It was a work thing.' She shuddered.

'What do you do for a job?'

'I'm a photographer, but I also work part-time for a detective agency.'

I raised my brow. 'That sounds intriguing. Tell me more?'

'It's not something I can talk about.'

Annie scowled and glanced towards the door. 'Oh, blimey,

that's all I need, the sleazeball.'

I looked around to see who Annie referred to and let out a groan. I might have guessed. This time I wasn't so lucky because the guy caught sight of me and made his way to the bar. Richard greeted me like a long-lost friend and bent to place a sloppy kiss on Annie's face, but I stood and grabbed his hand.

'Richard, so nice to see you. It's been ages. When we last met, you were trying to flush my head down the toilet. The good old days, eh? You haven't changed one bit. I'd love to stop and talk, but our taxi has arrived. Please send your wife my regards. I understand she's having a great time in Ibiza.'

Annie grabbed her coat from the back of her chair, and Jack leant over the bar and whispered something in her ear. We made our way outside and stood under the canopy.

'Thanks for the rescue,' Annie said.

'Look, you can tell me to mind my business, but you don't need to get mixed up with him. He's a married man, and don't you have a boyfriend?'

'It's not what you think. I can't go into the details, but it's work stuff. My boss would have my guts for garters if he knew I'd talked to a stranger about it.' Annie patted me on the arm. 'Don't worry. I'm going to get a taxi back to Jack's, so I'll be okay.'

I held out my hand. 'Well, it's been nice to meet you, and Jack is a lucky man. Stay safe and keep away from that slimeball.'

Annie stood on tiptoes and kissed me on the cheek. 'Thank you, Max, my knight in shining armour. It's been a pleasure to meet you, too. Your wife is one lucky lady.'

'No, I'm not married.' Oh, what was the point? It's not like I was trying to chat her up. Annie had a boyfriend, and I was at least ten years older than her.

As the taxi pulled away, I waved goodbye and walked back to the hotel. I made a mental note to text Tim in the morning to see how he got on, seeing as I'd disappeared without letting him know. I don't suppose he noticed, though. *What a good night. I must do this more often*, I mused.

9

KIRSTY

*O*ver the next few days, Dom and Emma took us on a guided tour around the island. We ate in marvellous tavernas frequented by the locals and hidden off the beaten track away from the tourist hotspots. The home-cooked cuisine tasted delicious, and we consumed copious amounts of wine. Before long, the waistband on my shorts pinched.

'I can't believe you're going home already. The days have gone too fast,' I said whilst Isabel packed her suitcase.

'I know. I miss the children terribly but would love to have stayed here a few more nights. Emma and Dom are wonderful people—do you think they'll let me visit again?'

'Without a doubt. Perhaps I'll organise a girl's holiday. I'm sure Henrietta would love to come along if she can tear herself away from her new love interest. You've not met Henri, have you?'

Isabel thought for a moment. 'Henrietta works for the detective agency, doesn't she? We've spoken on the phone, and she seems genuinely nice. You're so lucky to have such amazing friends. Richard and I only socialise with his friends. None of mine could tolerate him, so we lost contact over the years.'

She picked up her phone. 'Talking of making contact, Max sent me a wonderful reply. You're more than welcome to stay at the hotel in Cyprus as his guest. Just let him know when you intend to travel, and he'll arrange to have you collected from the airport.'

'I'm speechless. How kind. Such a generous offer.'

Max didn't seem the rude and arrogant oaf I came across at the airport. Maybe I'd judged him wrong? I forgot to mention this snippet of information to Isabel.

My friend swatted away a wasp that buzzed around the table.

'I spoke to my brother on the phone this morning. I worry about him because he's just separated from his wife, and my parents haven't been that supportive. Anyway, he met up with Max last night, and they saw Richard in the pub, drooling over some woman. Tim and Max avoided him until they went to another bar. Tim had the misfortune to bump into him on the dance floor, but he didn't hang around to talk. They've never seen eye-to-eye since Richard was a bully at school; although, he was quite the charmer when I first met him.'

Isabel took a notebook and pen out of her bag and wrote on the paper. 'Here are Max's contact details. Best you book your flight to Cyprus. How exciting.' Isabel sighed. 'Oh well, I'd better get ready to leave for the airport.'

EACH MORNING, I took a cup of coffee outside and wrote in my journal. The tension and anxiety drifted away, and I grew more relaxed. The house seemed quieter without Isabel, and Dom and Emma spent the days at work whilst I sunbathed by the pool with my nose deep in a book. Lucas sent me brief text messages to say his grandpapa was on the mend and flirting outrageously with a nurse who visited him daily. The woman had agreed to sit with Pablo so Lucas could go back to work. He was due to clean the pool at the end of the week, but I would be on a plane to Cyprus —a relief because I wanted to avoid further temptation. The memory of my time with Lucas made me horny.

❧

WE STOOD on the pavement outside the airport entrance, and my eyes welled with tears when Emma and Dom held me tightly in their arms. Even though I knew I'd see my friends again, I couldn't hold back the emotion—I hated goodbyes.

Whilst Dom got my cases out of the car, Emma whispered, 'I've got a feeling in my waters that next time we meet, you'll be in a relationship.'

She held my arms and frowned. 'Don't you dare put yourself down again. You're incredibly special and deserve to find love. Now, off you go before you make me cry.'

I stood on the pavement and watched the car speed off. Then I sniffed back my tears and made my way through to departures.

Yesterday, I'd received a polite email from Max. He'd arranged for a member of staff to pick me up from the airport, and my room would be ready when I arrived at the hotel. Margot, his mother, had agreed to meet me in the hotel bar at 6 pm and had made dinner reservations.

I felt extremely grateful for these kind gestures and slightly apprehensive about this new adventure. At least I wouldn't be completely on my own when I arrived. Max hadn't mentioned whether he was in Cyprus, and I didn't like to ask.

The temperature was a few degrees warmer than Ibiza, but the heat gave way to the cool sea breeze. Upon entering the hotel, I stood and studied the majestic surroundings.

The receptionist handed over my key and instructed a porter to take my luggage to the room—the penthouse suite. Wow, what did I do to deserve such treatment?

I stepped onto the balcony and took in the sea view and area. This had to be the nicest hotel room I'd ever stayed in. It seemed almost as big as my flat back home, and I couldn't believe my luck. Bright coloured cushions lay scattered across the king-size bed, a big-screen television hung on the wall in front of a plush velvet sofa, and vivid artwork decorated the walls.

The spacious and lavish bathroom made me long to soak in the clawfoot bathtub in the middle of the room. A gentle knock sounded, and I peered through the spyhole. A member of staff stood at the doorway, holding an ice bucket containing a bottle of something.

'Please accept this champagne as a gift from Mr Bright. He sends his apologies for not being able to greet you today and hopes the room is to your satisfaction. We would like to make your stay with us as enjoyable as possible, so please ask if you need anything. Mrs Bright looks forward to meeting you at the bar as arranged. Would you like me to unpack your luggage?'

'That won't be necessary, thank you. The room is exquisite. Do you know when Max, erm ... Mr Bright will be available? I would like to thank him in person for his generosity.'

'No, madam, but I could ask his secretary for you?'

I shook my head. 'No, that won't be necessary. I'll send him an email instead. Thank you for the champagne. Here, let me get you a tip.' I turned around to find my purse.

'No, that won't be necessary. You are Mr Bright's companion. Goodbye, madam.'

Companion? What was that supposed to mean?

With a shrug, I went to fill the bath.

Soon, the scent of lavender filled the air, and my body and mind felt more at ease when I immersed my shoulders under a thick layer of bubbles. Because I had to get ready to meet Margot Bright, I couldn't soak in the bath too long. We mixed in different circles, and I didn't come from a family of wealth, which left me anxious.

At 6 o'clock, I went to the bar. A lady—Margot, I presumed—turned around to greet me.

'Hello, darling. You must be Kirsty. Pleased to meet you. I'm Margot.' She held out her hand.

I almost curtsied because it felt as if I stood in the presence of royalty.

'Do come and sit next to me. What can I get you to drink?'

I glanced across at the menu. 'I'd love an espresso martini, thank you.'

'Make that two,' Margot said to the barperson. 'A shot of caffeine will give me some energy. I had the misfortune of going for a walk with a group of old farts this morning, and the conversation was so dull.'

She clapped her hands. 'I got so excited when Max phoned to say you'd planned to visit. You've been on holiday with Isabel in Ibiza, haven't you?'

I nodded, but Margot spoke again before I could reply. 'I've known Isabel since she was a baby and have been good friends with her mother. We had our first children around the same time. She's a lovely girl. Such a shame she didn't marry my son, Max, instead of the twit she's wed to now. Did she tell you she had a crush on Max when she was at school? It was as obvious as the nose on her face, but he was oblivious. Are you married?'

Hm. Isabel kept that fact quiet. I wonder why?

'No. Never met the right person, but I hope to one day.'

Margot picked up her glass and took a sip of the velvety liquid. 'My advice to you, dear, is the way to a man's heart is to keep him at arm's length and don't jump into bed with him straight away. Good old-fashioned courtship should do the trick.'

I smiled. 'Easier said than done. It's the way things are nowadays.'

Margot tutted and screwed up her nose. 'It's a shame my son Anthony's not here to meet you. His brother sent him to work at our hotel in Portugal. Banished him, more like. He's devilishly handsome. You'd make a lovely couple.'

'That's a shame. Perhaps we'll meet one day.' *But not if I have anything to do with it,* I thought.

'What about you? Isabel explained your husband passed away a couple of years ago. Do you think you'll re-marry?'

Margot twiddled with her napkin. 'No, never. I'm happy being on my own and am not sure my sons would feel too pleased if I tried to replace their father.'

'I'm sure they wouldn't see it like that. I should imagine they don't want you on your own for the rest of your life?'

Margot sat up straight. 'You're right. Gregory always said life is for the living, and if he passed away before me, he'd want me to meet someone else. That's fine, but I haven't had a relationship outside of my marriage and dread the thought of doing things in the bedroom with another man.'

She shuddered. 'The thought of undressing in front of someone else horrifies me. Every part of my body sags, even my wrinkles.'

'You're a stunning lady, and you have an amazing figure.' I glanced over her shoulder.

'And it looks like you have an admirer.'

'Who? What are you talking about?' Margot craned her neck.

I covered my mouth with the menu. 'There's a gentleman on his own seated behind you, who can't take his eyes off you. Don't turn around because he'll know we're talking about him.'

'Does he wear a blazer and cravat and have a white moustache?' Margot asked.

I nodded. 'That's the one—very dapper—looks quite the gentleman.'

A slow smile spread over her face and touched the corners of her eyes. 'That must be Mr Williams, who's vacationed at this hotel for several years now. He used to come here with his wife, but I believe she passed away eighteen months ago. He does look rather handsome, doesn't he?'

'Why don't I invite him over to join us?' I stood and waved the man over before Margot could protest.

A smile lit up his face whilst Mr Williams walked towards us with a spring in his step.

'Good evening, Mr Williams. Please meet my friend Kirsty. Would you care to join us?' A pale pink blush spread over Margot's cheeks. The gentleman took hold of my hand and gave it a gentle kiss.

'Please call me Ernest. It would delight me to join the company of two beautiful ladies.' As he spoke the words, he had eyes only for Margot. She lowered her gaze and blushed a deeper shade of pink.

'Can I get each of you a drink? How about a bottle of champagne? I have good news to celebrate,' Ernest said.

'That's truly kind of you. What are we celebrating?' I said.

'My daughter just gave birth to identical twin girls. My first grandchildren. I can't wait to meet them. Their arrival took us all by surprise—four weeks early—but mother and babies are healthy.' A smile warmed Ernest's eyes.

He glanced towards his hands, and the smile faded. 'I only wish my dear wife were alive today, as she would have made a wonderful grandmother.'

Margot leaned towards Ernest and patted him on the arm. 'Congratulations. This *is* a cause for celebration. I do envy you, though. I long to become a grandmother. Would you care to join us for dinner?'

'I'd be delighted, but I insist it's my treat. Let's order another bottle of champagne.

'Do you have any photos?' I asked.

'My daughter sent some over by WhatsApp. Only, I appear to have lost them. She insisted I buy one of those fancy phones before I came away, but I can't get used to the darn thing.'

I smiled. My dad was the same and couldn't get to grips with new technology. 'Let me look. I'm sure they're still on your phone.'

Within seconds, I gazed at a picture of two beautiful babies, and my stomach flipped. I passed the phone to Margot and let out a sigh. *Oh, how I long to have a child of my own.*

'What shall we call you now, grandpa or grandad?' Margot teased. 'Your granddaughters are beautiful. They look just like your late wife.'

'Yes, she was the most beautiful woman I've ever met ... until now,' Ernest said.

Margot's delight brought a shy smile to his lips. 'Please excuse me whilst I pop to the restroom. I'll be back in a jiffy,' Ernest said.

I raised my eyes and grinned. 'Well, it certainly looks as though the attraction goes both ways if I can judge by the sparkle in your eyes and the blush on your cheeks. It's a good job I'm here to chaperone the two of you.'

Margot fanned herself with the menu and frowned. 'Nonsense, he's just being friendly. Anyway, he's still grieving for his wife, as I am my dearest Gregory.'

'I'm not suggesting the two of you run off and get married, but it's obvious you share chemistry. Just see how things go. If nothing else, you may become good friends,' I said.

'I don't know about that, but he is rather handsome.' Margot grinned.

She jumped in her seat when Ernest said, 'Are you talking about me again?'

I almost choked on my drink, and Margot's face turned scarlet.

'Don't flatter yourself. Margot was talking about her son,' I said.

'Shall we make our way to the restaurant? I feel quite famished,' Margot said. 'Thank you,' she whispered as she stood.

The delicious food consisted of aromatic slices of baked lamb, served with seasoned potatoes and freshly baked bread. We devoured our meal in no time. I hadn't realised how hungry I was and couldn't resist the mouth-watering cubes of loukoumi, along with glasses filled to the brim with Brandy Sours.

My eyes grew heavy with tiredness and the effects of too much food and alcohol.

'I'll have to call it a night soon. It's been a long day.' I yawned.

'Oh, that is a shame,' Margot said. 'I'd rather hoped we could go to a few bars. The night is still young.'

'We can do that tomorrow if you don't have any plans? Anyway, I must change out of this dress. It feels quite snug after all that food. Thank you, Ernest. You're very generous.'

'You're welcome, my dear. Perhaps you'd like to join me for breakfast?'

'That's a marvellous idea. Shall we meet at 9 am?' Margot said, full of enthusiasm.

'It's a date.' Ernest blushed.

To me, Margot said, 'Before you go, I don't suppose you'd have an interest in aqua aerobics in the morning? We have a class at eleven. It's something I've wanted to do for quite a while but have never fancied it on my own.'

'That sounds great. I could do with some exercise, and I love aqua aerobics. What about you, Ernest?'

'Unfortunately, I've made plans to meet a friend for coffee, but perhaps I will come along and spectate if I get back in time. Although I haven't seen Miriam for a while, and we have lots to talk about. I believe you two know each other, Margot?'

Margot frowned and pursed her lips. 'Miriam Stearn? Yes, we belong to the same walking group. How do you two know one another?'

'We met here last year and kept in touch via email. Miriam is a wonderful lady, so friendly.'

'Too friendly,' Margot muttered.

'I'm sorry, I didn't quite catch that, dear,' Ernest said.

'Very friendly.' Margot's smile failed to reach her eyes.

Margot's jealous. She does *fancy him.* I covered my smile with a hand. The two of them would be perfect for each other. A slight nudge was all they needed.

10

MAX

*A*fter a long day yesterday, I escaped the office for a few hours to play a round of golf with Tim. As a result, I struggled to keep on top of the backlog of work I had to sort out before I flew to Cyprus. Happily, Tim handed in his notice and would come to work for me in a few weeks.

I poked my head around the office door. 'Rachel, could you stay a little later tonight? I want to clear my desk before I leave. Now my brother isn't in Cyprus to keep my mother company, I'd like to stay out there for longer.'

Stop kidding yourself. Mother has plenty of friends to keep her entertained. More likely, my extended visit has more to do with a certain lady currently in our penthouse suite.

'No problem, boss. I can stay as long as you like. I've picked up the dry-cleaning and ordered a taxi to take you to the airport tomorrow,' Rachel said. The woman deserved a pay rise. She'd been a loyal employee for fifteen years, and I didn't know what I'd do without her.

Unable to concentrate, I logged onto my Facebook account. Usually, I only checked my profile to keep up-to-date with the activity surrounding the hotels. But, today, I searched for Isabel Cartwright and clicked on her profile. Images of Kirsty and Isabel filled the screen. Both women were photogenic. However, Kirsty's natural beauty attracted me the most. Isabel had tagged Kirsty in the photos, so I clicked on her name. I longed to find out more about her. Disappointment washed over me when Facebook denied me access.

The desk phone rang and startled me from my daydream. Rachel said, 'Gabriella is calling. She said she's in town and wants to meet up to discuss new wines they have in stock.

I glanced at my mobile and saw several missed calls.

Gabriella and I had been friends with benefits for several years, but she'd moved out of the area, and we only saw each other every few months. This casual arrangement suited us both because neither of us wanted a relationship.

'Hello, handsome. You're hard to get hold of. I tried phoning your mobile, but you didn't pick up. Are you free to meet up tonight to discuss wine?'

Usually, the sound of her voice would give me a hard-on, but not today. Nothing stirred in my loins.

'Hi, Gabs. How are things? Sorry I didn't pick up. I had my phone on silent. Look, there's something I've meant to say but haven't. As much as I enjoy our time together, it's not fair for either of us to carry on. You're gorgeous, and the sex has been amazing, but you need to meet someone who deserves you.'

She giggled. 'That's a shame. Although I'd planned to say something similar to you tonight. I've met someone, and we're getting married next month. I wanted to tell you about the news in person, and if one thing led to another ... call it my last fling before I settle down.'

'Congratulations. Fantastic news. I wish you and your fiancé all the best. Sorry to rush off, but I need to go home and pack for my flight. Take care.'

I gazed at the image on my computer screen. *You don't realise how much of an effect you have on me, Kirsty Young.*

11

KIRSTY

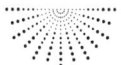

'*L*ook at the pair of you. What time did you get to sleep last night?' I said.

Margot and Ernest were noticeably quiet, and their eyes looked weary and bloodshot.

Ernest coughed and groaned. 'I think about four this morning.'

'Four o'clock! No wonder you've both got dark circles under your eyes. Why on Earth did you come down for breakfast? You should have had a lie-in.'

'We'd made plans with you and didn't want to let you down. Also, I'm meeting Miriam this morning.'

Margot tutted. 'It's a shame you didn't oversleep.'

'*Now, now*. Last night, I said you have nothing to worry about. Miriam and I are just friends, and I'm not attracted to her in the slightest,' Ernest said.

I glanced between the two of them and smiled. 'Unlike someone else I could mention. What did the two of you get up to after I went to bed?'

'A gentleman never kisses and tells.' Ernest's eyes glinted in amusement.

Margot gave him a gentle slap on the arm. 'Stop teasing. People will gossip. We went into town for a few drinks and ended up in a nightclub full of youngsters. The music was so loud we couldn't hear each other talk, so we ended up on the dance floor. Ernest bought me a glow-stick. Look, here it is.' Margot held out her wrist.

I chuckled. Bright pink plastic rested next to a Cartier bracelet. 'Well, I never. As soon as I turn my back, you turn into a pair of ravers. It sounds like you've got more energy than me. I'm glad you had fun. Next time, I'll come out with you if you don't mind me playing gooseberry?'

Margot signalled to the server to bring her more coffee. 'Ernest and I thought of returning to the club tonight. I'll be as right as rain once I've had a catnap this afternoon.'

'Yes, and me,' Ernest said. 'I rather enjoyed all that bopping around. I soon got the hang of it, although I prefer ballroom dancing. Regrettably, ladies, I must leave you. If I don't see you later, shall we meet in the bar around seven tonight? Goodbye for now.' He stood and gave us both a gentle peck on the cheek.

'Such a gentleman.' Margot sighed as he walked off.

I spooned yoghurt and honey into my mouth, and Margot nibbled a piece of cake. 'You two make such a lovely couple. I suppose aqua aerobics is out of the question now?' I said.

'Absolutely not. I need to get in shape.' Margot grabbed at non-existent fat around her stomach.

'You have an amazing figure, and by the sound of it, more energy than I do. If you prefer to cancel, I won't get upset, and we can re-arrange it for another day. I'm not going anywhere for a while.'

Margot shook her head. 'No, I've booked us a space, and the cold water will do me the world of good. I'll just flap my arms about to make it look like I'm joining in. Then we can go for a spot of lunch before I take an afternoon nap. My son's flight arrives this afternoon, and no doubt, he'll want to see me when he gets here. Perhaps I'll ask him to join us for dinner tonight if you don't mind?'

My stomach somersaulted. 'Anthony?'

'No, Max. He plans to stay for an extra few days. To keep an eye on me, no doubt. Although, he sounded quite cheerful when we spoke on the phone.'

I wasn't sure whether I wanted to spend time in the company of someone so obnoxious, but I didn't want to appear rude. After all, I was a guest in his hotel.

'That's fine by me. The more the merrier. Shall we make our way to the pool?'

'Yes, let's do. We don't want to arrive late, and I want to get a place at the back of the pool.'

By THE TIME WE ARRIVED, the pool was half-filled with eager women and men ready to start their morning workout. Briskly, Margot walked to the edge of the pool, her body hidden under a robe, and I felt body conscious because my breasts were on the verge of escaping my scanty bikini top. I'd picked up a hand towel instead of my body towel and this barely covered my bottom. 'I must buy myself a swimming costume before we do this again,' I said.

Margot looked me up and down. 'Nonsense, dear. You have a wonderful figure, so don't hide it. I wish I'd looked like you when I was your age—all the curves in all the right places. I was as thin as a rake until I had the boys. Now look at me.'

'You mustn't put yourself down. You have a figure any woman half your age would be proud of. And where have you been hiding those?' I pointed to her bosom.

Margot glanced at her chest and smiled. 'These were a 60th birthday present from Gregory. My breasts were never the same after I had children, but it wasn't until I had a bit of work done on my face that I got a boob job too. Only, now my décolletage resembles a dried-up piece of toast, so I always keep it covered.'

'I can't see anything wrong. We're all so self-critical.' I sighed. 'It's a subject I've been writing about in my journal for a while.'

A shrill whistle made me jump.

'Tell me all about your journal later,' Margot whispered.

I nodded and marched on the spot whilst the music blared. Within seconds, my eyes stung from the chlorine, which splashed on my face. *Why did I agree to do this?*

Once my eyes calmed down, I relaxed and had fun. The music sounded upbeat, and I kept up with the exercises. They weren't as easy as I'd thought, initially, and my muscles protested. Margot attempted all the exercises with ease and glided through the water like a graceful swan.

All too soon, the class ended, and we made our way to the edge of the pool.

'That was jolly good fun. We must do it again,' Margot said.

I glanced at the adjacent bar and glimpsed Ernest, who waved in our direction.

'Ernest didn't meet up with Miriam for long,' I said.

'My goodness, he can't see me like this.' Margot panicked and made a dash for the pool ladder and climbed out.

'Slow down,' I shouted, but it was too late. Margot tumbled to the floor and lay there, stunned for a few moments.

The instructor ran to her.

'Are you okay, Margot? Can you move?' I said.

'I'm fine. Pass me my robe before Ernest sees me.' When the instructor touched her wrist, she winced in agony.

'A doctor needs to check this. I think you may have broken the bone,' the instructor said.

'I'm sure it's only a sprain. No need to fuss,' Margot said. Her face turned ashen, and she looked as if she were about to pass out.

'Margot, are you all right?' Ernest called out with an expression of alarm.

'We think she's broken her wrist,' I called over.

Margot groaned. 'I'll be okay—it's just a sprain. The only thing hurt is my pride. I'm such a silly old fool for not being careful.'

With determination, she struggled to her feet and took a step. Then she swooned and collapsed into the arms of the instructor.

'I'll radio for an ambulance. She might have a concussion,' the instructor said.

'I'll go with Margot,' Ernest said.

Margot roused. 'That's awfully kind of you, but I'd prefer Kirsty to come with me. Perhaps you could let Max know when he gets here? Make sure you explain it's nothing to worry about. I'm sure everything will be fine.' She grimaced in pain.

'Can you sit with her whilst I change? The ambulance should arrive soon,' I said.

I took one look at Ernest's grief-stricken face and swallowed a lump in my throat when tears appeared in his eyes.

He leant towards me and whispered, 'This is all my fault—we shouldn't have stayed out so late, but we were having so much fun.'

I put my arm around his shoulders. 'Nonsense. It was an accident. Margot was in a bit of a rush to come and find you and slipped. That's all. Let me have your mobile number, and I'll phone you from the hospital when I have news.'

'Please do. Look after her for me. She's very precious,' he said.

Paramedics arrived and assisted Margot outside. Seated in the back of the ambulance, wrapped in a big blanket, Margot looked so vulnerable and frail.

I climbed in and sat next to her. She lowered the oxygen mask from her mouth.

'I feel such an idiot. Ernest won't want to know such a clumsy fool. He'd be better off with Miriam.'

'Stop talking nonsense. You just feel sorry for yourself. Ernest is extremely upset and concerned. He's asked me to phone from the hospital to give him an update. He feels responsible for keeping you out too late last night.'

'Well, that's poppycock—it was the other way round. I encouraged *him* to stay out. Poor man. I must reassure him he's not to blame when I see him next.'

'He's camped out in reception, waiting for Max to arrive, and I don't suppose he'll go anywhere until you get back. Have they given you anything for the pain?'

She nodded. 'Yes, and it's done the trick, whatever it was.' Her eyelids drooped, and the motion of the vehicle lulled her to sleep.

'Wake up. You mustn't fall asleep in case you've got a concussion,' I said, alarmed.

The medic patted my arm and gave me a reassuring smile. 'Don't worry, miss. We've ruled out a brain injury. And Mrs Bright didn't bang her head. I think it was the shock of the accident that caused her to faint, and a lack of sleep. We'll get her wrist strapped up in no time, and she'll be as right as rain; although, I can't say the same for the glow-stick.' He waved it about in the air, grinned, and winked at me.

I blushed and giggled and toyed with my hair. There's something about a man in a uniform.

1 2

MAX

The taxi driver dumped my luggage on the kerbside as I stood there and took in my surroundings. After a deep breath, I sighed. The gentle breeze took away the midday heat, and I couldn't remember the last time I'd arrived at the hotel this relaxed.

As soon as I stepped into the foyer, Mr Williams dashed to me with an expression of alarm.

'Good day, Mr Williams. Is everything okay? You look worried.'

'It's your mother, Mr Bright. She's had an accident and has been taken to hospital,' he said.

My heart sped up, and I made to turn around so I could jump into the taxi, which remained parked outside.

'Don't worry, though,' Mr Williams said. 'We think she's broken her wrist, and she should be back soon. I'm waiting for a call from Kirsty.' He waved his mobile around.

'Kirsty Young? Why did she go with Mother? What's she got to do with it?'

'They participated in aqua aerobics this morning. Afterwards, Margot slipped. I'll let her tell you all about the matter when you see her. Ah, Kirsty's ringing now.'

'Would you mind if I talk to her first?' I said. Ernest nodded and passed me the phone.

'Hello, I presume I'm talking to Kirsty? This is Max Bright. How is my mother?'

'Yes, Mr Bright, this is Kirsty, and your mother is going to be all right. As expected, she has a broken wrist and is waiting to have it put in a cast. We should arrive home within the hour, but she's exhausted from lack of sleep and the shock from the fall.'

'Lack of sleep? Aqua aerobics? Late night? This is your fault. How could you be so irresponsible? My mother's nearly seventy years old and should not be encouraged in this sort of behaviour. I hold you entirely responsible and shall see you when you get back.' I disconnected the call and passed the phone back to Mr Williams.

His face appeared bright red and outraged. 'How dare you?'

I stared at him and sneered. 'Pardon?'

'How dare you speak to Kirsty in such a manner? That was totally unacceptable. This had nothing to do with her. I was the one who stayed out with your mother—we went to a nightclub. She may be nearly seventy, but she is a fine and remarkable lady, who has the energy and the physique of a woman half her age. In fact, Kirsty retired to bed around ten o'clock and left us to it. As for aqua aerobics, your mother insisted Kirsty join her. Not the other way around. You owe that young lady an apology, and you would do well in remembering your manners and how to speak to a lady.' After this outburst, the anger drained from his face, and concern replaced the emotion. 'How is Margot? I hope she isn't in too much pain?'

Shame washed over me. Not only had I jumped to conclusions and spoken rudely to Kirsty, but I'd also upset Mr Williams. Obviously, he had feelings for my mother, and I shouldn't have been so quick to judge.

'Mr Williams, I'm so sorry. I feel extremely concerned for my mother, which isn't any excuse for the way I behaved. Mother can be wilful and enjoys a night out. She won't be coerced into doing anything she doesn't want to do. I'm grateful she has a friend such as yourself. You have every right to feel angry. I must apologise to Kirsty as soon as I get the chance.' I glanced at the floor, and my shoulders slumped.

'Apologies accepted, young man. You'll find Kirsty a wonderful lady, who's shown nothing but kindness towards Margot.'

§

THE TWO WOMEN under discussion arrived within the hour. Relief brought a smile to Ernest's lips. Mother looked tired and fragile when she walked towards us. Although when she saw Mr Williams, her smile broadened into a grin, and she waved her bright-pink plaster cast at him.

'Bad news, I'm afraid,' Mother said. 'They had to cut off my bracelet. We must go back to the club to get another one.' She chuckled. 'Not tonight, though. I feel quite exhausted. But I'm still on for drinks at the bar later if you are? You must join us, Max.'

'Only if you feel up to it, my dear. You must rest,' Mr Williams said.

'I'll be as right as rain after an afternoon nap. It's a bloody nuisance that I've broken the wrist that holds my drinking glass.' She giggled.

I glanced at Kirsty, who glared at me.

'Mr Williams, would you take my mother back to her room, please? I need a quiet word with Kirsty.'

'Yes, of course. Please call me Ernest. Mr Williams retired from the bank a long time ago.' Ernest took hold of Mother's arm and walked towards the lifts.

I rushed over to Kirsty when she turned to follow. 'Can we have a quiet word in my office? I owe you an apology.'

'Yes, but I hope it won't take long because I have a taxi booked for six and need to pack.'

I stood there, dumbstruck and in shock. Did this mean she was leaving?

13

KIRSTY

*M*ax closed the door behind me and gestured for me to take a seat. 'May I get you something to drink? Tea, coffee, or something stronger? I need a glass of wine. Would you care to join me?'

I nodded. After the day I'd had, a drink was just what I needed.

He leant back in his chair and ordered the wine from room service. I refused to make eye contact with him and sat and stared out of the window, which offered a glorious view—blue sky and sea, and lush, green palm trees. If this were my office, I wouldn't be able to work; although, judging by the pile of paperwork on the desk, Max didn't either.

You could cut the atmosphere with a knife. Max coughed to clear his throat. 'Please, accept my apologies for the way I spoke to you. I'm so sorry—there is no excuse. I tend to speak before I think when under stress. I felt extremely worried about Mother, and I overreacted. May I do anything to make amends? I understand if you still wish to leave, but please don't go on my account. I promise it won't happen again, and you're welcome to stay as our guest for as long as you like.' He sighed, and his dark eyes studied me with intensity whilst he waited for my response.

I lifted my chin and held his gaze. 'Look, thank you for the apology, but it would be better for me to leave. Our paths have crossed twice, and both times, you've been rude and obnoxious. It doesn't feel right to take advantage of the kind hospitality on offer from someone I find rather unpleasant.'

Max raised his brows. 'Twice? Ah, the airport. Yes, I was a jerk then as well. I'm sorry, no excuses but I've been under a lot of pressure lately. Please, would you reconsider? May I take you out for dinner tonight by way of an apology?'

I studied his face. Fine lines etched around his eyes, and he looked tired. We sat in stillness for a few moments before I nodded. 'Yes, okay, I'll cancel my taxi and meet you for dinner, but if you ever speak to me that way again, you'll find out how rude and obnoxious I can be.'

Max beamed with delight. His gaze shifted away from me, and he stood. 'Could we start again and forget we've ever met?' He held out his hand. 'My name is Maxwell Bright. Pleased to meet you.'

I took hold of his firm grip and my stomach somersaulted. My body betrayed me at his touch, even though this man didn't attract my mind. I snatched my hand away and shook my head.

'Well, you already know my name. Thank you again for your generous hospitality. Your hotel is magnificent, and my room is perfect. On that note, I must leave you. I need a shower, and my hair reeks of chlorine. I have plans to meet with your mother and Ernest at six. Will you be joining us?'

He nodded. 'Yes, pre-drinks before dinner would be nice. I'll book us a table for eight.'

He leant towards me and gave me a gentle kiss on both cheeks.

Butterflies fluttered around in my stomach at his touch. He smelt divine, and I had the urge to throw myself into his arms.

Get a grip ... he's not your type.

Back in my room, I stood under a hot shower and scrubbed the chlorine out of my hair.

My thoughts drifted to Max. I couldn't deny I found him handsome, but did I fancy him? When he replaced his angry scowl with a smile, his big brown eyes twinkled and his cheeks dimpled. When we stood next to each other, he towered over me —so strong. And when we touched, the chemistry was undeniable. Or was it?

My hand reached out and turned the dial on the shower. Freezing water cascaded over my body, and I gasped. For a few moments, I held myself beneath the punishing spray. It did no good, and I would have to put out this flame of desire in another way.

I JOLTED awake and sat upright when laughter and music drifted through the open window. My hair stuck to my face, and my mouth felt as dry as sand. I glanced at the clock and saw it was six already. Oh, goodness. I dialled through to the reception, and they reassured me they would pass a message to Margot and Ernest. With a sigh of relief, I straightened the bedcovers and saw my crystal wand waiting for me to put it back in its velvet surrounds. The flames of desire I'd felt in the shower had extinguished on their own accord, and I'd fallen asleep cradling my wand, taking comfort in the stillness and energy it provided.

After another quick shower, and a splash of make-up, I studied the contents of my wardrobe, undecided what to wear. It wasn't as if I were trying to impress anyone.

14

MAX

The afternoon passed in a blur. The pile of paperwork on my desk reduced when I absorbed myself in work, determined to take a few days break for my birthday. Though I didn't want to celebrate the occasion, Mother insisted she organise a party for the weekend, and most people on the guest list were her friends. Anthony would fly in from Portugal, and Roberto and Elena had made plans to stay too. Roberto had even booked us in for a round of golf on Sunday.

Showered and dressed, I picked up my keys and whistled a tune as I made my way to reception. The receptionists greeted me with polite nods, and the looks of alarm on their faces changed to broad grins once I engaged them in conversation. I passed the reception area and hesitated, then continued to the bar. It was 6.30 pm, and Mother and Ernest sat deep in conversation, huddled up together at the bar. With no sign of Kirsty, disappointment welled, but I pushed it away.

'Hello, Mother, Mr Williams ... Ernest. May I order drinks? How's your wrist? You look comfortable.'

Mother waved her plaster cast around. 'A bottle of champagne would be wonderful, my dear. Make it four glasses because Kirsty will join us soon. Are you still in the doghouse? Ernest told me everything.' Her eyes twinkled.

'I did behave rather rudely—no excuses. I've booked us a table in the restaurant as a way of saying sorry. Would you care to join us?' I said.

'That's truly kind of you,' Ernest said. 'However, Margot and I have plans for a stroll and shall eat at a restaurant along the seafront.'

Kirsty approached. My head spun, and I gazed at the vision of beauty walking towards me. She wore a figure-hugging maxi dress, which flattered her curves. Our eyes met.

'I can't wait for Kirsty to meet Anthony this weekend. They'd make a lovely couple, and what beautiful children they would have,' Mother said.

Ernest glanced across at me and wore a look of realisation when he recognised the disappointment etched on my features.

'Come now, Margot. Don't get carried away. Kirsty may have a suitor already.'

'No, she doesn't. She mentioned last night she's looking for Mr Right, and I think Anthony could be the one.'

Ernest addressed Max, 'What about you? Would you like to settle down and have a family?'

My smile died when Mother interrupted my intended reply.

'Nonsense. Max isn't interested in settling down. He's far too busy with the business. Although, I don't doubt you'd make a marvellous uncle one day.'

'Good evening, everyone,' Kirsty said. 'So sorry I'm late. I overslept. It must have been the aqua aerobics.' Her smile appeared strained.

15

KIRSTY

ax isn't interested in settling down and having children? When I overheard the conversation, my excitement plummeted into the depths of disappointment.

Why did that bother me? It wasn't as if I had any interest in him.

Ernest stood to greet me. 'So glad you could join us, Kirsty. Would you like a drink?'

'No, let me get these,' Max said. 'What would you prefer?' Our eyes locked for a moment, and my stomach flipped.

Margot picked up her glass and waved it under my nose. 'How about one of these? This Cosmopolitan tastes divine.'

I nodded, and a shy smile touched my eyes and warmth spread over my cheeks.

'We won't be joining you for dinner, dear. Ernest and I are off for a stroll by the sea. We'll see you at breakfast. I'll let Max tell you all about his birthday party tomorrow. Hopefully, you have made no plans?'

'Yes, you two enjoy yourselves, and remember our chat, Max. Fancy a bag of chips, dear?' Ernest said.

The older couple left, and an uncomfortable silence hung in

the air. Max shifted in his seat and cleared his throat. 'Mother appears to enjoy spending time with Ernest.'

'Yes, I believe they're fond of each other. Do you mind?'

'Not at all. I've told Mother I would be happy if she met someone. Although, I'm not sure whether Anthony will be. He's coming to the party tomorrow, so we'll see what he makes of their friendship.'

A couple of hotel guests, wearing matching Hawaiian shirts, stood next to Max, who scowled when they knocked into him. On the verge of saying something, he took a deep breath and gave me a smile. I stirred my cocktail and stabbed a maraschino cherry into the drink. When I bit into the cherry, Max's gaze fixated on my lips, and I blushed.

'I hope your brother doesn't mind. Ernest is such a gentleman. What did he mean when he said, "*remember our chat*"?'

'He gave me a stiff telling off for the way I spoke to you over the phone. I must apologise again. There are no excuses.'

'Don't worry. I've forgotten all about it. It must have been a shock for you. If it's any consolation, I can be quite rude without thinking.' I blushed when I realised my insinuation. 'Now it's my turn to buy you a drink as a thank you for your generous hospitality,' I added.

Max shook his head. 'No need. Tonight's on me. Tell me, what brings you to Cyprus?'

'It's one place I've never visited. My being on sabbatical makes this the perfect time. It's a beautiful country, and the people are so friendly,' I said. 'But I've only been here for a few days and haven't had time to explore properly.'

'I'd be happy to show you around if you'd like? I'd quite enjoy the chance to see more of the island. Usually, I'm stuck in my office. How long do you plan to stay? I should return to England on Monday but can fly back later in the week. I'd suggest going out this weekend, but I have to go to the *dreaded* party.'

I nodded. 'That would be wonderful, thank you. Only if you have time, though. Why dreadful? Don't you enjoy parties?'

Max tapped his forehead and sighed. 'Usually, but not my own. Mother insists I have a party for my birthday, even though most of the guests are her friends. Watch out … she's already said you and my brother would make a lovely couple.'

I reached out and stroked his arm. 'Don't worry. She's mentioned it to me as well. Isabel tells me he's quite the party boy. I believe our paths crossed at my firm's Christmas do. He won't remember me because he was drunk. He's handsome. Good looks must run in the family.' I grinned.

a blush crept up my neck after I absorbed the compliment. *Did she flirt with me?*

'Shall we make our way to the restaurant? I've booked us a table. Or would you prefer another drink at the bar?' I said.

Kirsty took another sip of her cocktail. 'This is rather tasty, although perhaps we ought to eat soon. I feel quite tipsy.'

As she stood, her foot caught in her handbag strap, and she stumbled into my arms. For a few moments, I held onto her whilst she gazed into my eyes. I had an overwhelming desire to smother her face in kisses.

'Whoops, that cocktail was stronger than I thought.' She giggled. 'Best I eat something soon, or I'll make a fool of myself.'

I held out my arm. 'We can't have that. Let me take your arm and escort you to the restaurant.'

Kirsty hiccupped. 'Thank you. What a gentleman. Just like Ernest.'

'Remember to tell him tomorrow that his pep talk worked. I don't want to be in his bad books again, or yours.'

'Especially on your birthday,' Kirsty said.

I stood still and looked towards the floor. 'Actually, I'm 43 today. Mother thought it would be better to have the party at the weekend because we have guests arriving from all over the place.'

'You should have said—I would have brought you a gift—happy birthday, Max.' She stood on tiptoes and brushed her soft lips against my cheek. I longed to bury my face in her hair, and the smell of her perfume intoxicated me.

In a whisper, I said, 'Your company is the only gift I desire.'

We sprang apart in alarm when my body responded to her touch.

Heat exploded in my cheeks. 'I'm so sorry. That was inappropriate,' I mumbled with my gaze downcast.

Kirsty lifted my chin. 'Don't apologise. I'm flattered, and these things happen. Let's get something to eat, and afterwards, you can take me dancing.' Kirsty giggled. 'We could always meet up with Ernest and your mother to make sure they come back at a sensible time. She mentioned she wanted to replace her glow-stick bracelet.'

The heat subsided from my face. 'Good idea. My mother can be a bit of a handful, and tomorrow will be a busy day. Although I'd rather spend time with just the two of us.'

1 7

KIRSTY

J couldn't deny I found Max attractive, and judging by the bulge in his trousers, the feelings were mutual. In a panic, I suggested we meet up with his mother, and disappointment washed over me when he agreed so readily. Although the food looked and smelt delicious, I'd lost my appetite and picked at the marinated lamb, chickpea, and capsicum.

Max lowered his knife and fork. 'I'm not that hungry, either. Let's go dancing. I know where to find my mother.'

We made our way to the bar, and the thudding music drowned out our voices.

I pointed towards the dance floor. 'Look, there they are.'

Margot and Ernest stood on the dance floor and waved their arms around, surrounded by a group of energetic clubbers. Their faces looked the picture of joy, and Margot's new glow-stick bracelet shone around her cast. Ernest caught sight of us and came shuffling over.

'I hope you've come to rescue me.' He puffed a breath. 'Your mother has far more stamina than I do. Bloody delightful music, though. Why don't you two join her whilst I get the drinks in?'

Max patted him on the back. 'I'll find us a table then help you with the drinks, as I'm not much of a dancer.'

'Nonsense. We have a table already, and I'll get Christina to fetch the drinks. Now, dance with Kirsty before she gets swept off her feet by one of these young men.' Ernest winked.

I took hold of Max's hand, and we wove our way onto the dance floor.

Margot shouted above the music. 'I didn't think this was your scene, Max. More like your brother's?'

Max frowned and gripped my hand. 'Well, it's my birthday, and I'm allowed to have some fun.'

'Certainly, dear. But don't forget we have a busy day planned for tomorrow. I need you up bright and early to greet all our guests,' Margot said.

I wagged my finger. 'Don't be a party pooper. We'll make sure we all get an early night—including you.'

Margot sniffed. 'I'm going to find Ernest. I could do with a drink.' She walked away with her nose in the air.

'That's it, off you go, Mother. Mustn't cramp your style.' Max scowled.

What was all that about? I'd only known Margot for a few days, and she seemed so warm and friendly, but her attitude towards Max could get quite frosty. *Oh well, family relationships can get complicated, and it's not my place to interfere.*

I glanced across at Max, who fidgeted his feet from side to side. He looked so out of place on the dance floor.

I grabbed his hand and pulled him towards me. 'Come on. Let's have one dance and go back to the bar.' He pulled me closer just as the beat of the music slowed.

'Phew, good timing. I'm not sure I could keep up with that fast a rhythm,' he said.

I laid my face on Max's chest. Oh boy, did he smell good, and his muscular torso felt rock-hard through his shirt. I grew giddy with lust and had an urge to rip off his clothes and devour him. Max nestled his face in my hair and held me tighter. I tilted my face towards him—lips parted—ready to welcome his embrace as he leant towards me.

A tap on my shoulder broke the spell. 'Come and get your drinks before the ice melts,' Margot said.

Max nodded, and regret filled his face. Deflated, we followed Margot back to the table.

'You two seem to have made up,' Ernest said with a mischievous twinkle in his eyes.

'Yes, we've put all that behind us, and I promise not to step out of line again,' Max said.

'I hope not. We don't want Kirsty to think bad manners run in the family. I've told Anthony all about her, and he can't wait to meet her,' Margot said.

I sighed. 'I'm sure Anthony is genuinely nice, but I don't feel sure I want to get fixed up with anybody at present. Anyway, it's Max's birthday, so he should receive all the attention.'

Margot shook her head in lofty disdain. *Why is she being so mean to Max? I thought the two of them got on well.*

I stifled a yawn. 'Well, I don't know about the rest of you, but I need to get some beauty sleep, ready for tomorrow. Shall we make our way back to the hotel?'

'No, let's stay for another drink,' Margot said.

'I don't think that's a good idea. You've had an eventful day, and we should call it a night too,' Ernest said.

We returned to the hotel in silence, and I sensed that Max felt deflated. 'Do you fancy a nightcap?' I asked in a whisper. 'We could pretend we're going to bed and sneak back to the bar? I want to buy you a birthday drink.'

His face lit up. 'Good idea. I'll meet you at the bar in five minutes, although I do have a lovely bottle of wine in my office if you want to go somewhere quieter?' He gazed at me with a twinkle in his eyes.

'I fancy a cocktail, so the bar sounds better,' I said. If we met in private, who knew where it might lead? I didn't want to get caught up in another holiday romance or one-night stand.

For the benefit of Margot and Ernest, I told Max, 'I'm going to grab a bottle of water from the bar, so I'll see you in the morning. Goodnight, and thank you for a lovely evening.'

Max winked, and I giggled when I walked away.

A few minutes later, Max sat next to me. 'Phew, that was a close call. Mother and Ernest just snuck out of the building, tittering like a pair of teenagers. Back off to that club, and no second guesses who instigated it.'

'The two of them are a right pair and well suited. Would you mind if your mother dated Ernest?' I said.

'Not at all. Mother loved Father, but she spent a lot of her time on her own and was lonely for most of their married life. My father was a workaholic, and I can't remember them ever taking a holiday for just the two of them. I spent more time with him than she did.'

'If you don't mind me saying so, Margot seemed abrupt with you earlier. I thought you two got on well?'

Max signalled to the barman. 'We do, most of the time. Anthony's her favourite, which doesn't bother me. My father and I shared the same birthday, and as I grew older, we usually went out for a meal with just the two of us. Although Mother misses him terribly, I think she resented the time we spent together, so she's never made a fuss of me on my birthday. The party gives her an excuse to impress her friends. Though I'm happy to go along with it if it makes her happy.'

So, Max's tough exterior was just a front. The man who sat next to me was sensitive and kind. 'I suppose that makes sense, but it's not your fault, and Margot shouldn't take out her frustration on you.'

Max sighed. 'It doesn't help that people say I'm the spitting image of my father. The likeness gives a constant reminder he's no longer with us, and now I have overall control of the business as well. I let it all go over my head. Mother has her faults, but she means the world to me, and her heart's in the right place.'

Max chewed his lower lip. 'Are your parents still together? Do you have any brothers or sisters?'

I shook my head. 'Mum passed away five years ago, and Dad lives with my older sister and her kids. We all get on okay, and I adore my nephew and niece. Dad would love it out here. He's always going on golfing trips with his mates. Do you play?'

'Yes and no. I'd love to play more golf. In fact, my friend Roberto has arranged for us to play on Sunday. You'll meet him and his wife Elena tomorrow.'

'Are you sure that's such a good idea to play the day after your party? Hangovers and hot weather make a lethal combination.'

'To be honest, I'm not a big drinker and will make sure I take plenty of water with me.' Max glanced at his watch. 'On that note, I suppose we'd better call it a night. I need my beauty sleep for tomorrow.' He laughed.

'Same goes for me. I need all the help I can get at my age,' I said.

Max leant over, brushed a strand of hair away from my face, and took hold of my hand and gave it a gentle kiss. 'You don't need any help and are perfect the way you are.'

I giggled, and my insides melted at his touch. 'I bet you say that to all the girls.'

'No, only the ones I'm attracted to,' he said.

For a moment, we looked into each other's eyes, and then I lowered my gaze. Part of me wanted to kiss him, and another part wanted to run away. Reality slapped me in the face—Max wasn't right for me. He didn't want to settle down and have children, and I wasn't interested in a one-night stand. I leant across and gave him a peck on his cheek. 'You flatter me, although I think it's the cocktails talking.' I laughed. 'Thank you for a lovely evening. I'll see you at the party.' I stood up to leave.

'Kirsty, tomorrow night ...'

'Yes?'

'Erm, tomorrow night, the party starts at seven,' he said.

'Oh, okay, I'll see you then.' I'd thought he was going to say something else. Whilst I walked away, I glanced over my shoulder. Max sat at the bar and stared into space with a pained expression. He glanced up, and our eyes locked. He waved. *Just my luck. I meet somebody who.* … Okay, I fancied the pants off him, but we also had a deeper connection.

1 8

MAX

*S*o much for getting a good night's sleep. My phone
pinged at four with a text from Mother. She'd cancelled
our lunch date with the excuse her wrist pained her and she
needed to rest before the party. She didn't realise I'd seen her
sneak out, and I presumed she sent the message when they'd got
back. I tossed and turned for another couple of hours and, eventually, got out of bed at six. It would be a long day.

I could have kicked myself. Why didn't I just ask Kirsty if she
would be my date for the party? The main reason I looked
forward to it now was that Kirsty would be there. I wanted an
excuse to spend more time with her and keep her away from my
brother. Last night, I'd tried to tell her I found her attractive, but
she didn't take me seriously. *Perhaps I'm not her type. Well, I can't
sit here and feel sorry for myself all day—I have a party to organise.* The
first guests weren't due to arrive until 9 am, so I had plenty of
time to visit the gym.

The hotel sprawled in stillness, and only one other guest occu-
pied the gym. I greeted the lady with a smile, and she took this as
an invitation to approach. It felt too early to engage in conversation, so I turned away and put on my headphones. The treadmills
overlooked the swimming pool, and somebody swam up and

down the lanes. I squinted to see if I recognised the guest but could only make out the colour of her hair, which was the same as Kirsty's. I needed to get my eyes tested. Glasses seemed inevitable, but I had a reluctance to wearing them. Not because of vanity because I didn't like sunglasses either. My mind drifted to thoughts of Kirsty. Tonight, at the party, I'd ask her on a proper date, and not just as a tour guide. I picked up the pace on the treadmill and jogged with enthusiasm, and before I realised it, eight o'clock arrived.

Blimey, Ernest was up bright and early for someone who'd stayed out till four. He wore swimming trunks, ready for an early-morning swim, and appeared full of energy. He glanced up and waved, but his attention stayed focused on the person at the far end of the pool. The swimmer made her way to Ernest and climbed out. My jaw dropped, and I almost fell off the treadmill. Kirsty wore a bikini that barely covered her voluptuous body. My lower regions responded with a surge of desire whilst I stood there, captivated by her beauty. Ernest pointed towards the gym, and Kirsty glanced up. A look of alarm spread over her face, and she grabbed hold of her towel and wrapped it around herself. She waved and dashed away. I could have kicked myself, again. If only I'd worn glasses, I would have recognised Kirsty and joined her in the pool. *That's it. When I get back to England, I'll book an appointment to see if I'm eligible for laser eye surgery.*

THE FIRST GUESTS TO arrive were Roberto and Elena. They walked into the hotel with their arms draped around each other like a pair of honeymooners.

Roberto grabbed me in a big man hug. I asked, 'Where did you park the helicopter?'

'We came by car today. I can't afford to fly with a hangover. If you're free, I can take you out in the chopper next weekend. I'll give you a tour of the island.'

'That would be great, thanks. Would you mind if I brought a guest?'

Elena kissed me on both cheeks and smiled. 'Who's the lucky lady?'

I grinned. 'Kirsty. She's a guest at the hotel. You'll meet her at the party.'

'I thought you didn't mix business with pleasure?' Roberta said.

'No, it's not like that. She's a friend of a friend, and I promised her a tour of the island.'

I stopped and stared. 'Talk of the devil—she's over by the bar.'

Roberto followed my gaze. 'The brunette? Wow, she's a stunner.'

Elena said to Roberto, 'Put your tongue away.' Then she nodded at me. 'You'll have to introduce us.'

Kirsty waved and walked towards the lifts.

I panicked and shouted out, 'Hey, Kirsty, come and meet my friends.'

She walked towards us, and her face lit up with a warm smile. I said, 'These are my dearest friends, Roberto and Elena, who live in Cyprus.'

She held out her hand. 'Pleased to meet you. Are you here for the party?'

Elena nodded. 'Yes, and I get to spend a weekend away from the kids.'

Kirsty frowned. 'Sorry, I've got to dash. I've booked a hair appointment and am late. I'll see you at the party?'

I couldn't help but stop and stare whilst she walked away.

Elena teased, 'Friend of a friend? You have the hots for her, Maxwell. I don't blame you. She's gorgeous, and judging by the blush on her face, the feelings are mutual. Call it a woman's intuition.'

I sighed. 'If only that were true. Last night, I said I was attracted to her, and she laughed it off. Anyway, Mother has plans to set her up with Anthony.'

'Anthony? As if that will happen. I know he's your brother, but he's such a player. If you like Kirsty, then ask her out on a date,' Elena said.

'Yes, and tell her she's welcome to join us next week. She can sit up front with me in the chopper,' Roberto said.

Playfully, Elena tapped him on the arm. 'Behave yourself. Any more of that and we'll be sleeping in separate rooms. Perhaps I should cancel my weekend plans and chaperone you?'

Roberto kissed her on the top of her head. 'Only teasing, my darling. You know I only have eyes for one woman. We could fly by and collect you from the conference on Saturday if you can get away earlier. The award ceremony is at lunchtime?'

'It's an idea. Let me think about it. Anyway, let's unpack. And I want a long soak in the bath with no interruptions. I'll see if they have any appointments at the hair salon,' Elena said.

Roberto put the room key card in his wallet and picked up his hand-luggage. 'Well, I'm redundant for the afternoon. Fancy a drink at the bar later?'

I nodded. Anthony entered the lobby with a young woman by his side.

'My goodness, I hope she's brought ID. She doesn't look much older than my teenage niece, and I think she's forgotten to wear a skirt.' Elena laughed.

'Now, now, don't be bitchy, dearest. It doesn't suit you,' Roberto said.

I chuckled. 'Mother won't be impressed, but at least it'll stop her from playing matchmaker. I suppose I'd better hang about here and wait for the other guests to arrive. Let me know when you're free for that drink?'

Anthony strutted across the foyer like royalty. When he looked around for attention, the only person who acknowledged him was the receptionist, with a hostile glare. Presumably, another victim to his wanton ways. The young woman followed him with her eyes downcast.

'Good morning, Brother. Happy birthday for yesterday. I

brought you a present.' Anthony glanced towards his female companion and snorted. 'Not this delightful specimen. It was a bottle of your favourite vodka, although we drank it at the airport. Sorry about that, old chap.'

Which would explain the toxic fumes that filled the surrounding air. His guest could barely stand up, and her sun-kissed skin looked pale and drawn. Up close, she appeared to be in her late twenties rather than a teenager. I felt sorry for her and touched her on the arm gently.

'Hello, I'm Max. Let's find you a bottle of water, and I'll ask a member of staff to take you to your room whilst I have a word with my brother.'

She nodded, mumbled a thank you, and stumbled off with the receptionist.

'Look, Anthony, I don't want to give you a lecture, but Mother will be disappointed if you get up to your old tricks tonight. Promise me you'll stay on your best behaviour. I don't want you to embarrass Mother in front of her guests.'

'Blah, blah, blah ... all you do is nag. You're not my father. I've come here for a party, not a wake. Scouts honour, though, I promise to behave. No need to lock me up and throw away the key. Anyway, the reason I brought a guest was because I knew the party would be filled with stuffy old bags.' Anthony sneered in contempt.

'I can't understand what's become of you. Have you always been such a sexist pig and I just haven't noticed it? Father would turn in his grave if he could see the way you treat women. Our parents raised us to treat people with respect and dignity. What went wrong?' *Perhaps I'll get Ernest to give him a lecture on manners.*

For a moment, Anthony's eyes glazed over, and he looked dejected.

'What's wrong, Brother? I know I can be a bit of an ogre some-times, but I'm always here for you. Talk to me.'

Tears trickled down his face. 'First, *she* broke my heart, then Dad died. The only way I've coped is by drinking and partying. I don't mean to be such a prick, but I can't help myself.' He looked so vulnerable, and no longer the cocky person who'd swaggered into the hotel.

Who was she? I reached out, folded my arms around him, and whispered, 'I miss him, too. Why don't we find some time before you fly back to Portugal and have a proper chat? Let's see if we can sort you out. For now, you'd better check on your guest.'

Anthony nodded. 'Her name's Fleur. We've had a bit of a thing going on every time I've stayed in Portugal, and since I'm living there now, we've seen more of each other. I like her.' Anthony hiccupped. 'Sorry I drank your birthday present.'

I ruffled his hair. 'Don't worry. You can buy me another. Go and get some rest, and I'll see you later.'

Throughout the rest of the morning, guests filtered into the hotel. Around lunchtime, they had all checked in, and I could breathe a sigh of relief. Mother hadn't made an appearance, so I sent her a text and disappeared to my room. I stripped off my clothes and stood under a cold shower for a few moments, then laid on the bed and savoured the peace and tranquillity. I hadn't felt this relaxed in such a long time. With my thoughts consumed by images of Kirsty, I drifted off to sleep.

*W*hy did I get so embarrassed when I saw Max at the swimming pool? It didn't bother me when I paraded around in a bikini in front of Lucas, nor anyone else. Then, to make matters worse, I bumped into him again on my way to the hairdressers, and I looked as if I'd been dragged out of a hedge backwards. When his friend mentioned a weekend away from the kids, it hit a raw nerve with me, so I spoke abruptly and rushed off. I'd have to apologise to Elena when I saw her next.

At the half-empty hair salon, the receptionist sat with her arms draped across the counter and read a magazine whilst she blew bubbles with her gum. She glanced up at me and pointed to an empty chair. 'Take a seat. Someone will be with you in one moment.'

A flamboyant hairstylist greeted me with a smile. 'You must be Kirsty? My name is Dee, and I'll be taking care of you today. Oh, my goodness, you're even more beautiful up close. I can see why Mr Bright is smitten with you.'

Shocked, I said, 'I hardly know the man.'

'Tell me off if I'm talking out of line. I saw the two of you together in Whispers last night. I've known Max for fifteen years and have never seen him look at another woman the way he looked at you on the dance floor. It was as though there were no one else in the room.' She sighed. 'The girls here all have a crush on him, even moody pants over there, and she doesn't like anyone. How on Earth did you get him to go to a nightclub?'

I shook my head and shrugged.

'We've tried to get him to go to Whispers every time he comes in for a haircut. Mind you, it's the first time I've seen Margot there, too, and she looks like she's got a new suitor—Mr Williams?' Dee grinned.

I laughed. 'It's not my place to gossip, although Ernest is such a lovely man. Are you going to the party tonight?'

Dee said, 'Try to keep me away. It'll be the first opportunity we get to see Max let his hair down. That's if his brother behaves himself. Anyway, tell me more about you. How did the two of you meet?'

'It's not like that. My friend mentioned that friends of her family owned a chain of hotels and she contacted Max. I'm on sabbatical and have never been to Cyprus, so here I am. Margot has taken me under her wing, and Max and I went out for dinner last night. They're a lovely family.'

Dee raised her eyebrows. 'Girl, you really can't tell when a man has the hots for you? I'm only teasing. How long are you here for?'

'At least another week. I haven't quite decided where I'm going next, and Max plans to take me on a tour of the island next weekend, so I'm in no rush to go anywhere. Have you ever met any of Max's girlfriends?'

Dee smiled. 'No, I've never known him to be in a relationship, other than with Elena, but that was years ago.'

'Elena? I met somebody called Elena this morning, along with her husband Roberto.'

'Yep, that's the one. They weren't really an item. She tried to get Max to settle down with her but gave up and married his friend instead. Isn't she stunning? So down to Earth.'

Dee leant towards me and whispered, 'Elena and Max had a

night out recently, and she stayed over ... got the tongues wagging in the morning. Although, I'm sure nothing went on, as she's happily married. Mind you, I wouldn't throw Roberto out of my bed—he's such a hunk.'

For a moment, a pang of jealousy swept over me, and I brushed it to one side. I'm sure nothing untoward would have gone on between Max and Elena even if they did have a history. They appeared friendly enough around each other, so it must be just gossip.

'Have you always worked and lived in Cyprus?' I asked.

'No, the Brights employed me as a junior hairdresser at the hotel salon in South Talling when I left school, and Mr Bright Senior set me up with my salon here in Cyprus about ten years ago. My mum used to be his secretary but stopped working for him when I was born. Mr Bright kept in touch with her until he died. He was a lovely man—so generous. He sent me a birthday card and a gift voucher every year. I've always thought he had a soft spot for my mum.'

Dee placed a gown around my shoulders, inspected the ends of my hair, and led me to the washbasin. After a hair wash and scalp massage, I returned to the chair with a towel wrapped around my head.

I caught her eye in the mirror's reflection. 'What did your dad have to say about Mr Bright?

'I wouldn't know. I've never met my father. My mum raised me on my own, and I suppose Mr Bright was the closest person to a father-figure I had.'

Dee glanced towards the receptionist when the phone rang and rang and rang. I studied her face in the mirror. Alarm bells went off—surely not—was I the only one to think this? The family likeness seemed obvious. Dee had the same hair colouring and brown eyes as Max. Could Mr Bright be her father? It wasn't my place to ask, so I changed the subject.

'One of my best friends runs a hair salon in South Talling,' I said.

'What's the name of the salon? I might know it,' Dee said.

'It's called Indulge.'

'I know the one. Darius owns it. He's such an amazing hair-dresser—I've followed him on Insta ever since he was on that TV program—he should have won it. I wanted to work in his salon when I first started out, but they didn't have any vacancies. Then Mr Bright sorted me out with a job at the hotel, and the rest is history.'

'Do you have someone special in your life?' I asked.

Dee spritzed my hair, and I gasped when tears formed and her lower lip trembled. She took a deep breath.

'Not anymore. I was engaged to the love of my life, but he died just over two years ago in a bike accident. Today would have been our second wedding anniversary and his 35th birthday.'

The tears spilt onto her cheeks. 'Not only that, but I miscarried our baby shortly after his death. It was a little girl. The doctors said the shock caused it.'

Tears rolled down Dee's face, and her shoulders shook whilst she sobbed quietly. I got out of the chair, grabbed a box of tissues, and put my arms around her.

'You poor thing, that's terrible. Let's get you a cuppa, and you can tell me all about him. What was his name?'

She nodded and hiccupped. 'Thank you. He was called Jacob. I'm so sorry I've had a meltdown in front of you.'

I patted her on the arm and gave her a half-smile. 'You go out the back, and I'll come and find you. I'll just tell your receptionist that you need to take a break.'

'Don't worry. She won't notice I've gone, and my next client isn't due for another hour. The other stylist will be back soon, so she can take over,' Dee said.

As the kettle boiled, I noticed a wall covered with photos of Dee and, presumably, Jacob. 'Is this Jacob?' I said.

Dee nodded. 'Yes, I put the pictures up when he was alive and haven't had the strength to take them down, even though it breaks my heart when I look at them, especially on an anniversary. None of my friends will talk about him because they think I'll get upset, but I don't want his memory to fade.'

Her tears continued to flow, and sobs wracked her body. I cradled her in my arms and stroked her hair the same way as a mother with a child until the sobs subsided. 'Tell me all about him. How did the two of you meet?'

'A charity fundraiser. Jacob's little sister was diagnosed with leukaemia, and he raised money to support the charity by getting his hair shaved off.'

She pointed to a photo on the wall. 'This was the day we first met—just look at his hair—it was so long.'

'He's good-looking. I can see why you were attracted to him,' I said.

Between fresh bursts of tears, Dee told me how Jacob was too shy to ask her out on a date, so she made the first move. They'd only been together for six months when she fell pregnant, and Jacob proposed. Tragedy struck when he was on the way to collect the wedding rings from the jeweller, and a coach bus ploughed into him.

'I didn't get the chance to say goodbye, and his family turned their backs on me. They didn't like the fact I wasn't a catholic and said I brought shame on the family by falling pregnant out of wedlock. I wasn't allowed to go to the funeral.'

I gasped. 'That's terrible. What did they say when you lost the baby?'

Dee scowled and took a deep breath. 'His mother wrote me a nasty letter and said it was my fault her son died, and she was glad I'd lost our baby. She called me a whore and said I deserved only bad things to happen in my life. I forgive her, though.'

'How can you forgive such a vile person? I've never heard of anything so cruel.'

'I pity her more than anything. When she wrote the letter, she was grieving the loss of her son, and her daughter was receiving treatment for leukaemia. It must have messed with her head.'

'I know, but really? I'm not sure I could have been as forgiving,' I said.

Dee gazed at the photos, then glanced back at me. 'Margot arranged for me to have counselling and got someone in to run the salon. She helped me put my life back together, then her husband died, and we supported each other. I felt so angry for such a long time until I realised I was holding on to too much negative energy and couldn't move on with my life until I'd let it go.'

I couldn't imagine what Dee had gone through, and it didn't surprise me that Margot had been so supportive. Although, it sounded like they were there for each other in the end.

'What happened to Jacob's sister?' I asked.

'Sophie's been given a clean bill of health, and I've given her a job at the salon. She fell out with her mum after the way she treated me and hasn't forgiven her. I feel as though I'm her big sister and have taken her under my wing.'

Dee walked over to the wall of photos, kissed her finger, and touched one of Jacob's pictures. 'Sophie is the only person in my life who wants to talk about him, and we have our own private ceremony on the anniversary of his death. She'll pop by later to put up some photos of her and Jacob, and no doubt, to check up on me to make sure I'm okay. You'll meet her at the party tonight. Thank you for listening. I feel so much better now. Usually, I try to take the day off on our anniversary but couldn't today because it's Max's party and we're booked up later. I thought I'd be able to cope if I kept myself busy, but it just goes to show that you shouldn't bottle things up.'

I took a sip of my coffee, grateful I'd been able to support this poor and unfortunate soul.

'I know what you mean. I've suffered nothing like the loss you have but bottled up my emotions for years until I started journaling. It's been so therapeutic—such a great way for me to identify any issues that hold me back,' I said.

'How does that work? Isn't that just another way of saying

you keep a diary? I always had one on the go when I was younger.'

'Not quite. I write about any issues I feel might have a negative effect on me. Then I question my behaviour patterns and try to work out the cause. If somebody pisses me off, I write that in my journal and get it out of my system. I also write about the positive things I want to bring into my life, such as love and children. Although I may have left it too late to have kids.'

'Nonsense. You're only a few years older than me and have plenty of time yet. You and Max will make gorgeous children,' Dee said.

I laughed. 'I'm ten years older than you, and all I keep hearing is that it's difficult for women to conceive at my age. It would help if I could find myself a man who wanted to settle down with me.'

'Max?' Dee asked.

'According to Margot, he doesn't want a wife or children. Although she plans to fix me up with her other son, who really isn't my type.'

'I wouldn't worry about that. He's here with a woman, and if his Instagram stories are anything to go by, he's smitten with her,' Dee said.

'That's good. I won't have to avoid him all night. Well, I suppose I'd better let you go back to work, but I'm around for a while if you need a chat. Things will get easier as time passes, but don't be afraid to talk about Jacob. I look forward to meeting Sophie tonight. It sounds as though she takes after her big brother.'

Dee's eyes welled with fresh tears. She stood and gave me a hug. 'Thank you so much for your kindness. I don't think you realise how much you've helped. I'll sit here for a bit and will spend some alone time with Jacob. See you tonight?' She forced a smile.

Deep in thought, I walked out of the salon. Life was too short for regrets. Tonight, I would let Max know I found him attractive, too.

20

MAX

By eight, the party was in full swing. Mother's friends knew how to enjoy themselves and had sat around the bar for the past two hours whilst they drank copious amounts of alcohol. My brother introduced Mother to Fleur, and they appeared to get on well. Mr & Mrs Fitzpatrick, and their single daughter Felicity, trapped me at the bar. Felicity stood there mortified when her parents suggested the two of us *singletons* go on a date. They made their excuses and left me and Felicity on our own.

She clenched her fists nervously. 'Sorry about my parents. They can be so embarrassing.' Felicity stared at her shoes.

'Don't apologise. You have nothing to be sorry for,' I said.

'They're always trying to fix me up with any single Tom, Dick, or Harry. Don't get me wrong, you're a lovely bloke, just not my type.' Felicity nodded and beamed. 'Now, *she* is.'

Her eyes lit up, and I turned around to see who Felicity referred to.

Roberto and Elena made their way over to us.

In a whisper, I said, 'I'll introduce you. Although, sorry to disappoint you, but she's happily married.'

'That's a damn shame. Please don't tell me the sex goddess walking over here is married, too? She's definitely my type.'

I laughed. 'Sorry to disappoint you again, that's *my* friend. Why don't I introduce you to Marissa, our receptionist, when she gets here? I'm sure she'd love to meet you. Let me order you another drink and I'll introduce you to everyone.'

Kirsty came and stood next to me. She wore a deep-blue figure-hugging dress that brought out the colour in her eyes, and the smell of her perfume took over my senses. I found myself temporarily tongue-tied when I went to make the introductions. 'You look absolutely stunning,' I whispered in her ear.

'So do you,' she said with a sparkle in her eyes. Something about her had changed. She seemed more at ease and confident around me.

'Everyone, this is Felicity. She's here with her parents, my mother's friends.' I said.

One by one, the gang introduced themselves, and I soon relaxed and enjoyed myself as we stood around the bar and drank cocktails and champagne. At around ten o'clock, Dee and the rest of the girls from the hair salon joined us, and finally, my brother and Fleur arrived after they'd escaped the company of my mother.

'Sorry we're late. I had an exhausting day and fell asleep,' Dee said.

I gave her a hug and kissed her cheek. 'Don't worry. You're here now, and that's all that matters.'

The party atmosphere was contagious, and as soon as the DJ played his first tune, the girls giggled and laughed all the way to the dance floor. Kirsty attempted to drag me along with her.

'It's too soon,' I said. 'Let me have a few more drinks to unwind.' I laughed.

She wagged her finger and wiggled her hips. 'Okay, I'll let you off this time, but you owe me a dance.'

My eyes followed her to the dance floor, and I couldn't take my gaze off her as her body moved to the beat of the music.

'Put your tongue back in. You're drooling,' my brother said. 'Although, I can see the attraction. She's a stunner.'

'Keep your hands to yourself. She's my date and, anyway, you're here with Fleur,' I said.

'Well, we aren't official yet, so you never know. I might try to charm Kirsty away from you.'

My shoulders tensed, and I clenched my fists, but before I could retort, Roberto glared at Anthony and put his hand on my shoulder. 'Don't worry about him. He's winding you up, aren't you?' he said.

Anthony nodded and smirked. 'Course I am, Brother, but if things don't work out between you two, let me know, and I'll take her off your hands as Roberto did with Elena.'

Roberto scowled. 'Show some respect, little man. That's my wife you're talking about.' Now it was my turn to put a restraining hand on Roberto's shoulder.

'Behave, Anthony, and steady on with the booze. We don't want to upset anyone tonight,' I said.

Roberto had never liked my brother, and the feeling was mutual, but tonight they would have to put their differences to one side. After all, it was my birthday party.

Fortunately, the women made their way back over to the bar to replenish their drinks, and Fleur distracted my brother before he could do further damage.

Dee stood next to me and reached into her bag.

'Happy birthday, Max. I didn't get you much for your big day, but I thought you might like this.' She handed me a photograph in a frame. The picture showed my father, Anthony, and myself. Dad had his arms draped around us whilst we stood outside the hotel in South Talling.

'I remember when this was taken,' I said. 'It was my first day at work after I graduated, and Anthony worked at the hotel part-time. I don't think I've seen this photo before, though. How did you come across it?'

'I found it in an old box of pictures my mum had. I think she took the photo on her camera but must have forgotten to give it to Mr Bright, and I thought you might like it, so I got a copy blown up,' Dee said.

I gave her a kiss on the cheek. 'Thank you. It's a lovely, thoughtful gift. I'll hang it on the wall in my office.'

'You're welcome.' Dee hugged me. 'I miss your father, too,' she whispered. I glanced across at Kirsty, who wore a puzzled expression.

'Thanks again for this. I'll put it in my office before it gets damaged, and then I owe somebody a dance,' I said.

On the way to my office, party guests stopped me for a chat, and it took me a while to put the photo under the safety of lock and key and make my way back. When I glanced at the dance floor, alarm bells rang at the sight before me. Kirsty was wrapped in my brother's arms. He whispered into her ear, and she pulled away and slapped him on the arm, although she appeared to enjoy the attention.

Fleur was nowhere in sight. My mother was right ... they made a perfect couple, but I would not stand by and watch the pair of them get it on.

I couldn't sneak off because it was my party, so I went to Roberto and Elena and feigned a migraine.

'I think it's all the excitement of the party, and I'm not used to it. I suppose I'd better say goodnight to my mother and then I'll slip off quietly. I'm sure they won't notice I'm gone,' I said.

'What about Kirsty? I thought you were going to ask her out on a date?' Elena said.

'So did I, but it looks as though Mother was correct, and she's better off with Anthony.

Elena gave me a knowing glance. 'Don't jump to conclusions. They are just having a dance, and I'm sure your headache will go once she comes back.'

I bit my bottom lip and slammed my hand on the bar. 'I'm not in the mood to hang about and watch my brother in action. Why would Kirsty be interested in me when she could be with the life and soul of the party? Look, I'm going before they come over. Can you say I've got a migraine, please, and I'll see you in the morning?'

'You deserve better,' Roberto said with a sigh and nodded.

Mother sat at the bar with Ernest and her captive audience whilst she regaled them with her stories.

'What have you done with my daughter?' shouted a red-faced and glassy-eyed Mr Fitzpatrick. 'I hope the pair of you are on your best behaviour. I was just saying to your mother how funny it would be if we ended up related.'

'Sorry to disappoint you, but I don't think I'm her type. Don't worry, though. She's in excellent hands. Marissa is a lovely woman and will take care of Felicity,' I said.

His red face turned a deeper shade of beetroot and before he could reply, I gave him a curt nod and whispered to my mother that I was going to make polite excuses and leave. She brushed me to one side.

'Max is such a party pooper and is leaving us, and the night is so young,' she said.

'Leave the poor man alone,' Ernest said. 'He can't help it if he doesn't feel well. I blame it on all these flashing discotheque lights —they're enough to trigger a migraine. It used to happen to me all the time.'

'Thanks,' I said. 'You're probably right, and I haven't slept well lately.'

'Neither have I, but that's because I've been out raving with this one.' Mother pointed towards Ernest. 'Who's up for joining us later at Whispers, once this party's finished? We can all get matching glow-stick bracelets.' Margot broke out into fits of giggles and nearly fell out of her chair.

'Be careful, Mother. You don't want to fall and break any more bones,' I said.

'Don't worry. I'll look after her,' Ernest said.

Ernest gazed at my mother, and I tapped him on the shoulder. 'Could I have a quiet word before I slip off?'

He nodded and followed me around the corner of the bar to a quieter area.

'Thank you for spending so much time with Mother. I know this is a recent development, but I'd like you to know that if things were to progress, I wouldn't object. In fact, it would make my day. Mother has been a bit of a lost soul since Father passed away and deserves to find happiness. Although, I believe she was lonely before he died—he was such a workaholic.'

Ernest took a deep breath and coughed to clear his throat. 'When my wife passed away, I vowed I would never look at another woman. Until I met your mother. I have the utmost respect for Margot, and I hope that now I have your seal of approval, you won't mind if I court her properly. She's an incredibly special lady.'

'You have my blessing, although she can be a bit of a handful, so don't let her lead you astray.' I laughed.

Ernest slapped me on the back. 'No danger of that, young man. I've got her cards marked. Now, off you go and sleep off that migraine. I expect Kirsty will be disappointed to see you leave?'

'I wouldn't count on it. She's otherwise engaged on the dance floor with my brother.'

Ernest's gazed followed mine, and a look of concern spread over his face.

I straightened my back. 'Don't worry. I don't need a woman in my life. Work keeps me far too busy, and I don't have enough time for pleasure.'

'We all need the love of a wonderful woman and, mark my words, Kirsty has definitely got a soft spot for you,' Ernest said.

I gave him a wistful look. 'But my brother's more fun. Goodnight. See you tomorrow.'

Fortunately, I could now escape unnoticed around the back of the bar, and I sloped off into the night. Hopes and dreams of a new romance shattered in pieces.

21

KIRSTY

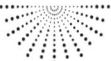

I must have stayed on the dance floor for over an hour. Every time I went to talk to Max, one of the girls dragged me back and insisted I dance to their favourite song. Fleur's shoes pinched her feet, so she went back to her room to change.

Anthony held out a hand. 'Come here, gorgeous girl. I could do with some female advice before Fleur comes back.'

He pulled me closer to him and placed a hand on my bottom.

'Cheeky, hands off.' I laughed.

'Whoops, my bad. It's a habit. I won't do it again. I'd better not upset the birthday boy.'

'Or your girlfriend,' I said.

'About girlfriends, I was thinking of asking Fleur to move in with me when we get back to Portugal. A part of me wants to make it official and propose to her, but I don't know whether it's too soon. I've known her for a while and get on well with her son, but I don't know if it's the right thing to do when there's a child involved. I don't want to cock things up. What do you think I should do?'

The tempo of the music slowed, and we swayed in tune to the beat.

'Do you love her?' I asked.

We stopped dancing, and Anthony gazed into my eyes. 'Yes, and it scares the living daylights out of me.'

'Why? Does she know?'

Anthony shook his head. 'No. What if I tell her and she doesn't feel the same? I'll look like a fool.'

'Sometimes in life you have to take a chance. Call it women's intuition, but I think she loves you too. I know it's a cliché, but life is too short, and you must do what feels right.'

He nodded and grinned. 'You're right. I'll ask her to marry me tonight. I know it's Max's party, but the timing feels good. Thanks, Kirsty. My brother is a lucky man. Now, I suppose I'd better let you find him.'

Arm in arm, we walked off the dance floor. Anthony went to tell Margot his good news. I looked around for Max but couldn't see him.

Roberto and Elena appeared to hold a heated conversation and stopped talking when I stood next to them. 'Have you seen Max?' I asked.

'He's not feeling great and went back to his room,' Roberto said.

'Yes, a migraine. He asked us to tell you because he didn't want to interrupt you and Anthony. You two seemed to get on rather well,' Elena said.

Alarm bells went off ... she was being frosty with me.

'He wanted a bit of advice,' I said. 'I can't say anything, but all will be revealed later.' I smiled.

Roberto guffawed. 'I bet it will. You looked rather cosy on the dance floor, and Max wasn't impressed.'

That didn't sound good. I prepared to defend myself, but I'd done nothing wrong. And who were they to judge? I bit my tongue and smiled. 'Perhaps I should find him to see how he is?' I said.

Elena shook her head. 'I wouldn't bother if I were you. Max

won't be in the right frame of mind to listen. I suggest you leave it until tomorrow.'

Did he actually have a migraine? Or had he jumped to conclusions when I danced with his brother?

In frustration, I sighed. 'Well, I'll call it a night now. I'm not in the mood to stick around either.'

I went to say goodnight to Margot and Ernest. Margot grabbed me in a hug, which startled me. 'Anthony has proposed to Fleur, and she said yes! I'm going to be a grandmother.' She squealed in excitement.

'Anthony didn't tell me Fleur was pregnant,' I said.

'She's not, but they plan to start a family as soon as possible.' Margot grinned.

'That's fantastic news. I'm thrilled for you and would stay to celebrate, but I'm going to call it a night because I feel quite tired. Shall we meet for breakfast?'

'Make it lunch, dear. Us oldies are going to Whispers after this party finishes.'

Ernest's shoulders drooped, and he yawned. The poor man looked shattered. 'Yes, dearest. We have to show these youngsters how it's done,' he said.

Dee and her gang danced energetically to Abba's *Dancing Queen* on the packed dance floor. 'I think Dee and the girls from the salon are going, too,' I said.

Margot flinched. 'Oh, I'm sure they won't want to be seen with old fuddy-duddies like us.'

Ernest smiled. 'Make your mind up, dear. One minute we're old ravers and the next we're fuddy-duddies. What's it to be?'

'Dee's lovely and is very fond of your family. How did you two meet?' I said.

Margot sipped her champagne and tilted her nose. 'It's a long story and something I don't want to think about tonight. I'll save that conversation for another day.'

She knows Mr Bright is Dee's father. It's not my place to pry, but if Margot wants to talk to me, I'm all ears.

I said my goodnights and headed to the foyer. On the way to the lifts, I saw lights shining underneath Max's office door. I knocked but nobody answered, so I turned the handle, and the door swung open. Max sat at his desk, eyes downcast whilst he stared at a framed photo. Tears cascaded down his face, and he didn't notice me straight away. I rushed over to him. 'What's the matter?' I glanced at the photograph, which showed his father with Max and Anthony. 'Do you want to talk about it?' I asked.

Max looked up, and scorn replaced the expression of grief.

'I don't want to keep you away from Anthony,' he said.

That's it. I've had enough of being judged for one night. I turned around and stormed off. When I got to the door, I glanced back at Max, who sat there with a stony expression, and shouted, 'For the record, there is nothing going on between me and Anthony. If you had asked me instead of jumping to conclusions, I could have explained what was going on. Your brother asked me for some advice about Fleur. He's fallen in love with her and wanted to know whether it was too soon to propose.'

Max sat there with his mouth wide open, too stunned to reply.

Our eyes locked. 'Oh, for the record, Fleur said yes. They've turned your birthday party into an engagement party whilst you sit here and feel sorry for yourself. You really are the most frustrating man I've ever come across.'

I didn't hang about for his reaction and slammed the door on my way out. A part of me wanted to run up to my room and pack my bags and leave, but another part wanted to curl up into a ball and cry. I shook my head. I'd do neither. Max Bright was history, and I didn't need someone like him in my life. I got as far as my room before the tears trickled down my cheeks. Every time I thought my life was getting on track, things went pear-shaped. I missed my friends, especially Henri, who always knew what to say to make me feel better. I glanced at my watch and reached for my phone. It was 8 o'clock in England, and hopefully, Henri would be at home, even though it was a Saturday night. I dialled her number, and she answered on the first ring.

'Hello, Danny,' she said.

'Sorry to disappoint you, but it's me,' I said.

She laughed. 'No, it's good to hear from you. What a lovely surprise. Danny's in London and I'm waiting for a call from him. I forgot you had a new mobile number. How's things?'

I burst into tears.

'Oh, my goodness, whatever is the matter?' she said.

I grabbed a box of tissues, blew my nose, and hiccupped. 'I miss you and want to come home.' Fresh tears poured down my face.

'That's not like you. What's going on? Tell me,' Henri said.

'I've had it up to my back teeth with men. Why am I so bothered about finding Mr Right when all I keep doing is meeting Mr Wrong or Mr Complicated?'

'Who are you talking about? I thought Lucas was just a brief holiday fling,' Henri said.

'He was and no, not Lucas, it's Max,' I said.

'Do you mean the Max, as in Maxwell Bright, who owns the hotel? Isabel came into the office this week and told me she'd contacted a friend, who'd sorted out a room for you. She showed me a picture of him. He looks rather scrummy.'

'That's the one. He may be scrummy, but he's the most obnoxious, frustrating person I've ever come across. One minute he's telling me he's attracted to me, and the next, he's accusing me of getting it on with his brother. How dare he? How could he even think I would do something like that? I've given him a second chance already, so that's it. He doesn't deserve someone like me.'

When somebody coughed behind me, I almost dropped the phone. 'You're right, I don't,' Max said.

Heat spread over my face. 'Sorry, Henri. May I call you back in a minute? I need to get rid of an unwelcome visitor.' I put the phone down and spun around. 'How dare you come into my room without permission?'

'Well, technically, I'm still in the corridor. You didn't shut your door properly, and it swung open when I knocked.'

I folded my arms and glared at Max. 'Well, it's your hotel. I'm surprised you didn't just march right on in. You're not a bloody vampire that has to be invited in.'

He stepped into the room and closed the door behind him. 'I would never be that disrespectful. I wanted to apologise for my behaviour.'

'Again,' I muttered.

'Yes, again. And before you did something rash such as book a flight home. I went to the bar, and Anthony shared his good news. If it makes you feel any better, my mother gave me a right earful when I told her I'd upset you again.'

Max glanced at his feet. 'I feel so ashamed and understand I've ruined everything between us. I'm such an idiot, but hopefully, one day, you'll forgive me, and we can be friends. I'll be out of your hair tomorrow because I've moved my flight forward and will go to the airport from the golf course, so you won't have to bump into me. Goodnight, Kirsty, and I *am* terribly sorry.'

Before I could reply, he left and closed the door.

'Good riddance,' I muttered.

Who needed a man in their life? I sat on my bed, and fresh tears trickled down my cheeks.

Get a grip on yourself. No man is worth tears.

I picked up my journal. I could have phoned Henri back, but this was something I needed to come to terms with myself. After I'd poured my feelings onto the pages, I re-read what had come to the surface. Was I partly to blame? Did I give off the wrong signals around men? I always knew I was a flirt and, on reflection, understood why Max could have gotten the wrong impression. If I'd explained things calmly instead of storming off, I wouldn't be sitting here feeling sorry for myself. I'd only known Max for a short while, and he had issues with his brother. My turn to apologise.

*E*ventually, at around three, I fell asleep. And, after a fitful night, the shrill sound of the hotel phone woke me. I grabbed the receiver.

'Good morning,' Elena said in a bright and breezy voice.

'I was checking to make sure you were okay and wondered if you wanted to meet for breakfast?'

My stomach growled in response. 'Yes, that would be nice. Give me twenty minutes to get ready and I'll come and find you.'

Guests checking in and out filled the foyer. Dee stood at the salon door. She looked up and beckoned me over.

'Morning. You look delicate,' I said.

Her eyes were red-rimmed, and she looked unkempt. 'I've only had two hours' sleep and I'm hanging,' she said. 'Where did you disappear to? We looked around for you, but you had gone. So had Max.' Her face broke out in a grin, and she grimaced. 'Ouch, it hurts to smile. Well, did you get it on with Max?'

I shook my head. 'No, nothing like that. We had a misunderstanding. Let's just say that ship has sailed.'

Dee let out a groan. 'Oh, no. You two are perfect for each other. Anyone can see that. Look, I'm busy all day and then I'm going home to crash, so do you fancy meeting up for a drink in the week?'

'That would be nice. I'm off to meet Elena now, so let me know when you're free. I hope you feel better soon, and don't forget to drink plenty of water.'

Dee saluted. 'Yes, boss. Have a good day, and I'll message you about that drink.'

I walked past a few guests I recognised from the party. They all appeared the worse for wear, and a few of them nodded and smiled at me.

Elena sat at a restaurant table and waved. She showed no signs of a hangover, and her skin looked flawless whilst her eyes sparkled. I commented on this.

'I stopped drinking early, unlike my husband, who woke up like a bear with a sore head. He's gone off to play golf this morning with Max. Although the pair of them were awake until the early hours and polished off a bottle of Jack Daniels between them.'

Feigning innocence, I glanced across and held her gaze. 'I thought Max had a migraine?'

'Roberto explained everything. I owe you an apology. When I saw how close you and Anthony were on the dance floor, and how upset Max was, I misread the situation and shouldn't have jumped to conclusions. I don't know you that well, and Max is mortified that he upset you again.'

I shrugged. 'It bothered me at first, and I had a right go at Max. Then, on reflection, I realised how the situation could have been misread easily. I planned to apologise to him today but understand he's off to the airport as soon as he finishes golf, so I suppose it will have to wait until next weekend.'

Elena paused until the waiter walked away from the table. 'Oh dear, he's not coming back next week,' she said. 'He was only coming for the helicopter tour and thought you wouldn't want to see him, so he cancelled. Let me message Roberto to see if I can get Max to change his mind. After breakfast, how about the two of us spend the morning at the spa? My treat as an apology? It would be good to spend some time with each other.'

I gave her a half-hearted smile. 'That's a wonderful idea, although you've got nothing to apologise for and don't have to treat me.'

Elena chuckled. 'I insist. Anyway, Roberto's paying—I have his credit card. He was in the doghouse last night. I hate it when he has too much to drink, because he turns into an arrogant pig.' She sighed. 'Oh well, I suppose he's allowed to let his hair down occasionally. Men.'

AT THE SPA, Elena and I chose a couple's treatment so we could spend more time together. We laid on identical couches, dressed in fluffy white dressing gowns whilst tranquil music played and the scent of lavender, blended with other essential oils, wafted over us. Our faces were smothered in honey and oats, and cooling cucumber covered our eyes. The more I got to know Elena, the more I warmed to her. She was down-to-earth and a good listener. I never intended to pour my heart out, but bit by bit, she peeled away at my layers.

'You should be a therapist. Look, you've made me cry, and the cucumber is going to slip off,' I said.

Elena reached out and touched my arm. 'Why don't you give Max another chance? He must like you, judging by the way he reacted last night. Yes, he can be stubborn and moody, but he has a big heart, and he'd make a great husband and father.'

Dread filled my stomach. Not this conversation, again. 'Don't get any ideas. I'm forty years old, single, and too old to have kids,' I said.

'Nonsense. I was thirty-eight when I had my daughter and forty when I gave birth to my son. Roberto and I tried for years to have children and it never worked out, so we stopped trying.

Then I fell pregnant. Why are women told to take contraceptives until they've been through menopause?'

I peeled the cucumber slices away from my eyes and sat upright. 'I suppose you're right. Although you have to have sex to fall pregnant.'

'Not necessarily. Have you ever considered a sperm donor?'

I shook my head. 'No. I don't want a baby if I'm not in a proper relationship.'

'Why not? There are plenty of single women out there who go it alone. Max wants children …'

'Not according to Margot.'

'Take what she says with a pinch of salt. She's only worried that somebody could knock her off her throne if Max found himself a wife.'

'You're not a fan of Margot then?'

'No. I like her, but I don't appreciate the way she takes Max for granted.' Elena took a sip of her rose-hip tea. 'Max and I had a bit of a thing before I met Roberto. Margot was always polite to me, although she frowned upon our relationship and made it obvious.'

I nodded. 'I get on well with Margot, but I wonder what it would have been like if I'd dated Max. Oh, well, now we'll never know.'

The therapists returned to the room to cleanse our faces. I drifted off to sleep for a few moments whilst my head and shoulders were massaged. Elena's groans brought me back to wakefulness. I glanced at her and saw that she was also getting a head massage. For a moment, I'd thought she was in the throes of an orgasm, and I chuckled with relief. Although always happy to talk about sex with my friends, I didn't want to share such a moment with them. The therapists left the room so we could get dressed.

'Blimey, you enjoyed that head massage.' I laughed.

'Sorry if I was too loud. I can't help but groan with pleasure when somebody massages my head. You should hear me when I have an orgasm. It's a good job we don't have neighbours. Max always refused to have sex with me at one of his hotels in case the staff overheard us.'

I frowned. Why did Elena have to comment about Max? That happened a long time ago, and I didn't want to hear about their old relationship. Did she still have feelings for him? I changed the subject. 'Aren't you worried the kids or the nanny will hear you?'

'No, that's all been sorted. Roberto got our bedroom sound-proofed a long time ago. Anyway, we don't have the time or the energy to have much sex nowadays, so it's not such an issue.' Her face grew serious. 'To be honest, Roberto hardly touches me nowadays.' Elena's eyes filled with tears. 'I don't think he finds me attractive anymore. Or, perhaps, he's got a mistress?'

She let out a sob. 'We had a blazing row about it last night. Whenever he has too much to drink, he can't perform. I'd hoped this weekend would give us the opportunity to rekindle our romance, and I even bought new underwear for the occasion, but it's still got tags on in the suitcase.'

I stood and wrapped my arm around her shoulders. 'I can tell by the way Roberto looks at you he's madly in love, so perhaps he has a problem down below? A friend of mine suffered from erec-tile dysfunction, brought on by stress, tiredness, and too much alcohol. Roberto may need to see a doctor.'

Elena shook her head. 'No, he's a proud man who will see it as a weakness, so he'd rather bury his head in the sand and not talk about it.'

'Don't give up on him. There are plenty of things he can do for himself to see if things improve before he sees a doctor. My friend quit smoking, took up exercise, and cut down on alcohol. He still works long hours but just started yoga, and that helps. I can imagine Roberto's job can be quite demanding?'

Elena frowned. 'Did your friend see a doctor?'

'No. Once he understood the problem, he changed his lifestyle, and things improved. Now, I'm told, he and his partner have an extremely healthy sex life. Although, they're about to adopt two young children and things could change.'

'Thanks, Kirsty. This all makes sense. I'll talk to Roberto when we get home and will see if he's prepared to do anything about it. Or I'll talk to a divorce lawyer. Things can't go on like this. Shall we grab some lunch? I could order a nice bottle of wine because I don't have to drive home.'

Elena reached into her handbag and took out her phone. 'Blast it. Roberto hasn't read my message, and Max never takes his phone onto the golf course. I hope he reads it before Max flies back to England.'

'Any chance you can give me Max's number? I only have his email. At least that way I can send him a text to apologise. I may not get the chance to see him again before I move on. Although I'd love to stay in Cyprus for a few more weeks.'

Elena clapped her hands. 'Don't leave me. You'll have to come and stay with me one weekend, and I can send a car to pick you up. Vineyards surround our house, and we could go on lovely walks. It's a beautiful location, but remote. Sometimes, I get quite lonely when Roberto goes away on a business trip. And though I have a nanny to help with the kids, I miss having my friends around me.'

I nodded. 'I know what you mean. I miss my friends, too. Coming away has given me time to think, and I've realised I've always taken them for granted. I may fly back home for a bit before I go off on my travels again.'

When we left the spa room, Elena linked arms with me and smiled. I grinned when I realised I'd found a good friend in her.

23

MAX

Sunshine beat down on us whilst we headed to the clubhouse. I played a rubbish game of golf and Roberto won hands down. He slapped me on the back. 'Your mind wasn't on the game today.'

I shook my head. 'I know. Gone are the days when I can drink all night, stay up late, and still play an early-morning round of golf. I blame it on you. Did you keep me out on purpose so you could finally win?'

'Not at all. I felt sorry for us because we're both in the doghouse with our women, and I still am. Hopefully, Elena will have calmed by the time I get back. Are you sure you can't postpone your flight home? We could go out for a meal later, and perhaps you could ask Kirsty to join us?'

If only it were that easy. 'No, I don't think so. I've already set up meetings for tomorrow, so I need to get back. Anyway, I don't think Kirsty will be so ready to forgive me this time. I behaved like a jealous fool.'

Roberto shook his head. 'Don't be so harsh on yourself. You don't know each other too well, and we all jumped to the same conclusions.'

I nodded. 'You're right. I'll let the dust settle and will send her an email in a couple of days, but I don't think she'll want to go on another date with me.'

We sat at the bar, and the barmaid's eyes lit up when she saw Roberto. She pouted and adjusted her blouse to expose more of her voluptuous cleavage. My mouth drooled when she placed a cold bottle of beer in front of me, and I downed the contents and ordered another.

I nodded towards the barmaid and nudged Roberto. 'She's got the hots for you.'

'I could do with a bit of fun. Maybe I'll get her number.' Roberto winked.

'No way I'll sit back and watch you flirt with another woman. Elena would kill me if she found out. You behave yourself.'

Roberto sat up straighter and ran his fingers through his curly black hair. 'It's nice to know I've still got it. Things haven't been great between Elena and me.'

'That's no excuse. Whatever difficulties you're going through, don't throw your marriage away for a bit of fun. Elena deserves more respect, and you need to sort out your relationship. If you're unfaithful, Elena will never forgive you. Think of your children, too. What I'd give to have a wife and kids.'

Roberto sat in silence for a while and looked like a scolded child. 'You're right. I love Elena with all my heart, and it would destroy me if she left me. You'd better pay the bar tab, and I promise not to look at another woman ever again.'

'I'm not saying don't look, just don't be unfaithful, even if it's only swapping numbers. Enough said, let's grab a bite to eat before I head to the airport.'

Later, when I settled the tab, the barmaid handed me a piece of paper and asked me to pass it to Roberto. I smiled politely and gave it back to her. 'Sorry to disappoint you, but my friend is happily married with children. I'm sure your boss, who happens to be a good friend of mine, won't be impressed if he finds out you proposition the guests, especially the married ones.'

The woman glared at me, and anger distorted her attractive features.

'A word of advice,' I said. 'You're an incredibly attractive young lady, but you need to have more respect for yourself and you'll soon attract the right man.' I placed a generous tip on the bar and left before she replied.

Roberto stuffed the last bite of a clubhouse sandwich into his mouth, sat back, and patted his stomach. 'That hit the spot. Elena won't let me eat white bread and chips at home.'

I laughed. 'Once in a while won't hurt, but you have to take better care of yourself. We aren't getting any younger, and you have a young family to support. I'll be back in Cyprus in a few weeks, so I could come and stay at yours for the weekend and play a few games of tennis on your court. When was the last time you used it?'

'I don't get the time. Either I'm at work or out in the helicopter. So many of my friends and customers want a guided tour of the island, and it takes up a lot of my spare hours. Although, I enjoy it, so I always oblige. It's a shame you had to cancel next weekend. I used to swim every morning, too, but I don't seem to have the energy to do that either.'

I placed my napkin on the table and sighed. 'It sounds like you're in danger of turning your hobby into a business, but if that's what you want then why don't you get a manager in to run the wineries, or at least employ someone who can take over some of your workload? You've built your business empire, and now it's established, you can take more time for yourself and the family. And you must take care of your health. Look at my father —he died too soon, and he spent all his life at work, and see where it got him.'

Roberto nodded. 'I've felt stressed, and I must admit, I do worry about my health. My father died from a heart attack when I was eighteen. He was only forty-nine, nearly the same age as I am now. What if it's in the genes? Though I passed my medical when

I applied for my helicopter's pilot licence, I was fitter back then. I want to be around to see my children grow up.'

We made our way outside and walked towards the car park. 'First things first,' I said. 'Get a full medical check, cut out cigars, and stop eating rubbish food behind Elena's back. As for the helicopter, it's your choice, but I would limit it to personal use. Already, you've earned enough to retire. Although, I still want you to take me out next time I'm in Cyprus.' Max smiled. 'How about you pick me up when I'm back?'

Roberto nodded. 'That sounds like a good plan. You'll never guess what ... Elena wants me to do bloody yoga, but it's not my sort of thing.'

'Yep, me as well. She suggested it a few weeks ago, and I dismissed it. Though it's good to keep an open mind, and now I think I'll give it a try. Perhaps Elena would show us how to do it when I come and stay.'

Roberto snorted. 'I'm not sure about that, but I'll clear some space at work, and we'll make a long weekend of it. It's been so good to talk. I haven't even told Elena my worries. You're a good friend. On that note, I suppose I'd better let you get to the airport, and I'll make it up to Elena. I'll ring for a taxi. Oh, darn it, my battery's gone flat.'

I glanced at my phone. 'I can't get a signal here, so I'll get a member of staff to call for us to save us waiting out here in the heat. One more drink for the road?'

A few hours later, I rested back in the aeroplane seat and my mind drifted to thoughts of Kirsty. She stirred so many emotions in me, and I wished I could turn back time and put things right between us.

24

KIRSTY

After the excitement of the weekend, things settled into a quiet routine, and I spent the next few days either at the gym or relaxing by the pool with my nose stuck in a book. Elena kept in touch with texts and arranged for me to stay with them. She had a work conference the following weekend, so we planned my visit for the week after. Ernest and Margot had become inseparable, though they still invited me for dinner every night. I accepted gladly but felt like a gooseberry.

Dee and I made plans to go for a meal on Wednesday night, and as she didn't work on Thursdays, I had no doubt we would end up at Whispers. After the disastrous weekend, I needed some fun. Max hadn't replied to my email, so I assumed he didn't want to bother. Oh well, I had plenty of friends and didn't need another. As luck would have it, he wasn't due to come to Cyprus for a couple of weeks, and I wasn't sure if I'd be around. However, I didn't think I was ready to leave such a beautiful country, and I'd met some amazing people. I felt reluctant to take advantage of Max's generosity for much longer, even though I expected to pay for my food and drinks, so I mentioned my concerns to Margot at dinner.

'Don't worry, my dear. You can stay as long as you like. I enjoy your company and would miss you terribly if you were to leave.' Margot patted her mouth with a napkin. 'The hotel is quieter at this time of the year, so we have plenty of room. However, if you want a change of scenery, you could rent my flat for a few weeks. My last tenant left a month ago, and it's stood empty ever since. It's within walking distance of the shops and bars, and we could meet up every day. Of course, you would have full use of the hotel facilities.'

She leant across the table and took hold of my hand. 'We've known each other for only a few weeks, but you're like the daughter I never had, and I'm so grateful you want to spend time with me.'

A lump formed in my throat. 'I'm fond of you, too, and I'll miss you terribly when I leave. I would feel happier if I could pay my way. So, yes, I'd love to rent your flat. On another note, I need to watch my weight, and the hotel food is so delicious, my waistbands have grown rather snug.' I laughed. 'I'm not much of a cook, so no doubt the weight will drop off once I have to fend for myself. Salads are my speciality.'

Margot patted her abdomen. 'I know what you mean. I rarely eat three meals a day, but Ernest insists we do, and I've developed a bit of a belly.'

'Nonsense. You have a wonderful figure. By the way, where is Ernest?'

Margot waved her hand around. 'On the phone to his daughter.' Her face grew serious. 'I need some advice on a delicate matter.'

I nodded. 'Talk to me.'

She covered her mouth with her hand and whispered, 'It's about S.E.X.'

'Okay. What do you want to know?'

'Last night, Ernest asked if we could be more than just friends. He's invited me to visit his family next weekend in England. I said yes, but the thing is, they've only got one spare guest room, so we'll have to share. I'm not sure if I'm ready to share a bed with another man, and I haven't had *you-know-what* since I was in my fifties. What do I do?'

Oh blimey, I'm not used to these sorts of conversations with a mother figure. 'Talk to Ernest. I'm sure he'll understand how you feel. You're fond of each other and could take your relationship to the next step before you fly to England.'

Margot's eyes widened. 'Oh, my goodness, I'm not sure I'm ready for that. Isn't it too soon?'

A blush spread over her face, and she fanned herself with the menu. 'I struggled to have sex after I went through menopause, and eventually, Gregory gave up. Things weren't quite the same in certain departments. How should I put it? They were quite dry. Anyway, he wasn't bothered because his mistress was much younger than me.'

I reached across the table and squeezed her hand. 'His mistress? Poor you. How long had you known? Oh, dear me ... please don't cry.'

She shook her head and reached into her purse for a tissue. 'I don't know what's wrong with me. I'm all over the place with my emotions. Never mind. It's history. Anyway, Ernest will be back soon, and I don't want him to see me upset.'

I glanced at my watch and nodded. 'I'm here if you want to talk. What are your plans for tomorrow? We could have a girl's day out and have lunch and go shopping. I need a new outfit for when I go out with Dee tomorrow night.'

Margot flinched. 'Yes, that sounds wonderful, and afterwards, I'll show you the flat so you can decide if you want it.'

I handed her my vanity mirror and tissue. 'Freshen up your lipstick.' Ernest entered the restaurant. 'I'm going to go back to my room to order room service and could do with an early night. We'll have a proper chat tomorrow, and you can tell me everything.'

꙳

BACK IN MY ROOM, I ordered a chicken and avocado salad and couldn't resist adding a bottle of wine. Fortunately, I had a fridge in my room and didn't have to drink it all in one night. Who was I kidding? The food should arrive within the hour, which gave me enough time to run a sumptuous bubble bath and relax. Since I'd arrived in Cyprus, I'd not had the urge to pleasure myself, even though Max had ignited a fire in my belly and the flames hadn't extinguished. Come to think of it, I did feel quite horny, so I reached into my bedside cabinet and took out my vibrator. I always bought waterproof sex toys, as I enjoyed masturbating in the bath, which was something I'd done since I first discovered my pleasure. Because I shared a bedroom with my sister, the bathroom was the only place of privacy I could find.

I leant back in the bath, and whilst the jets from the spa massaged my back, I focused my attention on my hidden pleasure. My body responded to the warmth of the water and the intensity of the vibrations. In no time at all, sensations built, but I didn't want a release from this roller-coaster ride so soon. I cast the vibrator to one side, and with one hand, gently circled my clitoris, and with the other, I pinched my erect nipples. It did no good. I no longer had control, and my body wasn't prepared to prolong the journey. Within moments, the volcano erupted. I let out a satisfied cry, and the tension left me. Pure ecstasy consumed me.

A knock on the door brought me back to my senses, and I jumped out of the bath and wrapped my body in a fluffy white towel. Room service already? I checked my watch and realised I'd lain in the bath for nearly an hour. I peered through the peephole and opened the door to the waiter. He pushed the trolley into the room and glanced towards the bathroom, where the door was wide open. His face lit up in a broad grin when he caught sight of my vibrator, which rested on the edge of the bath. My face flushed crimson, and I grabbed my purse to give him a tip.

'Have a good evening, madam, and please let me know if you need anything. And I mean *anything*,' he said.

I held his gaze for a few seconds. 'No, thank you. I have more than enough to satisfy me.' Now it was his turn for his face to flush scarlet.

৯৯

THE CHICKEN SALAD TASTED DELICIOUS, and I washed it down with several glasses of wine. However, I craved something sweet and contemplated a trip to the hotel shop to buy chocolate. Then I remembered I'd bought a box of pistachio-flavoured loukoumi for my sister. If I opened it, I'd be tempted to eat it all, and my clothes were snug already. I had to work hard to keep the weight off, but it hadn't been such a problem until now. Oh well, a few pieces of Cypriot delight wouldn't hurt.

My thoughts drifted to Margot and her situation with Ernest. Initially, I planned to suggest we visit a shop that sold sex toys, amongst other things, but I felt unsure how to broach the subject. I'd known Margot for only a few weeks, and we weren't close enough to have the same sorts of conversations I'd have with my other girlfriends. I could suggest she bought herself a dildo, but how would she react? A few friends were going through menopause, and some complained about dryness. Was there a remedy? My mum never discussed her menopause, so I couldn't offer Margot any advice. Unless ... I picked up my iPad and typed into the search engine, 'tips for sex over 60'. The results showed so many sites to choose from, all offering similar advice. I remembered Henri subscribed to the *Ageing Gracefully* magazine, so I clicked on their website to see if they had any articles on the subject. Sure enough, I found plenty to read, and the magazine offered back issues for sale. Also, customers could sign up for an overseas subscription. I skimmed through the articles until I came across a post that mentioned vaginal dryness. I'd heard about the condition but didn't know why it could happen. Apparently, it was because of a drop in oestrogen levels, and our bodies produced less moisture when we grew older. Poor Margot must have felt too embarrassed to talk about it with anyone and accepted she could no longer have sex. The article suggested you use a water-based lubricant to make sex more comfortable, and I felt sure we could get this in town. Perhaps I could email Margot the link to the article, so she'd have time to read it before we went shopping. I wondered if she'd ever watched *Grace and Frankie* on Netflix? It was one of my favourite TV shows and featured two women who set up a business with vibrators designed for women over seventy. Did such things exist?

I clicked on my emails to send the link and felt disappointed to see that Max hadn't yet replied. Fuelled with a few glasses of wine, I typed another message. How dare he ignore me after I'd tried to apologise?

KIRSTY

*M*argot greeted me with a wave and a broad smile. Ernest stood next to her with his chest puffed out and a sparkle in his eyes. Something had happened between them.

'Good morning,' he said. 'Don't worry. I'm not coming with you. I'm here to wave off my beautiful lady.'

'I don't mind if you want to come, but you might get bored following us around clothes shops all day,' I said.

'No, no, I'm going for a swim and will meet Miriam for a spot of lunch.'

'Have a lovely time, my dear, and say hello to Miriam for me,' Margot said.

I studied Margot's face—not one trace of sarcasm—oh, I couldn't wait to get Margot on her own so I could interrogate her.

Margot stood on tiptoe and gave Ernest a kiss on the lips. The look of adoration on his face warmed my heart.

As soon as the taxi driver started the engine, I launched into my interrogation. 'Have you got something to tell me? The pair of you look madly in love with each other—did you have a sleepover?'

Margot blushed. 'Well, if you must know, yes. Ernest stayed

over last night but we didn't get up to you-know-what. We had quite a few kisses and cuddles, and it was amazing.'

'How did that come about?' I asked.

'Well, we went back to my room to grab a shawl because we had plans to go for our evening stroll, and it felt chilly. I'd left my laptop open on the table, and Ernest saw your email when it flashed up on the screen. Apparently, his late wife used to buy *Ageing Gracefully*, and Ernest loved to read it. Whilst I went to powder my nose, I suggested he read the article, and he put two and two together.'

The taxi driver adjusted his mirror and lowered the volume on the radio. Margot nodded towards the driver and put a finger to her lips.

'Okay, you can tell me later over a glass of wine. Or is it too early?' I said.

'Absolutely not. Let's start the day as we mean to go on. There's a marvellous bar I frequent around the corner from the shops. The taxi can drop us off there.'

§▲

THE BAR OWNER'S face lit up when he saw Margot, and he rushed over and gave her a hug. 'Hello, my darling. I haven't seen you for a few weeks. Where have you been hiding?'

'I've been otherwise engaged,' Margot said.

He held her hand and studied her fingers. 'Have you met another man? Are you cheating on me?'

'Yes, Kostas, and I'm sorry to say my heart is no longer yours.' Margot chuckled.

'Who is this man? I must meet him.' His gaze shifted towards me. 'But I see you have brought me a new friend. What's your name, beautiful lady?'

Before I could reply, a lady walked up behind Kostas and smacked him playfully with a tea towel. She wore an apron decorated with flowers, and a scarf covered her hair. 'Behave yourself,' she said. 'You're a married man.' She kissed Margot on both cheeks.

Margot said, 'This is Ariana, Kostas's wife, and this is my dear friend Kirsty. She's staying at the hotel and hopes to move into my flat for a few weeks. You'll be neighbours.'

Kostas winked. 'If you need help around the flat, I'm your man.'

'Don't worry,' Ariana said. 'He's harmless and flirts with all the ladies. If you ever need help, please ask. I'll give you my phone number before you leave. Let me take you to your table and bring you a bottle of your favourite wine, on the house.'

I followed Margot to a table at the front of the bar, which looked out onto the terrace. A few guests were already seated outside and gave Margot a wave after they caught sight of her.

'People in Cyprus are so friendly,' I said.

Margot nodded. 'Yes, which is why I spend most of my time here. I've made quite a few friends in Cyprus. I love Portugal, but the hotel is further out of town, which makes it harder to meet people.'

Suddenly, Margot picked up a menu and hid her face behind it.

'What's wrong? Who are you hiding from?' I said.

'Two nosey-parkers from the walking group. They saw me the other night with Ernest, and if they see me now, they'll want to know the ins and outs of a duck's derriere.'

I peered out of the window and watched two women look around and take seats. One of them caught my gaze and frowned before she returned her attention to her friend.

'They can't see you,' I said. 'Never mind them. What happened last night?'

Margot fanned herself with the menu and giggled. 'Well, you can imagine the shock and horror I felt when I realised what the article was about.'

'I'm so sorry. I meant it for you to read,' I said.

'Don't apologise. After I got over the initial embarrassment,

Ernest explained that his late wife had experienced a similar predicament. She suffered from atrophic vaginitis—see, he even knew the medical term for it. It was easy to talk to him about sex, and he was ever so understanding. He doesn't want to rush things between us and suggested we take one day at a time and get to know each other more. I never thought I would ever have sex again, especially at my age.' Margot rested her chin on her hand and sighed.

I smiled. 'You may be in for a pleasant surprise. Another article explained that women over sixty could enjoy sex more than in their younger years. Apparently, you're more body confident and less worried.'

'Don't bank on it, although Ernest encouraged me to get undressed in front of him, and it felt liberating. I never undressed in front of Gregory, and we never spoke about sex.' Tears welled in her eyes. 'I miss him terribly, and a part of me feels I'm being unfaithful, which is ironic considering he cheated on me for over thirty years.'

I took hold of her hand and gave it a squeeze. 'Why did you stay married to him?'

'Because of the children. They idolised their father, especially Max, and I didn't want them to find out that he was a cheating so and so, and that they have a half-sister.'

So, Margot *had* known about Dee since she was born. I nodded, 'Dee?'

'Yes, how did you know? Did she tell you?'

'No, when she told me about her relationship with Mr Bright, I noticed the resemblance between her and Max and worked it out. Her mum used to work for Mr Bright, didn't she?'

Margot scowled and tutted. 'Yes, Ruth was Gregory's secretary for over fifteen years before she left to have a baby. I was unaware of the affair until I found a receipt for a pram and cot. When I quizzed Gregory about it, he broke down and admitted he was the father of her child and was in love with Ruth. We came to an arrangement that he could continue the affair if he stayed married to me and his daughter never found out about their relationship. He agreed because he didn't want his sons to discover he was a cheat.'

I swallowed a lump in my throat. 'That's so sad. Poor Dee never knew who her father was or that she had two half-brothers.'

Kostas appeared with our wine and interrupted our conversation. He gave Margot a gentle pinch on the cheek and turned around and winked at me. After he poured the wine, he placed the bottle on the table. 'She's broken my heart,' he said as he walked away.

Margot took a sip of her wine. 'Kostas is such a lovely man. He may be a bit of a flirt, but he loves his wife. I only just found out that his family owns Whispers too—his brother runs it. I must tell him on the way out that I've been there a few times. Now, where were we? Ah, yes, Dee ... I wish I could turn back time so Dee knew her father. He supported her financially throughout her life and has left her well provided for. They were fond of each other, but there are times I wish she knew, especially after her fiancé died in that accident.'

I shuddered at such a sad story. 'Dee told me all about that and said how supportive you were. Why don't you tell her about her father? I'm sure she would understand.'

Margot took a sip of her wine, and we sat in silence for a few moments. 'It's difficult, and I don't think it's my place to break the news. It should be her mother's, although that's not possible because they don't talk to each other.'

'Dee mentioned nothing. What happened?'

'When Gregory died, Ruth went off the rails for a while. I suppose grief affects us all in different ways, and in her case, she developed a drinking habit. She became quite spiteful, especially towards Dee. Now she's met another man and is tee-total but wants nothing to do with her daughter.'

Ariana approached our table with a tray laden with bread and olives and placed it in front of us. I tore off a piece of bread and stuffed it into my mouth. 'That's so sad. She's had little luck in her life. It's up to you, but do you think you should tell her?'

Margot nodded. 'I'll give it some thought, but I'd want to tell my sons first. Enough about that subject, let's drink up and get to the shops.'

I took my phone out of my bag and handed it to Margot. She held the device at arm's length and squinted. 'I can't read that, dear. I've left my glasses back at the hotel.'

'It's a website for a shop called *Aphrodite*. Do you know where it is? It sells lingerie and other discreet items, and I'm sure they'll have exactly what you need.'

Margot blushed. 'I'm so glad you're with me because I'd never go there on my own.'

When we stood to leave, I felt off-balance and noticed Margot's cheeks looked flushed and her eyes shone with excitement. We bid our farewells to Kostas and Ariana with the promise of a return visit. After we stepped outside, the women from the walking group noticed Margot and invited us to join them. Margot declined and took great relish in their reactions when she explained we were on our way to *Aphrodite*.

Tastefully decorated, the boutique had discreet lighting, which shone on mannequins dressed in beautiful, luxurious lingerie. We browsed the store for a while, and I picked up a baby-doll nightie and matching underwear. 'These are beautiful. Why don't you treat yourself?' I said.

Margot scrunched her nose. 'Aren't I too old for them? I'd feel silly. They look uncomfortable, and the nightdress won't keep me warm.' She crossed her arms. 'You can't beat Marks & Spencer's underwear.'

'You're not too old,' I said. 'And imagine Ernest's reaction when he sees you in them.'

She tutted and sighed. 'I don't know if I'm confident enough. I never dressed up for Gregory.'

'It's up to you. But remember, you've started a new chapter in your life, and Ernest isn't Gregory. I know you loved him but ...'

'Enough said. You're right. Do they come in a different colour? Because I don't suit black.'

Towards the rear of the store, shelves stood stacked with a variety of sex toys, and I suggested Margot purchase a vibrator.

'No, dear. The underwear is enough for one day. Next time, perhaps,' she said.

I smiled and nodded. It was Margot's choice, and I'd nudged her out of her comfort zone already. Twenty minutes later, we left the store with bags full of lacey underwear and several bottles of lubricant and made our way to a big department store that housed a variety of fashion brands, beauty products, and home furnishings.

SEVERAL HOURS LATER, my good mood dissipated with each outfit I tried on in the changing room. Nothing suited me, and the fabrics stretched taut over my body. I studied the subtle changes in my shape in the mirror and flung dress after dress on the floor in frustration. Patiently, Margot sat outside the curtain and complimented me on each outfit whilst I fought back the urge to cry in despair. My weight was something I'd been able to control for an awfully long time and the stark realisation I'd piled on the pounds caused me anxiety. I didn't want to impose on Margot's good mood, so I made up an excuse for us to leave the store empty-handed.

Over lunch, I picked at my salad leaves whilst Margot tucked into a juicy burger and a plate of sweet-potato fries.

'You should have ordered the burger. It's delicious,' Margot said, and cheese dripped onto her plate.

'Not after realising how many pounds I've piled on since I left work,' I said.

'Nonsense, dear. You have an amazing figure,' Margot said.

'But nothing fitted. It's so frustrating to see how some people can eat what they like and never gain a pound whilst I only have to look at a cake to gain weight. You're so lucky.

'Why don't you buy a bigger dress size?' Margot asked.

The thought made me shudder, and I shook my head.

Margot studied my reaction with a look of concern. 'Just because I've always been slim and never had to watch my weight, doesn't mean that I'm lucky. When I was a teenager, my hair was quite short, and I looked like a boy. For years, I despised my flat chest and stick-like figure. When I got pregnant with the boys, I loved my bigger boobs and curvy hips, but the weight dropped off once I breastfed. Now I still look like a stick even though I've got bigger boobs. I'd love to have feminine curves like you. Now, stop staring at my fries and help yourself.' Margot laughed. 'Oh, I wish I had a daughter like you.'

The sweet-potato fries tasted delicious, and within moments, the bowl sat empty. I smacked my lips together and dabbed my mouth with a napkin. 'Dare I mention Dee?'

'You read my mind,' Margot said. 'She could have been the daughter I never had. How did we get things so wrong? She was an innocent child, and we used her as a bargaining chip. How will I ever make it up to her?'

'By telling her who her father is?' I said.

'Yes. I'll phone Max and tell him when we get back to the hotel. But how will I pluck up the courage to speak to Dee? What if she hates me?' She muffled her sobs into a napkin.

Though Margot was partly to blame by keeping this thirty-year-old secret, I couldn't help but pity her. After all, she'd stayed silent to keep her family together and protect her children, and she had to share her husband with another woman for all those years. An idea formed. 'Why don't you meet Dee and me tonight before we go out, and you can break the news then? I'll be there to intervene if things go wrong.'

'I couldn't do that. It would spoil your night out.' Margot shook her head.

'No time is a suitable time, but at least I can be a shoulder for

Dee if she needs one. No doubt the news will come as a bit of a shock,' I said.

'That's kind of you. I'll speak to Max first and see what he thinks before I make up my mind. Oh, my goodness, look at the time. We were going to look at the flat,' Margot said.

'Let's save the flat for another day. Perhaps at the weekend? We could bring along Ernest too, and he can meet Kostas.' We both laughed with relief, and the sombre mood lifted.

26

MAX

I put down the phone and shook my head in amazement. As soon as Mother spoke, I could tell by the tone of her voice that something was amiss, although I would never have guessed what. I had a half-sister. Dee was my half-sister.

Initially, I felt angry at Dee's mother. *How dare she keep this a secret all these years? My father deserved to know he had a daughter.* I wanted to drop everything and fly to Cyprus to console my mother when her sobs intensified. She took a deep breath, and the rest of the story tumbled out. I couldn't believe my own parents had conspired to spin such a web of deceit and had deprived an innocent child of a father and a family. How did my mother stay married to a cheat? My father, the man I idolised, had committed adultery for the best part of my life. Did my parents even love each other? Mother explained she would phone Anthony with the news as soon as our call ended. Her voice faltered, and she asked my permission to break the news to Dee. I agreed, although I wished I could have been there to support them both.

Mother reassured me she would be okay and said Kirsty would be there too. I needed time to digest the news so suggested

I call her back the next day. My poor mother. This was all Father's fault. He should never have cheated. Over the years, I felt an immense sense of pride when people compared me to my father and commented that I was a chip off the old block. But, now, I didn't feel so sure.

I had the urge to hear Kirsty's voice but remembered we'd only communicated by email or on Ernest's phone. Perhaps it was a good idea to not reach out to her, as no doubt, she was still angry with me. I wanted to know as soon as possible how Dee reacted to the news, although I didn't want to quiz my mother relentlessly. So, without hesitation, I opened the emails on my computer and searched for Kirsty's email address.

It surprised me to see two unopened messages from her, and I put my head in my hands in despair when I realised she'd tried to reach out to me with an apology, and I had blatantly ignored her. Any hope of a friendship lay shattered in pieces, and who could blame her?

Paperwork and stationery flew across the room after I lashed out in frustration. Then I crumpled to the floor, and tears flooded down my cheeks. A sense of loneliness consumed me.

A gentle tap on the door brought me to my senses, and I brushed the tears away. Before I had a chance to compose myself and respond, another knock sounded, and Tim opened the door.

'Oops, sorry, boss. I thought the office was empty, and I need to write something in the diary before I go.' His gaze drifted to the scattered paperwork on the floor. Tim walked into the office and closed the door behind him. He took a handkerchief from his pocket and passed it to me. 'What's wrong? Let me pour us a drink, and you can tell me all about it.'

I avoided his gaze and bent over to clear up the mess. 'No, don't worry. I'm fine.'

'No, you're not. It's not good to bottle things up. And, as they say, a problem shared is a problem halved. Let me sort this mess out, and you pour the drinks. I don't know where you've stashed the whiskey.'

As soon as everything was back in its rightful place, we sat at the desk, and I sipped the smooth, amber liquid. For a moment, I closed my eyes and took a deep breath.

Tim sat in silence, and concern filled his eyes whilst he waited for me to speak.

'It turns out my father had an affair with his secretary for over thirty years, and they had—have—a daughter, and I've known her for over fifteen years.'

'Who? Do I know her?'

'I don't think so. She moved to Cyprus a while back and runs the hair salon. My father set her up in business. I always felt curious as to why, and now I know.'

Tim shook his head in amazement when I told him the full story. After I got to the part about Kirsty, he looked at me in puzzlement.

'Kirsty Green again? Has something happened between the pair of you?'

I shook my head. 'I wish. I like her immensely, but I think I've burned my bridges and am so annoyed with myself.'

The whiskey hit the back of my throat, and I coughed and spluttered. After a deep breath, I told Tim the whole story, right from when Kirsty and I first met at the airport.

Tim gulped his drink and held out the glass for a refill. 'I can see why she's upset with you,' he said. 'I don't think I've ever seen you get so upset over a woman, not even at university when Lucy dumped you.'

'Kirsty has gotten under my skin, and I thought she was interested in me.' I sighed.

'It sounds like she was. Leave it a few days for the dust to settle and get in touch with her.'

'I haven't got her number.'

'That's easily sorted. I'll get it from Izzie,' Tim said.

'No, don't do that. I'll be in Cyprus next week and can apologise in person.'

'That sounds like a good idea, and it'll give her some time to calm down. Fancy a pint?'

My face felt flushed as the whiskey hit my empty stomach. 'I thought you had a date?'

'No, she cancelled. I think she got a better offer. Women, eh?'

*T*he taxi dropped us off at the hotel, and as we walked across the foyer, Dee came to meet us. 'Phew, that was a long day. I can't wait to go home, soak in the bath, and get ready for a night on the town.' She grinned.

I glanced across at Margot, who stood there with her eyes downcast. When she looked up, I noticed tears in her eyes, and she bit her bottom lip. 'Dee, there's something I want to talk to you about before you go home, and if you don't mind, I've asked Kirsty to join us?'

A puzzled expression settled on Dee's face. 'Shall we go into the salon? It's quieter than out here.'

Margot nodded, and the three of us made our way into the empty salon. Margot's face was pinched with tension, and Dee shuffled the furniture around so we could sit in comfort next to each other. 'Would you like a cup of tea or something stronger? I have wine in the fridge,' Dee said.

'We'd better have something stronger,' Margot said. Her nervous laugh made me cringe.

Dee looked at me and back at Margot. 'That sounds ominous. I'll get the wine, and you two make yourselves comfortable.'

As soon as Dee was out of earshot, Margot leant over and

spoke in a hushed voice. 'When I saw Dee, I knew I had to say something before I lost my nerve and chickened out.'

I nodded. 'I thought as much when I saw your reaction. It's probably for the best. Dee can decide whether she still wants to go out tonight.'

'I hope so because I didn't intend to spoil your night out,' Margot said.

'Don't worry. This is more important, and if at any point you want me to leave, just say the word.' I squeezed her arm for reassurance.

Dee swanned back into the room with a big smile and a brave face, but as she popped open the cork and poured the wine, her hands trembled. 'It's from Roberto's vineyard, so it should be good.'

Margot fidgeted in her seat and took a gulp of wine. She tapped her fingernails on the table and sipped more of her drink. After a deep breath, she said, 'I need to tell you something, although I don't know how to.'

'Is it about my father?' Dee asked.

Margot's eyes opened wide. 'Yes. H-how did you know?'

'That Mr Bright was my father? I've known for a while. I'm so sorry.' Dee sniffed and twiddled with her bracelet.

'You're sorry? It's I who must apologise. You had every right to know who your father was, and we had no right keeping it a secret from you. You poor girl.'

I swallowed a lump in my throat. 'Let me get a box of tissues.'

'There's some in the back, and you'd better get another bottle of wine,' Dee said.

On my return, I glanced out of the window. Ernest paced up and down and checked his watch repeatedly. 'Ernest is outside looking for you,' I said.

'He must be frantic with worry,' Margot said. 'I told him we were on our way back, and he wanted to meet me.'

'I'll let him know where you are. Shall I tell him you'll phone him later?' I said.

'Invite him in for a glass of wine. I don't mind,' Dee said.

Margot shook her head. 'No, this is a conversation between you and me. I have a lot of explaining to do and need to beg your forgiveness.'

Dee leant over and patted Margot's arm. 'You don't have to apologise for anything. After all, it was my mother who had the affair with your husband, and I understand why you kept it a secret. Although, I felt terribly upset when Anthony first told me.'

I spun around, and before I could help myself, I blurted out, 'Anthony? How did he know? Sorry ... not my place to ask. I'll go and meet Ernest.' I closed the door behind me and left the two women deep in conversation whilst they held each other's hands across the table.

I walked up behind Ernest and tapped him on the shoulder. He spun around, and his face fell when he realised it was me. 'Margot's here. She's in the hair salon,' I said.

'I didn't realise she had a hair appointment.' He raised his brow. 'Ah, I see ... Dee. Shall we get a drink at the bar, and you can put me in the picture?'

My throat felt parched, and my stomach growled after the bartender placed a bowl of tempting nuts and crisps in front of me, alongside a tall glass of lime and soda. Ernest's phone pinged. 'Drat, I think I've just received a message, but it's disappeared. I can't get used to this new phone. Here, can you see if you can find it for me, please?'

I smiled. 'Give it here. What's your passcode?'

'Passcode? What's that? Oh, do you mean four zeros?'

'Ernest, you must change your security settings in case your phone gets stolen. Don't tell me you use the word "password" when you log into your email?'

His face flushed. 'How did you know? Are you a mind reader?'

I shook my head and laughed. 'Tomorrow, we'll go through your settings to change your security details, and I'll show you how to use your mobile.' My heart fluttered when I read the name on the message. 'It's a text from Max.'

Ernest peered at the screen and smiled. 'He wanted to make sure Margot was okay because he won't arrive in Cyprus for a while. Ah, he's such a splendid chap, and he said he's so grateful I'm there for her.' He closed his eyes, smiled, and nodded. 'Always.'

'That's so cute.' I smiled. 'You are perfect for one another.' I swallowed a lump in my throat. Life wasn't fair. Why couldn't I meet someone and fall in love?

Margot and Dee joined us at the bar, full of giggles and eyes that gleamed.

'It looks like you've sorted things out?' I said.

'Yes, we have. Everything is out in the open, and it feels marvellous,' Margot said. 'Now, all we need to do is get to know more about each other. Dee suggested we all go out for a meal tonight to celebrate.'

'Sounds like a plan. I'm sure you have lots more to talk about, and I'd be interested to find out how Anthony knew,' Ernest said.

Margot raised her eyebrows. 'Apparently, Anthony found out about the affair several years ago. He confronted his father, who explained everything, including the fact he was Dee's father. Anthony agreed to keep the knowledge to himself to protect me. However, on a night out with Dee and the girls from the salon, he got drunk and blurted out the truth. Although he must have forgotten what he said because he never mentioned anything about it.'

SEVERAL HOURS LATER, I staggered to my room, kicked off my shoes, and flung myself onto the bed. Laughter and tears had filled the special night, and my heart felt full whilst I stared at the ceiling. Things had worked out for the best. I picked up my phone to call Henri but realised the time, and she'd probably be at

Harry's Bar after yoga. I logged on to my Facebook account and searched for Isabel. She'd posted lots of photos of our time in Ibiza, and then one entry caught my eye. Isabel had updated her status to single. Too late to phone her, I sent a brief message of congratulations. Finally, the rat had got what he deserved. This meant she would be my boss. At the thought of going back to work, I felt a heavy sensation in the pit of my stomach.

I'd received new friend requests, so I clicked on the link. A recent one came from Elena, which I accepted. Then my mouth fell open when I saw Max's name. After I'd studied the request, I realised it had arrived a few days ago, after my terse email. I settled my iPad on the bed and tapped my knuckles against my lips. After retrieving the iPad, I stared at the screen. My finger hovered over the button, and I let out a squeal and pressed 'accept'.

Curiosity led me to Max's timeline, and I sat transfixed at the post, dated the day previously. It showed a meme image.

I realised I was thinking of you, and I wondered how long you'd been on my mind. Then it occurred to me ... since I met you.
  yourtango.com

WAS THIS ABOUT ME? I jumped when *Messenger* pinged to notify me I'd received a message. Max sent it. My heart pounded whilst I opened it and shrank when I read, 'You and Max are now friends.' Were we? I dropped the iPad as if it were a lump of hot coal after a green button appeared next to his name. He was online.

2 8

MAX

a s soon as I saw that Kirsty had accepted my friend request, I felt the urge to run and jump around the room. My phone pinged to notify me that I had a new message, and I clicked on *Messenger*. The green circle shone out next to Kirsty's name, and I hesitated. *What do I say?* I pressed the 'thumbs up' button and snorted in mirth. *I'm not a teenage boy.*

The three circles remained invisible, so I sent another message. 'Hello, Kirsty. How are you?' Not much better, but hopefully, she would reply. My heart beat faster when three dots appeared.

Kirsty: Hi Max, all good thanks, how are you?

Max: Keeping busy. Thanks for accepting my friend request.

Kirsty: I nearly didn't after you ignored my emails.

WHOOPS, that told me. I hesitated and bit my nails.

Max: I can explain. Your messages ended up in my spam folder, so I didn't see them until yesterday. Then Mother phoned me about Dee, and I forgot to reply.

I HADN'T, I just didn't want her to know I'd given up any hope of a friendship.

Kirsty: No worries. You're forgiven ... again.

Max: Are we friends?

Kirsty: The jury is out on that one. I'll let you buy me dinner and then decide.

Max: And hopefully, one day, breakfast.

AARGH. I cringed. Thankfully, she replied with a laughing emoji.

Kirsty: Nice try, although if you behave yourself ...

Max: Don't go anywhere. I'll see you next week.

Kirsty: I won't. See you soon. Take care K xx

I JUMPED up and down and pumped my fist in the air. I was still in with a chance, only this time, it really was my last shot.

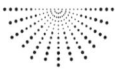

*L*ast night, I scrolled through Max's timeline until I drifted to sleep with a smile. When I woke up, I went for an early-morning swim and I managed about a hundred lengths in a daydream trance, as thoughts of Max preoccupied me.

Afterwards, I walked through to the restaurant to meet Margot & Ernest for breakfast. *Oh, I didn't realise Dee had planned to meet us, too.*

'Good morning, my dear. I've ordered you a pot of tea,' Margot said. 'We have some good news to share.'

'Are you two getting married?' I asked.

'Don't be silly, dear. It's far too soon. Although, one day.' She wiggled her fingers.

'No, the good news is that Dee has agreed to come with us to England. We've made plans to see Max, and Ernest's daughter Sarah, and then we shall spend a few days in Portugal with Anthony.'

My chest tightened at the thought of my family and friends. With false bravado, I smiled. 'I'm so happy for you all. What will I do without you?'

'You'll be fine. The time will fly by, and we'll be back before you know it,' Ernest said.

'Yes, and I'll get the girls from the salon to invite you along if they plan a night out,' Dee said.

'Don't worry. I've got plenty of books to keep me busy, and I can spend more time at the gym. I must get rid of these extra pounds. When will you leave?' I said.

'Tomorrow morning,' Margot said. 'It's last minute, I know, but Max sorted out a good deal on the flights. If you don't mind, I'll have to show you the flat when I get back. Can you put up with hotel food for another week?'

I nodded. 'It will give me time to plan where I'm off to next. I may even go back to England for a few weeks to see family and friends.'

'Well, don't go anywhere without saying goodbye,' Ernest said.

'Of course, I won't. I'll be here waiting for you when you return. Don't forget, I still need to sort out your phone.'

'No need to. Dee's going to set it up properly when we're on the plane. She's a wizard with technology,' Ernest said.

I turned away from his gaze and studied the menu. 'That's good.'

Dee leant towards Margot and gave her a gentle kiss on the cheek. Her eyes shone and her face beamed. 'Sorry I can't stop for breakfast, but I have to sort out the salon before we go.'

'If I don't see you before you leave, have a lovely time,' I said.

Throughout breakfast, I switched off from the conversation, which centred around Dee and their forthcoming trip. Under a heavy grey cloud, I toyed with my food and couldn't wait to leave the table. With slumped shoulders, I said goodbye to Margot and Ernest and returned to my room.

I needed to talk to a friend, but Henri was off on her yoga retreat, and it was too early to phone Emma. Perhaps Isabel would be awake?

The outward-bound ringing sounded for a few moments, and I was just about to hang up when Isabel's groggy voice answered.

'Morning. Hold on a sec ... kids, turn the TV down. I can't hear myself think.'

'Good morning. Have I caught you at an inconvenient time?'

'No, I'm awake, although I have a hangover. How're things?'

'Not great, but don't worry about me. Tell me the news? You changed your Facebook status.'

'I'm a free woman,' Isabel said. 'I've kicked him out of the house and the business and, oh my goodness, it feels amazing.'

'Hence the hangover?' I grinned.

'Yes.' Isabel chuckled. 'My brother stayed last night, just in case Richard came back. Max popped by, too, and we drank several bottles of wine to celebrate. I believe someone's got a crush on you?'

My stomach fluttered. 'Don't be silly. Last time we saw each other, we had an argument.'

'Yes, but he told me that was just a misunderstanding. In fact, Max couldn't stop talking about you. You'd better snap him up before I do because I'm a single woman now.' Isabel laughed. 'Only joking. I've had enough of men to last me a lifetime.'

Was she joking? As they say, no truer word said in jest. I bit my lip.

'I might come home soon for a few weeks to catch up with the girls and decide where I'm off to next,' I said.

'I could do with you back at the office now I've taken over. I need all the support I can get. It seems Richard was popular with quite a few members of staff.'

'You'll be fine, and if they give you any stick, fire them. I'd better go, and I'll call you again soon. Go back to bed.'

'I wish I could.' Isabel sighed. 'Let me know when you're coming home. Miss you.'

'Miss you too.'

Now what would I do? I'd become reliant on Margot and Ernest for company, and I didn't like the prospects of dinner for one every night.

Whilst on the phone, I'd received a WhatsApp message from Elena.

She'd invited me to her house the following weekend, and without hesitation, I accepted.

I wrote back with a brief explanation that I was free anytime due to spending the week on my own. Within seconds, Elena replied and suggested I stay for longer because Roberto was away on business from Monday. When I agreed, she arranged for a car to collect me. I couldn't expect the hotel to keep my room free, so I checked out on Monday morning.

30

KIRSTY

The magnificent house appeared pristine with white walls and black wrought-iron railings that circled the balcony. The structure stood in grandeur amongst a vibrant garden, and vivid flowers and bushes swayed in a gentle breeze. Palm trees surrounded a swimming pool, and in the corner, a cream parasol protected an outdoor bar area from the sun's rays.

Birds tweeted and a beach ball danced about on the surface of the azure water.

I rolled up my borrowed yoga mat and followed Elena into the house. Every morning since I'd arrived, we got up early and practised meditation and yoga. Elena proved the perfect hostess, and I felt at ease in her presence. During the daytime, we went for long walks, either through vineyards and countryside or beautiful beaches. Trips to the shops added more clothes to my expanding wardrobe, and I treated myself to perfume and jewellery. We laughed and chatted into the night, and her housekeeper and chef prepared tasty meals throughout the day. I didn't have to worry about my waistline because all the meals were nutritious and healthy. If not for the copious amounts of wine and spirits we drank, my visit would have felt like a stay at a health farm.

I couldn't believe Friday had arrived already, and Roberto would fly back from his work trip today.

'I've missed Roberto this time,' Elena said. 'We had a good chat before he left, and he's agreed to speak to a doctor, change his diet, and give up the cigars. He may even join us for yoga tomorrow.'

'That's good to hear. Often, we forget men have their own challenges as they grow older and just assume they're all right.'

'Yes. Max spoke to him before I had the chance, so he'd prepared to make changes already. We've agreed not to rush things in the bedroom department, but there are lots of other things we can do for pleasure.'

I groaned. 'Oh, I miss sex. Even though I can pleasure myself whenever I like, I miss the touch of a man. I thought it could have been Max, but it wasn't meant to be.' I sighed.

Elena shifted in her seat and stared at her hands. 'There's something I meant to tell you.' She stood and walked around the back of her chair.

'Go on,' I said.

The air filled with the sound of rotor blades, and Roberto's helicopter landed behind the house.

Elena said, 'Er, I'll tell you in a minute. Let's meet Roberto.'

Whilst we walked around the side of the house, two figures jumped out of the helicopter. I recognised Roberto, and he waved. The other person had his back to us as he reached into the cabin. He lifted a suitcase and turned around. My nipples hardened, and a flush of warmth spread from my groins at the sight of Max, who walked towards us. He wore khaki green cargo trousers, and a black fitted t-shirt clung to his muscular arms and body, and Ray-Ban 'Aviator' sunglasses covered his eyes. As the men approached, Max peered over his sunglasses and stopped walking.

31

MAX

$\mathcal{W}$hen I returned to the hotel on Wednesday, I couldn't concentrate on my paperwork, and my mind was in turmoil. Kirsty wasn't in any of the public areas. Although late in the afternoon, I presumed she must be in her room. Whilst I stood outside her door, I fidgeted with my clothes and brushed my hands through my hair. When I knocked, I received no answer. Perturbed, I knocked again, and silence greeted me. My mother wouldn't arrive back from Portugal until Saturday, and Kirsty had been on her own this week, so I went to look for her in the bar. Again, no sign. Eventually, I went to the reception to see if they knew where Kirsty had gone. A new member of staff I didn't recognise said she didn't know a Kirsty.

The receptionist tapped away on the keyboard and looked up from the computer screen. 'The Diamond Suite is empty. Kirsty Young checked out on Monday morning and settled her bill. She didn't leave a forwarding address or contact details. I'm sorry, but I can't help you.'

A sudden heaviness washed over me, and my heart sank. Slump-shouldered, I trudged to my room.

That's it. She's gone. Checked out of the hotel and my life.

I spent the next day in a trance and locked myself in the office.

I snapped at a few members of staff and cursed under my breath when they flinched and the colour drained from their faces.

When Roberto walked across the hotel foyer on Friday morning, a sigh escaped me. I could flee this prison of memories.

The helicopter ride dispelled my negative emotions, and I gazed out of the window at the picturesque landscape. The ride exhilarated, and by the time Roberto's house came into sight, I felt relaxed and energised. With gentle ease, Roberto guided the helicopter onto the landing pad.

'When's it my turn to fly? How about I take her out tomorrow?' I said.

'Absolutely not. This is my baby, and you haven't flown a helicopter for a long time. Take some more lessons, and then I'll have a rethink. Or buy your own bloody helicopter. You've got enough money.' Roberto laughed and slapped me on the back. 'Come on. Let's say hello to the girls.'

Girls? What's he talking about?

I peered over the top of my sunglasses at two women who walked towards us.

Under my breath, I muttered, 'You didn't tell me Kirsty would be here.'

Roberto gave me a cheeky grin. 'Did I not mention it? It must have slipped my mind.'

KIRSTY

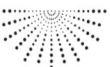

*T*he two men made their way towards us, and I hissed, 'You didn't tell me.'

'I was about to, but they got here earlier than I expected,' Elena said.

'Blimey, I look a right mess. I haven't had a shower yet.'

'You look beautiful. Check Max's face. He's like a love-struck puppy.'

Max grinned, rushed towards me, folded me into his arms, and whispered into my ear, 'I thought I would never see you again.'

I stepped away and frowned. 'Whatever gave you that idea? I told Marissa I'd be back after the weekend. I thought it made sense to check out in case the hotel wanted to use the room.'

Max shook his head. 'I should have explained when you first arrived that your room is only used for my friends and family, so you didn't have to check out. It gave me a fright.' He laughed and rubbed his chin.

Roberto and Elena studied our reactions.

'The pair of you set this up, didn't you?' I said.

They exchanged knowing glances with each other.

Elena said, 'It was coincidental at first, although we may have forgotten to mention anything, just in case you changed your minds about coming to stay. It's nearly lunchtime, so I'll let Roberto show Max to his room, and we can get ready. I've put you in the room next to Kirsty's. Our other guest rooms are being decorated.'

My face flushed. *That's funny — I didn't see any signs of decorating when Elena gave me a guided tour.*

'Where are my favourite godchildren?' Max asked.

'They've gone to stay with my parents for a few days, who've just come back from a four-month cruise. They'll come back on Sunday,' Elena said.

'That's good. I bought them a present and can't wait to see how much they've grown,' Max said. 'Right, show me to my room so I can unpack.'

Roberto said, 'I'll let Kirsty lead the way. I need a quick word with Elena.'

We walked through the house, and our footsteps tapped across the marble floor. We stood outside my bedroom door and gazed into each other's eyes. Max reached over and caressed my cheek. He leant towards me and kissed the top of my head.

'You don't know how pleased I am to see you,' he said. 'Now, go and get showered.' He scrunched his nose. 'Obviously, you had a good workout.'

Whilst he laughed, I slapped his arm playfully and headed into my room. Over my shoulder, I said, 'Yeah. I missed you too.'

❧

A SHORT WHILE LATER, the four of us sat around a table next to the outside bar. Our glasses stood filled to the brim with sparkling wine. Plates of grilled halloumi, home-baked bread, freshly prepared salad, and olives covered the table. Roberto raised his glass. 'Here's to a wonderful weekend with best friends. Tomorrow, I'll take us out in the helicopter for a tour of the island, and I've reserved a table for lunch. My friends have opened the restaurant especially for us as they are usually closed at this time of the year.'

'This is a bit early, isn't it?' Max said.

'They have relatives from England who always visit in October and stay with their brother, who lives on the other side of the island. We can fly over their town tomorrow, and I'll point out where they live,' Roberto said.

'How about you, Kirsty? Have you ever flown in a helicopter?' Max asked.

'No, it's something I've always wanted to do. Although, I must confess, I'm nervous,' I said.

'Roberto's an exemplary pilot, and you have nothing to worry about. I can sit next to you if it helps?' Max said.

'Yay, I get to sit in the front.' Elena smiled.

In no time at all, we'd emptied the plates and topped up our wine glasses. I felt lightheaded by the time the afternoon sun shone on us.

'Who fancies a swim?' Elena said.

Do I want Max to see me in a bikini? I barely fit in the ones I brought with me.

The others nodded, which left my doubts outnumbered, and we set off to get changed. I rushed to my room, threw on my bikini in record time, and muttered *thank you* when I jumped into an empty pool.

With my chin rested on the edge, I peered through my sunglasses and watched Max approach. He wore jade-green swimming trunks that fitted snugly around his taut waist, and my breath hitched when he adjusted his trunks and briefly displayed his V-shaped muscles. He hadn't noticed me in the pool and took a step back when he did.

Roberto and Elena charged past, and Roberto shouted, 'Last one in the pool's a wuss.'

Max shrugged with a bemused smile. 'That will be me, then.'

After a few macho swimming races, which Max won easily, Roberto challenged us to a water jousting duel, and Max scooped me onto his shoulders. He moved about the pool with ease, and I clung on for dear life. Elena's competitive streak became apparent, and constantly, she knocked me off Max's shoulders with the foam noodle. Finally, the two of us admitted defeat, and I swam to the surface of the pool, coughing and spluttering with my vision blurred from tears.

Max tapped me on the back, pushed my hair out of my face, and wiped the water from my face. My vision cleared, and I shivered. I gazed into his eyes, and he leant towards me and kissed me on the nose.

'That's enough for today. Let's warm up in the sun. You look like a drowned rat,' he said.

'Thanks. I've been called better things.' I laughed.

Max blushed. 'Oh, no. I didn't mean to offend you.'

'I know you didn't. You're my knight in shining armour.' I stood on tiptoes and gave him a gentle kiss on the lips.

MAX

A gentle kiss on the lips wasn't enough to satisfy the intense desire I felt around Kirsty. All afternoon, I watched her every move, and when she wrapped her legs around my neck, I couldn't concentrate. No wonder Roberto and Elena won the jousting challenge. My mind went into overdrive. How could I spend time alone with Kirsty? Elena answered my prayers when she suggested we go for a stroll along the beach whilst Roberto and she caught up with business affairs.

Kirsty met me outside her room, and she looked stunning in a simple white dress and sandals. The smell of her perfume wafted towards me, and her freckle-covered nose had turned a delicate shade of red after our afternoon in the sun.

I borrowed one of Roberto's cars, and we drove to the beach car park.

'I'd love to sit and watch the sunset,' Kirsty said.

'I'm sure we can, as we won't be eating for a while,' I said.

Side by side, we walked barefoot. The sand tickled our toes, and the waves washed them clean. Kirsty stumbled on a shell, and I reached out to steady her. She turned around and faced me and let out a burst of shaky laughter. 'That would have been embarrassing,' she said.

I smiled and pulled her trembling body into my arms. 'I've got you now,' I said.

We walked onward, and our hands were drawn to each other's until our fingers intertwined. I spun Kirsty around until she faced me again. 'There's something I've wanted to do since I met you. Do you mind if I kiss you?'

She nodded, and her lips parted to welcome my embrace.

We broke apart momentarily when a dog ran past and drops of ice-cold water splashed onto us.

The owner nodded and muttered an apology whilst Kirsty's musical laughter filled the air. This time, Kirsty pulled my face towards hers, and our lips collided again.

I let out a deep groan. 'I don't think I can control myself if we carry on,' I said.

'Me neither. There's a bar up ahead—shall we get a drink and wait for the sun to set?'

Blow the sunset. I want to take her home so we can be alone.

We sat on the dunes, and as the temperature dropped and the sky turned a vivid shade of orange, I wrapped my arms around Kirsty, and she rested her head against my body. I didn't want this moment to end, but when the sun dipped below the horizon, the air turned chillier.

'Time for us to head back now,' I said.

'Just one more kiss, and then we'll go.' She grinned.

WHEN WE ARRIVED BACK at the house, music and the smell of a barbeque greeted us. Our intimate bodies leaned against the car, and for a few moments, we stood with our arms wrapped around each other before our lips collided in a passionate embrace. Kirsty's hands explored my body, and I caressed her soft curves. A groan escaped my throat.

'We'd better find Roberto and Elena. They'll know we're back. The gate triggers a sensor.' I wiped a speck of sand from Kirsty's bare shoulder. 'Whilst we're still on our own, there's something I want to tell you. I've never wanted to be in a relationship, that is—'

'There you are. Dinner's ready,' Elena said. 'Roberto's in a flap in case the food is over-cooked. He's such a perfectionist with cooking on the barbeque.'

Kirsty patted my arm. 'You can tell me later, but I think I know what you'll say.'

KIRSTY

I could second guess what Max planned to say, and I didn't want to hear it. I didn't want him to break the magic spell. Whilst we sat on the beach and watched the sunset, I made up my mind. I wanted Max. I wanted to touch every part of his body and feel him inside me, and I'd never felt this sort of chemistry with anyone. Although it wouldn't be the sort of relationship I desired, I wouldn't be able to tear myself away from him if things were to carry on between us.

We followed Elena over to the table, and Roberto walked towards us with a plate of cooked meat in one hand and a set of tongs in the other. He wore a white chef's hat and an apron with the image of a naked man's muscular chest printed on it.

'Suits you.' I laughed.

'I don't like it. It's too tacky, and I had to persuade him to put a pair of shorts on,' Elena said.

'You always tell me I've got a great arse, and it turns you on when I wear just the apron,' Roberto said.

Elena blushed. 'Shush! Not when we have guests. Anyway, what did you two get up to?'

My face flushed, and I cast my gaze downwards. Max coughed, cleared his throat, and said, 'We went for a lovely romantic stroll along the beach, had a drink, and watched the sunset.'

'Romantic. Is there something you're not telling us?' Roberto said with a glint of mischief in his eyes.

'Leave them alone. I knew this weekend would sort things out between the pair of you,' Elena said. 'You make a lovely couple.'

'You're like one of Cupid's helpers, or that's what my friends back home would say,' I said.

'I like the sound of that. Perhaps I should start a dating agency?' Elena grinned.

Roberto served the food onto plates and frowned. 'Don't get any ideas because you've got enough on your plate already.'

Elena said, 'I was only joking. I'm trying to cut back on work, not add to it. How's that working out with you, Max?'

'Things got easier when Tim joined the company, and Mother is in a relationship, so I no longer have to keep flying over to Cyprus to check up on her. Plus, I have a new sister, who will keep an eye on her.'

'How did their trip to England go?' I said.

'Mother introduced Dee to her friends as the daughter she never knew existed. They agreed to tell people my father had a brief relationship with Dee's mother when they were on a temporary separation. Mother doesn't want to sully my father's reputation. Another web of deceit. But, I suppose, it's not hurting anyone, and Dee is over the moon with her new family. She's a lovely girl, and I've grown fond of her in the brief time we've known we're related, even though I've known her for a while.'

I held Max's hand under the table and squeezed.

'That's lovely to hear. Dee's such a nice girl, who's had some terrible luck in her life. It's great things have worked out for her. All she needs now is a good man in her life,' I said.

'Well, I shouldn't gossip—' Max said. '—but she got on well with Tim, and they went out for a meal. I tried to quiz him, but he wouldn't say anything. There's a bit of an age gap, and he's only recently separated from his wife.' Max shrugged. 'You can't help who you fall for.'

My heartbeat flickered when he held my gaze.

'Age is just a number,' Elena said. 'There's a nine-year differ-ence between Roberto and me. I expect we'll see Tim in Cyprus one day soon?'

'Probably. Already, he's hinted he feels ready to get involved with the other hotels, and to be honest, it would do me a favour. All this travelling is taking a toll. I don't know how my father coped all those years.'

'Do you forgive what he did to your mother?' Elena said.

'I can't say I totally forgive him. Infidelity is wrong. However, he must have had his reasons, and not all marriages are what they appear on the surface. It saddens me they kept the marriage together for the sake of appearances when Mother could have met somebody like Ernest sooner. I've never seen her this happy and full of love. She even gave me a hug last week, which is unheard of.'

It made sense why Max was so detached from relationships. I grew up surrounded by love and hugs, and a day never passed without my parents telling my sister and me they loved us.

Poor Max had grown up without such love and affection. Still, it was never too late, and Margot had time to put things right.

We ate in silence, deep in our thoughts, until Roberto slammed a bottle onto the table and roused us. 'Come on, guys. This is supposed to be an evening of fun. My number-one rule is you can't change the past, so don't look back. I'll clear the table whilst Elena tops up the drinks, and Max can sort out the music.'

'What about me? What can I do?' I asked.

'Make sure Max doesn't play any of that 80s rubbish. In fact, you can take care of the music and Max can pour the drinks. Elena, would you help me in the kitchen?'

'Yes, boss. I love it when you take control.' Elena slapped Roberto on the bottom.

Once Roberto and Elena had disappeared out of sight, Max

pulled me to my feet and his lips covered mine in a long, sensuous kiss that left me short of breath. I pulled my head back and gazed up at him before I returned his kiss with passion.

His hardness pressed against me, and the effect I had on him left me intoxicated. The hunger in his eyes was intense, and I longed to rip off his clothes and touch every part of his body. We were so absorbed in each other that we didn't realise we had company until Elena let out a gentle cough.

'So, this is what you get up to when we turn our backs?' Elena laughed and directed her gaze to Roberto. 'I won the bet, so you have to do the clearing up.' Her face beamed.

'Yes, you won fair and square,' Roberto said.

'Excuse me, but what bet?' Max sounded indignant at the comment.

'We're only teasing. I bet that you two would end up having a kiss within the hour, and Roberto thought it was too soon. I can almost see sparks fly with the amount of chemistry between you,' Elena said.

I put my hands on my hips and stood my ground. 'For your information, you both lost the bet because our first kiss was at the beach, so you both need to do the washing up, although maybe Max and I can come and help.'

'Thank you for the offer, but I'm sure our housekeeper will clear up in the morning. I'm going to have one more drink and get an early night. We have a long day tomorrow, and I need to keep my head clear. I can't wait to show you around the island,' Roberto said.

I glanced at my watch and stifled a yawn. 'I'll have one more drink and get an early night, too. I don't want to feel hungover tomorrow.'

Elena tutted. 'You two are lightweights. The night is young, and it's been ages since I had a night away from the children.'

'What rubbish. You were away last weekend, and then there was Max's party. Anyway, let's save the dancing for tomorrow night when I can let my hair down. Shall we leave these two lovebirds alone?' Roberto winked. 'My shoulders ache, and I could do with a massage.'

For a long moment, Max and I stared at each other in the moonlight. Elena and Roberto headed into the house.

Max buried his face in my hair and whispered, 'You're so beautiful, and I can't get enough of you.'

I licked my lips, and heat spread over my body. 'We should both get an early night.'

We stood outside our bedrooms, and nervous, I giggled. 'I'd invite you in, but my room's a mess.'

35

MAX

'Why don't you come into my room for a nightcap? I haven't unpacked yet,' I said.

The door slammed behind us, and I pushed Kirsty up against the wood and pressed my lips against hers. She nipped my lower lip, and our tongues collided. I groaned when her hands explored my body and unbuttoned my shirt. I kissed her delicate neck at the base of her throat, and she thrust her head backwards when my fingers pinched her erect nipples through the fabric of her dress.

In a powerful lift, I carried Kirsty to the bed and eased her on top of the pristine white bedsheets. I shrugged off my unbuttoned shirt, and our eyes locked in an intense gaze. I stood transfixed whilst Kirsty shimmied out of her dress to reveal delicate white underwear. For a moment, she covered her chest with both arms, then her face lit up in a playful grin, and she reached behind her body and unclasped her bra. Beautiful, full, ripe breasts tumbled out. Kirsty unclasped the buckle of my trousers and revealed snug-fitting boxer shorts, which failed to hide the effect she had on me. My hands reached out to touch her, but she pushed me away and our gazes locked again. I bit my lip and grew harder at the thought of what was about to happen.

Within moments, Kirsty took the tip of my erect manhood into her sultry mouth. The muscles in my buttocks tensed when her head rocked backwards and forwards, and I groaned whilst her tongue licked and teased the smooth surface of my cock. I pushed her away and stepped out of my trousers and shorts. Without the need for any words, she lay on the bed and beckoned me towards her with an intense stare. She fixed her gaze on my erection and shuffled around so her head rested at the bottom of the bed. I felt an urgency to feel myself deep inside her, but her intentions were clear.

KIRSTY

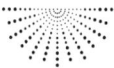

*B*utterfly kisses spread along my body as Max made his way to the top of the bed. His firm hands peeled away my briefs, and his long fingers explored the wetness in my hidden folds of desire. His rock-hard cock pressed against my body, and I adjusted my position to allow myself to take it in my mouth one more time.

Max groaned. 'I want to taste you.'

I grunted, unable to speak whilst my mouth savoured the taste of his manhood.

With expertise, he licked and sucked the entrance of my womanhood, and my legs trembled when his tongue probed the centre of my excitement.

Sensations spread throughout my body as we continued to taste and savour each other until I felt a familiar intensity build up. No longer able to concentrate on Max's pleasure, I broke away and arched my spine on the bed. Within moments, muscles contracted, and heat spread throughout my body whilst I screamed.

Max reached for his wallet on the bedside cabinet and took out a condom. 'I want to fuck you,' he said.

I took the condom out of his hands and rolled it over his erect manhood. 'No, I'm going to fuck you.' I straddled my legs over his hips.

He slipped into my drenched pussy with ease, and his hands rested on my hips as we moved together. A look of concern crossed his face. 'I won't last much longer.'

I leant towards his ear and nipped the lobe. In a whisper, I said, 'Don't worry. We've got all night.' His body bucked beneath me.

I curled up next to Max, and he stroked my body with his warm hands. He kissed the top of my head and laughed. 'I was excited about going for a ride in the helicopter this weekend but spending time with you beats that hands down.'

I gave Max a brief kiss on the lips. 'I'm more excited about the helicopter ride.'

'Give me a few minutes, and I'll change your mind,' he said. 'Although I could do with a shower. Do you fancy joining me?' Max winked.

True to his word, under the cascading water, our bodies collided in frantic passion, and once again, I screamed out when a powerful orgasm engulfed my body.

Max wrapped a fluffy white towel around me, and we sat on the bed whilst he dried my hair. A blush spread over my face after my stomach growled in hunger.

'I'll raid the kitchen fridge. I could do with something to eat, too,' he said.

'See if they have any peanut butter?' I said.

When Max left the room, I laid on the bed and studied my surroundings for a while. Then I sighed with contentment. I reached across to my handbag and took out my phone. Several missed calls from Henri displayed on the locked screen. A sense of alarm washed over me, and I sat up. I misdialled the passcode to my phone several times before I could dial her number. The phone rang twice, and when Henri answered, I heard voices in the background. 'What's wrong?' I said.

Max returned to the bedroom, carrying a tray laden with

peanut butter on toast and two mugs of tea. When he saw me, he stood by the door with a concerned frown. After a brief time-lapse, I had to repeat myself and cried out, 'What's happened?'

Henri's laughter filled the air, and she screeched, 'Danny's asked me to marry him, and I've said yes.'

My eyes filled with tears. 'That's fantastic news. I'm so happy for you both.'

'Will you be my bridesmaid?' Henri asked.

I burst into tears. 'Of course. Oh, I can't wait to see you so we can celebrate together. I miss you so much. I'm coming home next week.'

We chatted for a while until Danny interrupted the call. Henri said, 'My daughter's home.'

After the call, I wanted to go home but also didn't want to travel anymore. Max handed me a box of tissues and a cup of tea. 'It sounds like you've had some good news?'

'My best friend's getting married,' I said.

He pulled me to my feet and wrapped his arms around me. 'That's great.'

The tone of his voice indicated he had no interest in the news. *What did I expect from someone who doesn't want to get married?*

The subject closed when he patted the bed beside him. 'Come and eat your toast before it gets soggy. Mind you, don't get crumbs in the bed.' Max laughed.

I shook my head. 'I've lost my appetite, but thanks for going to all that trouble.' I stood to leave, and Max grabbed my arm and looked puzzled.

'Are you okay? Why don't you stay the night?' he said.

'No, thanks. I'll call it a night. We have an early start in the morning, and at least I'll get a decent night's sleep in my bed.'

Max's shoulders slumped, and he lowered his head. I could just about hear his reply when he mumbled goodnight.

37

MAX

At one in the morning, I lay in bed and stared into the darkness. The chirps and clicks of insects filled the air. After Kirsty had left so abruptly, I struggled to get to sleep. Throughout the night, I listened to her move around her bedroom and contemplated whether it would be a good idea to knock on her door and pick up where we'd left off. The thought excited me, but I saw sense. We needed our sleep. I picked my brains to work out what I'd done to upset her. *Women ... I can't understand them sometimes.* Eventually, I fell asleep. The shrill sound of my alarm woke me up at seven. I heard the shower pump in action next door and knew Kirsty was awake. The thought of her naked body made me rock-hard, and I jumped under a cold shower to douse the flames of desire.

In haste, I dressed and made my way to the kitchen for breakfast. Elena and Roberto were there already, and the smell of freshly cooked bacon wafted through the air.

Roberto nudged Elena, 'You'd better put some extra bacon on for lover-boy. He worked up an appetite, judging by the sounds coming from his bedroom last night.'

Elena flicked him with a tea towel and scowled. 'Shush, you

promised not to say anything, and we don't want to embarrass our guests.'

'You'd better put some extra bacon on for me,' Kirsty said from behind me. She wore a bright-green summer dress that clung to her body and had tied her hair in a ponytail. Around her delicate neck, she wore a gold chain and a letter K charm, which rested against her chest. My eyes settled on her ample cleavage until the sound of Elena's apologetic voice brought me back to my senses.

'I'm so sorry about Roberto. He can be so indiscreet.'

Kirsty responded with an infectious giggle, which lightened the mood. 'There's no need to apologise. I can get vocal in the bedroom. At least you both know your match-making was a success.'

Roberto grinned. 'That's a relief. I thought I'd be in the doghouse with Elena all day. Do you both want a glass of freshly squeezed orange juice? I went out to the market this morning and picked up a sack of oranges especially.'

'And some freshly baked, mouth-watering-delicious bread,' Elena said. 'We have a fresh fruit salad and yoghurt in the fridge if you prefer.'

'A bacon sarnie sounds great—I could eat a horse. It must be all the exercise I had last night.' Kirsty glanced across at me and winked.

Roberto smirked. 'Look, you've made the poor man blush.'

Kirsty sat next to me at the table and squeezed my thigh. She leant towards me and whispered, 'Mmmm, you smell gorgeous.' Then she sucked in her breath. 'I'm sorry I ran off last night.'

I gave her a gentle kiss on her lips. 'It doesn't matter. We both needed our sleep. You look stunning, by the way. I can't wait to spend more time with you on our own. And please don't leave me ...' The word *ever* was on the tip of my tongue.

Over breakfast, Roberto regaled us with the story about how he came to purchase his pride and joy. Although the Bell helicopter was nearly thirty years old, he'd kept it in immaculate condition and had a full set of inspection records. The previous owner, now deceased, had hardly used it, and the craft had remained protected in the hangar for most of the time. The previous owner's son didn't hold a pilot's licence and grew anxious at the thought of flying, so he wanted to get rid of it. Roberto put in an offer 100,000 euros below the asking price and was amazed when the young man accepted.

Roberto's phone rang. When he picked up his mobile, his face flushed. He paced up and down and slammed the phone on the table. 'That was the police. Some scumbags have broken into the winery and caused a lot of damage. They've smashed bottles all over the place and tried to break open the till. I need to make a police report so we can claim on the insurance. That's put paid to our plans today. Now I'll have to wait for a glazier to come in and fix the broken window.'

Elena stroked his back. 'Calm down. I'll come with you, and we can phone Georgios and get him to wait for the glazier. After all, we pay him to manage the winery.'

His shoulders relaxed. 'Yes, yes, you're right, my darling. He can arrange for the cleaners to come in as well. It's bloody frustrating, but that's why we have insurance.' Roberto explained to Kirsty and me, 'The scoundrels couldn't get to the good bottles of wine because we keep them under lock and key behind a steel door. We display only the cheaper bottles in the store. This is the third time it's happened to us in as many years. I'll catch the buggers, though, because I've installed hidden cameras everywhere.'

'Is there anything we can do to help?' I said.

'No, you stay here. We will be back within the hour. Here're the keys to the chopper.' He passed them to me. 'Show Kirsty around, but promise not to fly her. I'll let you start the engine, though.'

I could think of other things I'd rather do with Kirsty, but the look of excitement on her face told me she'd be happy to have a tour of the helicopter.

'Okay, we'll clear the breakfast plates away and then ...' I smiled and saluted. 'Today, ma'am, I'll be your captain.'

KIRSTY

*L*ast night, I'd overreacted when I mentioned Henri's news. When I got back to my room, sleep evaded me, so I picked up my journal and wrote. It wasn't Max's fault; I'd shut the conversation down before it had gotten started, and I'm sure he would have been more than happy to listen if I'd continued instead. Two words jumped off the page: *jealous* and *never*.

I chewed the top of my pen and threw the journal onto the bed. Then I stood and paced and picked up clothes discarded on the floor.

To calm my anxious mind, I sat on the floor and took deep breaths, but I couldn't concentrate and words spun around and around.

I reached across to the journal and opened it. I had to be honest with myself, especially when I journaled my thoughts. My cheeks flushed when I read back the words on the page.

I'm jealous of Henri. Why is it she can fall in love—again—and meet somebody who wants to spend the rest of their life with her? Okay, things didn't work out with her and Pete, but they have two beautiful children.

And now she's met Danny, who's absolutely besotted with her. I'll never meet someone like Danny, who would sweep me off my feet. Someone I could spend the rest of my life with.

How could I be such a terrible friend and resent her happiness?

Tears escaped my eyes and dripped onto the pages. I shook my head and said, 'Right, Kirsty Young. That's enough. Time to pull yourself together and stop feeling sorry for yourself.'

After that self-admonition, I crossed my legs and took a moment to compose myself. My hands rested on my lap, and I inhaled several deep breaths. This time, my affirmation became, *I am worthy of love.*

Exhausted, I crawled under my covers and a sense of calm washed over me, and I fell into a deep and restful sleep.

Before my alarm went off, I woke up and opened the blinds. The sky had turned a delicate shade of orange and birds rested in the tree outside my window. I strode to the shower and savoured the hot water that cascaded over my aching body. Whilst I rubbed *Neal's Yard Wild Rose Oil* into my skin, I whistled a tune, and within no time, I felt ready for the day.

Whilst I walked along the hallway, Roberto's deep voice bellowed out. I cringed—he'd heard us last night. Oh well, I'd better pull up my big girl's knickers and face the music.

Max sat at the breakfast table with his mouth open and an expression of alarm, which turned into a slow smile when I joined the conversation. I had the urge to drag him back to the bedroom and pick up where we left off the previous night, but my stomach let out a loud growl and the smell of grilled bacon overwhelmed me.

We tucked into bacon sandwiches, washed down with cups of hot, strong coffee, but the news of the burglary at the winery interrupted breakfast. Once we sat alone, Max and I gazed at each other and he leant over and kissed me. 'Do you want to see the helicopter, or would you rather do something else?' he said.

I gave him a brief peck on the lips and stood. 'Come on. Let's see this helicopter. I promise I'll make it up to you later.'

A light breeze danced around my legs and lifted the skirt of my dress, and Max whistled when my underwear made a brief appearance. 'Should I go back and change?' I said.

'Only if you want to, but you look beautiful.' Max took hold of my hand and twirled me around.

Sunlight reflected from the helicopter blades when we drew closer, and Max donned his sunglasses. My stomach flipped when I followed behind him and studied his muscular torso.

Max opened the door, and I climbed inside. His eyes sparkled like a child with a new toy. 'It's ages since I've sat in the pilot's seat,' he said.

I covered my ears with headphones and shrieked when Max's voice tickled my ears. 'Good morning, ma'am. This is your captain speaking. Before we take off, let me talk you through the controls.'

'What's that between your legs?' My face turned a deep shade of red when I realised my double entendre.

Max stifled a laugh. 'That's the control stick.'

I shuddered. 'I'm not sure I'm going to like this. What if the engine stops working?'

Max squeezed my knee. 'You've got nothing to worry about. Roberto is an extremely experienced pilot, and safety checks are always carried out before we set off. Look, all these gauges, switches, and caution lights play an important role in keeping us safe. Mark my words, once we're up in the air, you'll love it.'

'It all looks too complicated to me. I'm only glad we'll be sitting in the back so I can shut my eyes if I don't like it. Roberto said you could start the engine?'

'He was only saying that to impress you. He'd have my guts for garters if I started her up.'

My heartbeat thumped in my chest, and I took a few deep

breaths. Max appeared completely relaxed, so I shouldn't worry. I had an idea, and my face broke into a mischievous grin. 'Do you belong to the Mile High Club?'

He looked at me, aghast. 'Certainly not. You can just about get one person in a plane toilet cubicle, let alone two. Although there's more room in first-class.' He shook his head. 'No, not my thing.'

I glanced over at the back seats. 'Is there a special club for helicopters?'

'Well, technically, you join the Mile High Club when you're aboard an aircraft in flight, so I suppose this could apply to a helicopter, although make sure it's not with the pilot.' He chuckled.

'Do you belong to the club?' he said.

'A lady doesn't kiss and tell. But, no, I don't. I'm not sure if it's my thing either. Although, if it were on a private jet plane, then never say never. Anyway, I don't suppose there's a lot of room in the back of these things.'

'You'd be surprised. Shall we sit in the back and see how roomy it is?'

Max climbed in behind me, and my stomach somersaulted when he brushed his hands across my derriere, accidentally. *Or was it not an accident?*

The space was cramped in the back, and Max's long legs drifted over to my side of the cabin. Max rested his hand on my bare leg and stroked it. The temperature rose, and I fanned myself with the safety card.

I trailed my finger towards my cleavage. 'Oh my, it's hot in here,' I said and tilted my head towards Max and licked my parted lips. Max's gaze went to my lips, and he glanced towards my parted legs. He put his hand behind my neck, pulled me closer, and groaned. 'I know what I want to do to you right now,' he said.

I pulled away from his embrace. 'I know what I want to do to you too.' My hand rested on the bulge that pressed hard against his trousers.

Our kiss deepened and I let out a gasp when his fingers pushed my underwear to one side and discovered my hidden pleasure.

Gently, I nipped his bottom lip. 'Do you think we could?'

'There's only one way to find out.' Max unzipped his trousers and revealed his rock-hard length.

Thank goodness I've been practising yoga this week, I mused as I climbed onto Max's lap.

'Oh, fuck it, I've left the condoms in my wallet on the kitchen table.'

'Well, I don't mind if you don't, and I think I'm too old to fall pregnant. Anyway, my period finished last week so we should be okay.'

He slipped inside my moist entrance with ease, and I gasped when he penetrated me completely. There wasn't a lot of space to move about, and I cried out after a cramp tightened my calf. 'Shall we stop?' Max said.

'No, keep going, don't worry about me.'

I gyrated up and down and sensed Max was close to his climax when he arched his back and let out a deep groan.

My body responded, but before I could reach my release, Max's face contorted, and he shuddered. 'I'm so sorry, you didn't come, did you?' He groaned and covered his face with his hands.

I eased his palms away from his cheeks and kissed him. 'Please, don't say sorry. That was special, and sometimes I take longer to get there. And I've still got cramp.' I laughed. 'Oh, God. We'll leave a mess on the back seat.'

We ran indoors, hand in hand, giggling like naughty children. Just in time because the electronic gates opened.

After a quick freshen-up in the bathroom, Max and I joined Elena and Roberto back at the helicopter.

'Any luck with catching the burglars?' Max asked.

Roberto stuck his chest out and stood tall. 'Oh yes. Oh yes, indeed. The police are on their way to arrest the morons as we speak. The idiots sat right in front of the camera, took off their masks, and guzzled down a bottle of wine. Then they threw the bottle on the floor and went on a rampage. I recognised one of them—the son of a competitor, who's tried to put me out of business for years.'

Elena sighed. 'Bloody idiots. They'll get what's coming to them. Anyway, let's forget about it and enjoy the day. Did you give Kirsty a guided tour of the helicopter?'

'Only a quick one,' Max said.

I snorted and laughed. 'Oh, I wouldn't say that. It was an incredibly in-depth tour, and it got me quite excited.'

Roberto raised his eyebrows in a puzzled frown. 'Well, I'm going to run all the safety checks and then we'll be ready to go.'

3 9

MAX

The magnificent view from the air showed lush green landscapes nestled against the deep blue sea. Roberto circled over his vineyards and began the guided tour. He mentioned familiar names and pointed out homes and businesses. Kirsty relaxed the grip on my hand and absorbed the information fed to her through her earpiece. Roberto regaled us with the history of Cyprus and offered his version of the historical conflict between the North and the South. I could only half-concentrate because my mind kept drifting to Kirsty.

The feelings that ran through my body were ones I'd never encountered before, and when I glanced at the beautiful goddess who sat next to me, I knew I'd fallen in love.

The tour continued for the next forty minutes until Roberto pointed out a pristine white building surrounded by palm trees and a near-empty car park. Two tiny figures stood outside and waved when we made our approach. With gentle ease, Roberto landed the helicopter. Then the magic fell apart after Kirsty stepped onto the hot tarmac and spoke words I didn't want to hear. 'That was incredible,' she said. 'I'm so glad I got the chance to do this before I go home on Monday.'

'Home? I thought you had plans to rent Mother's flat for a while?' I said.

'No, these last few weeks have been amazing, but I miss my friends and family. Although, I may take Margot up on the offer if I return.'

Elena wagged her finger. 'Not if, *when*. We've become such good friends in such a short time, and I'll miss you.'

Kirsty opened her arms. 'Come here. Of course I'll come back to visit. I'm still on leave from work, but Isabel sent me a text and asked if I could help for a few weeks now things have gotten complicated. Anyway, I don't want to think of that now whilst I'm still on vacation.'

Kirsty looked over Elena's shoulder, our eyes met, and she gave me a half-smile.

I hadn't realised we'd only spend a brief time together. I'd rearranged some appointments, and Tim was due to fly out to Cyprus next week to learn the ropes. All of which meant I wouldn't get back to England for another week, and I'd planned to travel to Portugal to look after the affairs of the hotel whilst Anthony visited his fiancée's family in France. I'd hoped I could persuade Kirsty to come with me so we could spend more time together. Her plans would mean two whole weeks apart, and that's if she didn't go off on her travels elsewhere. She'd mentioned Australia.

Roberto's friends welcomed us into their lavish restaurant, and we followed them to a table that presided in the centre of the room. Colourful plates of meze, and a variety of wines, covered the white tablecloths. The staff encouraged us to take our seats.

Conversation flowed as easily as the wine, and in no time, we demolished plates of continually replenished food until Roberto held up his hand. 'Thank you, but no more for us, or the helicopter will have trouble taking off.'

About to eat another tasty morsel, Kirsty held still, her hand suspended mid-air, and her eyes opened wide in horror.

I squeezed her leg and leant over to her. In a whisper, I said,

'He's only joking. Helicopters can lift heavier weights than the four of us. Elena's watching Roberto's diet.'

'That's a relief.' She chuckled. 'This food is so tasty, and I could have made room for more.' Kirsty popped a meatball into her mouth.

❧

BACK IN THE HELICOPTER, I fastened my seatbelt across my lap and relaxed into my seat. Kirsty sat transfixed and gazed out of the window whilst Roberto took a different route home. Once again, he provided us with a guided tour full of stories that captivated his audience. Secretly, I felt thrilled when we flew over my hotel, and I realised how impressive it looked from the air.

Kirsty must have read my mind. 'Oh, my goodness, doesn't the hotel look superb? You can't appreciate its vastness from the ground.'

'I'm rather proud of it. You'll have to visit our hotel in Portugal one day,' I said.

'That sounds like a good idea. I'll add it to my wish list,' Kirsty said.

After we'd landed, Kirsty covered her mouth to stifle a yawn. 'I could do with a siesta after all that excitement,' she said. 'Would you join me?' She stroked my thigh and gazed at me through her lashes.

After such a gastro feast, I would have benefited from an after-noon's nap, but I knew exactly what she had on her mind. Without hesitation, I nodded. We had little time remaining together, and I wouldn't pass up the opportunity to spend every minute of the day with her.

Without urgency, we explored each other's bodies, and after a while, we collided in unison and Kirsty screamed out my name. She draped her arm over my chest, which glistened with sweat, and pinched my nipple. 'Do you think we'll be able to meet up in England?' she said.

'Well, I'll be in Cyprus for the rest of the week and then Portugal, so I don't know.'

She put her finger on my lips. 'Well, you know how to get hold of me. Let me know when you're next free. I suppose we'd better get ready for tonight.' She kissed me and climbed from the bed. Whilst she walked towards the bathroom, I savoured her nakedness.

'I'm borrowing this towel,' she said. 'There's no point getting dressed. See you in a bit.' Kirsty sauntered out of the room.

She hadn't let me finish my sentence. I'd wanted to suggest she cancel her flight home and stay with me for the next two weeks. After which, we could fly back to South Talling together.

*T*he door closed behind me, and I threw myself onto the bed and stared at the ceiling. After a moment, I shook my head. *No, not this time. Don't you dare wallow in self-pity. You made your bed, and now you've got to lie in it.*

When I jumped into bed with Max, I'd known the stakes, so I shouldn't have expected a different outcome when I suggested we meet up in England. I wouldn't allow his excuses to impede the rest of the time we had together. Fed up but determined, I went to the wardrobe and rifled through the contents until I settled on an outfit for the evening—a dark-grey calf-length strappy dress with slits up the sides and a plunging neckline trimmed with lace. I'd bought it earlier in the week when Elena and I went shopping and planned to wear it back in England, perhaps on my next night out at the Base? It struck me as over the top for this evening, but I needed to gain control of my emotions, and this dress made me feel powerful. I put on black matching underwear and studied myself in the full-length mirror. For once, I liked what I saw. My bronzed, sun-kissed skin glowed. Okay, my stomach didn't lie as flat as it used to, and small indentations marked my thighs, but overall, I looked good and couldn't wait to see Max's reaction. My aim was to leave him with the memory of a night he would never forget.

When I made my way to the patio, Max sat deep in conversation with Elena, and his eyes lit up like fireworks whilst I walked towards him. Elena whistled and nudged Max in the ribs. 'Check you out, gorgeous girl. That dress looks fabulous. You have a figure to die for,' she said, as she strolled indoors.

Max stood and pulled a chair from under the table. 'Wow, you look amazing ... stunning ... beautiful,' he said.

I flicked my hair and pouted. 'You should see what I'm wearing underneath.'

Max groaned. 'What are you doing to me? You've put me under your spell.'

Roberto approached the table. 'Nice dress.' He nodded in my direction. 'Now, where's my wife? I'm starving.'

'I thought she'd gone inside to find you,' I said.

At that moment, the door opened, and Elena breezed back outside, carrying a tray laden with drinks.

She'd changed into a designer figure-hugging dress that clung to her curves, and Roberto wolf-whistled. 'Weren't you wearing a cream dress?'

'Yes, but I spilt wine over it so had to change.' She gave me a sheepish look. 'That's a lie. I changed because Kirsty looks so stunning, and I felt like a frump next to her.'

'Well, you looked amazing in your other dress as well. In fact, you'd look gorgeous in a sackcloth. What are we like?' I chuckled.

Roberto took charge of the wine and poured us each a glass. 'Are you not drinking?'

Max asked when Roberto topped up his empty glass with sparkling water.

'No, I've given what you said some thought. The thing is, I know everything I need to know about the wine business and have made more than enough money to retire tomorrow. So why don't I?'

A frown creased Elena's brow. 'Because you have a family to provide for, and I still have to work.'

'No, you don't. You're always saying I need to spend more time with my family, so why don't we retire together? We will still own the winery and can leave it in the capable hands of our manager and hire an assistant to help. We have so many options and could even travel the world.'

Elena shook her head. 'What about the kids? Ada has just started school, and Andreas has settled into the nursery. We can't simply whisk them away from their home.'

'Look, it's something to think about. I don't mean we'll sell up everything and leave it all behind. We can hire a tutor, and the nanny can come with us, too. Don't you want to visit Kirsty in England?'

'Of course, I would love to.' Elena beamed.

Max cleared his throat. 'May I make a suggestion?' Three pairs of eyes studied him in anticipation.

'You don't have to retire. Just take a break from the wine business. You'd both get bored if you gave up work this early in life. Roberto, you're sitting on a talent that needs to be expanded on. You were so passionate when you gave us the tour of the island, and bloody good at it, too. I was against the idea at first, but you could turn it into a part-time business venture.'

Roberto's face lit up with a broad grin.

Max said, 'And as for you, Elena, you need some independence away from the kids … and Roberto. You're not cut out to be a sales rep, although you're good at it, and you work brilliantly with people. I've thought for a while that I need a new marketing director. It would only be a part-time position, based in Cyprus, and you would be perfect for the role.'

Elena's eyes widened, and she grinned. 'Tell me more.'

Max took a sip of his wine. 'Well, one aspect would be to wine and dine our special guests, and you can stay at the hotel whilst doing so. Another task would be to raise our profile on social media, which you can do from home or at the hotel.'

'That sounds like the perfect job for Elena,' Roberto said. 'She's always on her phone and would jump at the chance to stay at your hotel. Just a thought, though, what if I were to offer exclusive tours only to your hotel guests?'

Elena clapped her hands. 'Oh, yes, I could sort out the advertising and social media, then wine and dine the guests when they returned from the tour.' She glanced at me. 'We can't leave Kirsty out. Do you have a job for her?'

Max looked at his hands. 'Kirsty doesn't need a job. She's got one waiting for her when she goes back to England. Anyway, that's enough about work. I'll give you time to think, and we can talk about it next week. Let's make the most of our last night together.'

All right, Max, I get the hint ... you don't want me in your life.

Elena's housekeeper had prepared a wonderful array of food ready to get cooked, and my mouth salivated when delicious aromas wafted over to us. Roberto turned juicy *souvlakia* and *shaftalia* on the barbeque whilst sipping from a bottle of spring water. One thing I wasn't looking forward to when I returned to England were rushed meal deals for one, or chicken salads, which were my go-to staples most nights.

'Remind me to swim extra laps in the morning.' I soaked up the meat juices with bread.

'Max and Roberto are going to join us for yoga,' Elena said.

I glanced across at Max, who wore a bemused look. 'When did I sign up for that?'

'Roberto said he'd only do it if you did,' Elena said.

Roberto stood. 'I don't need yoga—I'm flexible enough. Look, I can touch my toes.' When he bent over, he grimaced in pain, and his hands dangled by his knees. 'Perhaps I'm not.' He rubbed his back.

I relaxed back into my chair and swayed my head to the sounds of Daniel Caesar. I glanced up at the star-lit sky and closed my eyes for a moment.

Gently, Max shook my arm. 'Wake up, sleepyhead. Shall we go to bed?'

Roberto and Elena were nowhere to be seen.

'Oh, my goodness, did I fall asleep? What time is it?' I said.

'Nearly midnight.'

'Why didn't you wake me up sooner?'

'You looked so peaceful, and I didn't want to disturb you.'

'Did I snore?'

'Yes, but don't worry, the other two had gone to bed, so didn't hear you. Anyway, it's something I'll have to get used to if we're to share a bed together,' Max said.

'Well, I suppose we'd best make our way to bed. How about we get up early and see the sunrise?'

'Who said we'll get any sleep?' Max said, his eyes dark with lust.

*N*aked but for a sheet draped over him, Max sat on the mattress. I stood at the foot of the bed, fully clothed and, for a moment, contemplated tantalising him with a strip-tease. Only I felt knackered, so I yanked my dress over my head. His eyes flittered about as he studied my underwear-clad body, and I smiled when the contours of the sheet shifted.

I crawled onto the bed and straddled his torso. My hair tickled his face when our lips collided and our tongues explored each other's mouths.

Max reached behind my back, unclasped my bra, and sucked on my erect nipples, moving from one side to the other. With his other hand, he fumbled around until his fingers came to rest on my hidden bud. When the pressure of his touch intensified, I gasped and arched my back.

Max groaned. 'You're so wet, I just want to be inside you.'

I climbed off him and shifted to my hands and knees. 'Why don't you, then?'

He reached into the bedside cabinet and retrieved a condom. Within seconds, it covered his blood-filled shaft, and he thrust deep inside me.

Max grasped hold of my hips, and our bodies slapped together as we rocked backwards and forwards.

I threw my head backwards and shouted out his name whilst sensations swept over my body.

'I don't think I can hold on much longer,' he said in a pained voice.

'I'm nearly there, but can you touch me again?' I said.

Once more, his fingers found the centre of my desire and circled around and around. I bit into the pillow to stifle my screams, but it did no good. With my head thrust backwards, I bellowed his name, and the volcano inside me erupted. Max gripped my hips, and with one last thrust, surrendered to his orgasm.

'If I smoked, this would be the moment I'd light up a cigarette.' Max laughed.

'Me too. That was amazing.'

'At one point, I thought you were trying to suffocate yourself.'

'I know, I thought after this morning's commentary, I'd try to be quiet.' I giggled.

'There's no need. It's such a turn-on to hear you cry out in pleasure.'

'I'll remember that next time.'

With the anticipation of a repeat performance in the night, we fell asleep in each other's arms.

J couldn't get enough of this beautiful woman who lay in my arms, and my mind filled with thoughts about how I could see her again ... sooner rather than later. Within moments, she fell fast asleep, and I smiled when she let out a gentle snore. My eyelids grew heavy, and within no time, I drifted off.

Some hours later, sunlight peeked through the blinds, and the birds tweeted outside our window.

We sat up, startled when the bedroom door thrust open and two excited children squealed in delight and shouted out my name. 'Uncle Max, Uncle Max, where are our presents? Who's that in your bed?' Ada said.

Elena followed behind, out of breath. 'I'm so sorry, Max. My mother dropped the kids off early and I told them you were here. I didn't mean for them to wake you.'

'Why's that lady got no clothes on?' A wide-eyed Andreas wanted to know.

'Kids, this is my friend Kirsty. Let us get dressed, and we'll come down for breakfast.'

Ada crossed her arms and scowled. 'And our presents,' she said.

'Yes, and your presents, too, but only if you're a good girl and help your mummy with the breakfast.'

'Yes, Uncle Max. I love you.' Ada took hold of her brother's hand. 'Come on, Andreas. You can help me; otherwise, you won't get a present.'

'Phew, that could have been a close call,' I said.

Kirsty lifted the bedsheet, which had covered our modesty. 'Yes, and that will have to wait. Oh, my God, those kids are so cute.'

'Aren't they just. Have you ever wanted kids?' I said.

Kirsty nodded. 'Yes, but it was never meant to be.'

My eyes glazed. 'We'd make beautiful children.'

Kirsty gave me a playful slap on the arm. 'Come on, Mr Broody. You have two little children waiting for you downstairs and for their presents. Anyway, your mother told me you don't want kids.'

'She said what?'

'Forget I said anything. I'd better have a quick shower. See you downstairs.'

Where did Mother get the idea I didn't want children? We've never had a conversation on the subject. I'll have words with her when I see her.

Downstairs, Ada and Andreas sat at the table and unwrapped the gifts my secretary had chosen for them in England. Andreas shrieked and jumped off his chair to play with his new bright-red fire-engine truck whilst Ada cradled her baby doll in her arms. 'Her name's Annabel, but I like the name Kirsty,' she said.

Elena suggested, 'Why don't you call her Kirsty-Annabel, then?'

Kirsty walked into the room and sat next to Ada. 'That's such a pretty name, although I think Ada is prettier,' she said.

Ada tapped Kirsty on the arm. 'Have you got a second name?'

Kirsty laughed. 'You will never believe this, but my middle name is Anna. Kids used to call me Kay at school because my surname is Young, so it spells out K. A. Y.'

Ada put the doll on the table and folded her arms. 'That's silly. Your name is Kirsty. I hope you told them off. Stupid kids.'

Roberto looked up from his newspaper. 'Now, now, Ada. You mustn't call people stupid.'

'Sorry, Daddy. Silly children.'

Andreas sat back in his chair and shouted out 'nee-naw' as he pushed the fire engine around the table.

Ada put her fingers on her lips. 'Shush. You'll wake the baby up. Kirsty, will you hold her whilst I go for a pee-pee?'

'Well, I suppose yoga is out of the question now the kids are back?' I said.

'Not at all—Ada and Andreas often join in when I practice yoga. They'll be able to teach you a thing or two,' Elena said.

Kirsty cradled the baby doll in her arms and rocked it gently. 'I can't believe I'm going home tomorrow. I'll miss all this, even though I'm homesick.'

'Catch up with everyone, then come back?' Elena said.

Kirsty shook her head. 'I'm not sure what I'll do next. Anyway, you could come and visit me in England before I go off on my travels again.'

I nodded. 'Yes, you're always welcome as a guest at the hotel. Stay as long as you like, and I'll show you the sights. Let me know when you're free, and I'll clear a space in my diary.' I glanced at Kirsty to make eye contact, but she diverted her attention when Ada returned from the bathroom.

Ada pinched her nose with her fingers. 'Eew, I think baby Kirsty has done a poo-poo.'

Roberto let out a belly laugh. 'Darn it, I thought I got away with that one. Sorry, folks. Those sausages we had last night gave me terrible wind.'

'Pew-yew, Daddy—Mr Smelly Pants. You stink,' Ada said.

'You stink, you stink, you stink,' Andreas sang whilst he pushed the fire engine over my arms, which rested on the table.

'Come on, kids. Put down your toys. Breakfast's ready,' Elena said.

Ada thrust her doll at Kirsty. 'Can you hold her again so I can eat my scrambled eggs?'

I reached out my arms. 'Pass baby Kirsty over to me. I'll look after her so Kirsty can eat her breakfast, too.'

'Aww, you look so cute,' Roberto said.

Elena glared at him and put her hands on her hips. 'Don't be a tease, and please stop farting at the breakfast table. Where are your manners?'

After we'd rested from the meal, we marched outside, carrying our yoga mats. Dressed in swimwear, the kids soon lost interest in the yoga class. The sun rose higher in the sky, and the little ones donned their life jackets and jumped into the pool. Unable to resist, we abandoned the exercises and joined them. Ada monopolised Kirsty for the rest of the day, and I felt slightly put out that I hadn't spent any alone time with her. Roberto arranged to fly me back to the hotel later that day, and before I knew it, I stood on the tarmac with my bag packed, ready to leave. Whilst Roberto went through the safety checks on the helicopter, the children clung to my legs and begged me not to go.

'Come on, kids, that's enough. You'll see Uncle Max soon, and if you're good, we may even go to see him in England,' Elena said.

Ada let go of my legs and tugged on Kirsty's dress. 'Will we see you too?' Her big, beautiful eyes gazed up at Kirsty.

Kirsty crouched and wiped away a tear, which had trickled down Ada's cheek. She kissed her and said, 'Of course you can see me in England. Make sure you bring baby Kirsty, too.'

Elena said, 'Come on, kids. Let's go indoors so Max and Kirsty can say goodbye.'

Kirsty tiptoed towards me and kissed me on the lips. 'Thank you for such an amazing weekend. It's been incredibly special. Take care of yourself, Max.'

That doesn't sound good. No 'see you soon' or 'when can we meet up again'.

Before I replied, Roberto shouted out that the chopper was ready to fly. Kirsty gave me another kiss and turned to walk off.

'Wait, I ... err ... um, I'd like to see you again,' I said.

'Come on, Max,' Roberto shouted. 'The winds are picking up, and I want to set off.'

Kirsty waved over her shoulder. 'Phone me when you're free. Safe journey.'

4 3

KIRSTY

*T*he next morning, Elena and I stood at the airport entrance and hugged.

'You make sure you keep in touch and look after Max for me,' I said.

Elena frowned. 'I know what you said last night, but please don't give up hope. Max has never been in a serious relationship, so you may have to do some of the running.'

'I don't think so, but if he gets in touch, I'll meet up with him. Anyway, he's busy. I'm busy. We're all busy. It was nice whilst it lasted, but I shan't sit indoors, waiting for the phone to ring. Oh, bugger it, I forgot to give him my number.'

Elena smiled and hugged me again. 'Don't worry. I'll send him a text. Dammit, here comes a parking attendant. Look, I must dash, but message me when you get home. Miss you already.' She blew me a kiss.

❦

GREY SKIES DASHED fat raindrops against the plane window, and I waited for disembarkation instructions from the cabin crew. The journey home passed in the blink of an eye, and I'd spent most of it asleep. The weekend's activities had caught up with me. I'd sent Margot and Ernest a text to say goodbye and apologised for not seeing them in person.

It's not goodbye but au revoir, Ernest texted in response.

My phone pinged, and my stomach clenched when I studied the unknown Cypriot number. My heart sank a little as I read the message from Dee.

Margot just told me you're back in England. I'm coming over in a fortnight, so can we meet up?

I replied, *That would be lovely. Let me know when you get here, and we'll arrange something.*

Another message flashed on the screen. This one came from my sister, already parked in the car park. She'd sent me the details of where to find her.

I checked Facebook Messenger. Max had been active two minutes previously, and my fingers hovered over the buttons. After a deep breath, I typed in a brief message.

Hi, Max. Thanks for a wonderful weekend. I'm back in England, and it's raining. I miss Cyprus already. Don't work too hard—K xxx.

ON THE DRIVE back to South Talling, I told my sister all about my travels but didn't mention my brief dalliances with Lucas and Max. She always lectured me on my moral standards, and I had no wish to hear her opinions on the matter. Anyway, Eloise could hardly talk because she'd fallen pregnant in her teens. My dad insisted she and Ben got married when they were twenty, and their second child was born within wedlock ... just.

Rosie, my niece, waited at the front door of my flat, and her face broke out in a big grin when I stepped out of the car. She flung herself at me and wrapped her arms around my torso. 'I've missed you so much, Aunty Kirsty.'

'I've missed you too. Thank you so much for looking after my flat.'

'It's spotless, and I've tidied up and even sorted your kitchen cupboards. They were a bit, erm ...'

I cringed. 'Don't remind me. They were an embarrassment. I meant to sort them out before I left, but I ran out of time. Thanks for doing that.'

Rosie smiled. 'They're all sparkling clean, and I've thrown away the herbs and spices that had gone five years out of date.'

'Whoops, I bought them when I went through my *learning-to-cook* phase. It didn't last long.'

'I'll make us a cuppa whilst you unpack and then we'd better get back. Ben will want his dinner,' Eloise said.

'Mum, I've told you time and time again that dad needs to learn how to cook his own meals. I want to hear all about Aunty Kirsty's travels. What are Cypriot men like? And who was that picture of the hunk by the pool when you were in Ibiza?'

'Shush,' I said and cringed. 'I don't want your mum to hear. I'll tell you another time when we're on our own.'

I reached into my hand luggage and took out a box gift-wrapped with a red ribbon. 'I got this for you as a thank you for looking after my flat.'

Rosie unwrapped the package, and her eyes lit up when she unscrewed the lid on the bottle. 'OMG, Aunty Kirsty. How did you know *Jo Malone* was my favourite perfume?'

'I guessed. You always make a beeline for it when we go out shopping.'

'I love it. I've never been able to afford to buy it for myself, though. It's out of my price range, being just a poor student. So, who was the hunk in the photo?'

'He's called Lucas, and he's such a lovely young man. He looks after Emma and Dom's pool.'

'Did you do the deed?' Rosie giggled.

'What deed?' Eloise plonked three mugs of tea onto the table and glanced at the perfume. 'That's nice. Did you bring anything back for me?'

'Yes, a bottle of vodka and a box of Loukoumi,' I said.

'What's Loukini when it's at home?'

'It's otherwise known as Cypriot Delight.' I chuckled.

'Well, why didn't you just call it that?' Eloise said. 'I'm going outside for a quick ciggie before we set off. You'll have to show me the photos another time.'

'I wish Mum would quit smoking. The car will reek of cigarettes on the way home, and then she'll eat a bag of mints to hide the stench. Dad will have a hissy if he finds out she still smokes. Anyway, enough about that. Did you meet any other *Cypriot Delights*?'

'Behave yourself.' I laughed. 'For the record, the only Cypriot Delights I sampled came in a small package and were covered in nuts.'

'Sounds like some men I've met at university.' We broke out into fits of giggles, which quickly subsided when my sister returned from her cigarette break.

By the time I'd spoken to my dad on the phone, texted Henri and Isabel, and unpacked my suitcases, I felt exhausted. I climbed into bed and pulled the covers over my fatigued body. Just as I nodded off, my phone pinged.

Goodnight, darling. Glad you arrived home safely. I miss you already. Max xxx.

Short and sweet, but the butterflies danced around my belly.

Goodnight, you gorgeous man, I murmured.

THE NEXT DAY, I arranged to meet Henri at Harry's Bar after she'd finished work.

A loud cheer greeted me when I entered. Familiar faces smiled.

I'd only been away for six weeks but still burst into tears at the sight of my best friends.

Henri gasped in alarm. 'Whatever's the matter?'

'It's just me being silly. I've missed you all.' I gulped and studied the man with a protective arm draped around Henri's shoulder. 'Hello Danny, how are you?'

He was bloody gorgeous, and I could see why Henri had fallen for him. He kissed me on the cheek. Oh, my, he smelled great too. Not as nice as Max, though.

'Let me get you a drink,' he said.

'Just a lime and soda, please.' I smiled.

'What? No vodka?' Darius asked.

'No, I'm giving my liver a break for a few days. Come here and give me a hug.' I gestured for him to step closer.

'Only if you promise not to cry on me. You'll streak my tan. Just look at you.' He wagged his finger up and down. 'I've got tan envy. That's it, Paul, we need to book a holiday before the children get here. I need to get a proper tan.'

'What do you mean by children?' I said.

Paul nudged Darius out of the way and gave me a hug. 'We've missed you too, Kirsty. We have some fantastic news. Darius and I are going to adopt two children. The adoption agency matched us with a four-year-old girl and her two-year-old brother.'

I swallowed the lump that formed in my throat. 'That's the best news. I'm so happy for you both. What else have I missed?'

Our heads turned towards the door when two more familiar figures walked in, hand in hand. Maggie rushed over to greet me whilst John hung back and waited for me to say hello. Maggie wore a figure-hugging dress, and John looked rather handsome in pressed trousers and a checked shirt. I'd grown so used to seeing them in white overalls with their hair covered by blue netting that it took me by surprise to see how well they scrubbed up. Maggie's eyes sparkled, and John adopted a big, soppy grin. 'We've missed you, Kirsty,' Maggie said.

'I've missed you, too. Something is different? You look positively glowing.' I studied her.

Maggie whispered, 'Let's just say things are spicing up in the boudoir.'

'Oh, that sounds interesting. You'll have to tell me more about it when we're on our own,' I said.

'Isabel sends her apologies. She's caught up at work and will speak to you tomorrow,' Henri said.

Our group sat around a table at the front of the restaurant, and I told everyone about my time in Ibiza and Cyprus.

'Who was that hunk on Instagram? I wouldn't kick him out of bed,' Darius said.

Paul glared at him. 'Behave. Mind you, I wouldn't either.' He laughed.

Harry, the restaurant owner and Henri's future son-in-law, came to the table to take food orders. It felt lovely being back home, but my mind kept drifting to Max.

'So, did you meet anyone special?' Maggie asked.

Henri's eyes widened whilst she waited for my reply.

'Yes. A wonderful man called Max.'

Darius clapped. 'Tell us more. What's he like? Is he a fit Cypriot?'

'No, English born and bred. In fact, you may know him. His family owns the Brightside chain of hotels.'

Paul raised his eyebrows. 'Do you mean Max Bright? Our paths have crossed. He's a bit of a tyrant.'

My body tensed, and I clenched my fists. 'I thought so at first, but when you get to know him, he's kind and funny and so devoted to his family.'

'Sounds like you're smitten. When will you see him again?' Maggie said.

I shrugged. 'Who knows? He's busy with work, and I have no expectations. Anyway, I'm sorry to be such a party pooper, but I feel drained. It must be the jet lag.' I chuckled. 'I'm going to love you and leave you, and I'll see you when I get back from my sister's.'

I blew kisses at my wonderful group of friends and made my way home to my empty flat.

$\mathcal{T}$im picked up things quickly and soon learnt the ropes within the hotel business, which pleased me. Mother and Ernest returned from an extended stay in Portugal, and Tim often joined them for an evening meal, along with Dee, with whom he'd become absolutely smitten. I envied his new romance and the way Mother welcomed him into the family fold. Even though he was my childhood friend, and Mother knew him from old, she frequently referred to him as her future son-in-law. Usually, I declined their invitation to join them for dinner because I felt like a spare part with the blossoming romances all around me.

Kirsty and I messaged each other lots, but I saw no indications she wanted to see me again when I returned to England. With Isabel under a lot of pressure due to the change in management and staff rebelling against their new leadership, Kirsty returned to work for a few weeks to support Isabel and, in her words, 'kick some ass.'

Elena and I met up to discuss her new job within the hotel, and her enthusiasm thrilled me, as did her ideas for improving visibility and reputation. Roberto advertised for her replacement in the winery, to seek someone who could assist the manager, who was more than happy to take on extra responsibility after the promise of a generous pay increase.

Roberto went to see his GP for another health check and felt delighted when he discovered he'd lost over 6 kg. Elena reported things had improved in the bedroom department, and she and Roberto had booked a mini-break to the North without the kids. She referred to the holiday as her second honeymoon. We discussed their visit to England and decided the family would travel over at the beginning of December to see the Christmas lights. I promised to take the children to meet Father Christmas. They had also arranged a brief trip to Lapland to see the reindeers, although the thought of snow horrified Roberto, and already, he'd gone shopping for winter thermals.

Tim would stay on in Cyprus for a few more days, once I left for Portugal, which scored me a few brownie points with my half-sister. I'd grown protective over her in a short time and had joked to Tim that he would get the sack if he upset her.

He reassured me there was no chance and confided he was falling in love.

When I arrived in Portugal, the appearance of the hotel impressed me. Everything appeared spick and span, and my brother stood behind the reception desk and greeted everyone with a bright smile. Fleur agreed to work at the hotel, whilst her son attended school, and became an asset to the company. We discussed plans for her to join the marketing team under Elena's wing and that she could, therefore, work from home as well as at the hotel.

Finally, Anthony and I met up on our own for a long-overdue catch-up following his breakdown on the day of my party.

He sat at the bar, nursing a half-pint of lager shandy, and shook my hand with gusto when I joined him.

'I've got something to tell you, but you mustn't breathe a word of it to anyone. Promise?'

'Scout's honour,' I said.

'We got married last weekend.'

'Oh, no. Does Mother know?'

'Of course. That's why she and Ernest stayed in Portugal for a few extra days. They were the witnesses. But that's not the news. Fleur's pregnant. It's the only reason Mother agreed to such a quick wedding.'

'Thanks for the invite.'

Anthony looked down at his hands, which lay folded in his lap. 'Sorry. I really wanted to invite you, but it was done in such a rush, and Mother said you wouldn't mind.'

Mother, again.

'No, don't worry. You know I'm not a fan of weddings. Congratulations to you both, and I'm thrilled to bits you're going to make me an uncle.'

'Well, it's early days, and that's why Fleur doesn't want anyone to know yet.'

Tears welled in my eyes. 'Come here and give your brother a hug. I hope you know I'm immensely proud of you. There's something I've meant to ask. On the day of my party, you mentioned another woman? What was that all about?'

Anthony shuddered. 'Somebody I thought I loved. She's a married woman, a few years older than me, and we met at a party in London. We started seeing each other, and I fell madly in love. She promised to divorce her husband, and we planned to set up a home together. We had even discussed getting married and found a flat. Before we signed the lease, she changed her mind. Her husband reminded her that she'd signed a prenuptial agreement, which meant she wouldn't be entitled to anything from the divorce settlement. By all accounts, they have a marriage of convenience.'

I sipped my wine and studied his face, which showed no sign of the sadness that haunted his eyes when I last saw him.

'Anyway, that's all in the past,' he said. 'As Fleur says, always look forward, never back.'

He took a sip of his shandy. 'Mother's happy with Ernest. Do you think they'll get married one day?'

'Yes. Ernest is old-school, and Mother has fallen in love with him. I'm happy for them. I didn't realise how tough things must have been for her all those years. What with father's absence and infidelity. Remind me why you didn't warn me about Dee?'

'Look, we all know you were Father's favourite, and I'm Mother's. You worshipped the ground Father walked on, and I didn't want to shatter your illusions. I buried my head in the sand and hoped it would all go away. Unbeknownst to me, Mother knew about Dee already.'

I prodded Anthony in the arm and laughed. 'You have competition regarding being Mother's favourite child.'

'Don't I know it. All I hear is Dee this, Dee that. I'll be Mother's number-one child again once I make her a grandmother.' Fleur entered the bar area. Anthony said, 'Don't forget, no mention of the baby.'

'Mum's the word,' I said.

Fleur greeted me with a kiss on both cheeks. Pregnancy suited her, and she glowed. A shy, blond-haired boy hid behind her skirt. I crouched to his level and held out my hand. 'And you must be Beau? I'm your Uncle Max. Do you work in the hotel, too?'

The boy grinned. 'No, silly. I go to school. I'm only six.'

'Six? I thought you were at least sixteen. Can I get you a drink? How about a Coca-Cola ice-cream float?' Beau glanced towards his mum with an expectant expression. Fleur raised her eyebrows.

'No, thank you. Mummy says fizzy drink rots your teeth— look.' He pointed to the gap in his incisors.

My eyes creased with a smile. This was something our mother used to say to us when we were younger, and I didn't have any fillings.

'Mummy knows best. What can I get you instead?'

'Could I have a glass of milk with a straw, please?'

'Of course. Coming right up. Can I get you two a drink?' I nodded towards Anthony.

'No, thanks. We have a flight to catch, and I need to grab our suitcases from the flat. In fact, can we leave Beau with you for ten minutes? It would be better if Fleur came with me because you know what I'm like. I'm bound to forget something.'

Fleur kissed Beau on the top of his head and told him to be good for his Uncle Max.

I patted the chair next to me. 'Come and sit here and you can tell me all about yourself.

He climbed onto the stool, and his eyes lit up when he spotted the ice-cream menu. After a sigh, he sipped his milk.

'Your drink looks so good. I think I'll order one instead of this yucky glass of wine,' I said.

Beau beamed. 'Yes, and your teeth will be strong like mine, apart from the one the tooth fairy took away. My girlfriend Maisie has lost two of her teeth. Have you got a girlfriend, Uncle Max?'

My eyes opened wide and for a moment, and I felt too stunned to reply. I wasn't used to being interrogated by a six-year-old.

'Not yet. I've met a beautiful lady, but I don't think she wants to be my girlfriend. I need your advice. What should I do?'

Beau took a big slurp of his milk, pinched his chin, and nodded. 'Well, my girlfriend likes me because she says I'm funny and I share my sweets with her. So that's what you need to do.'

If only things were so simple. I'd buy a sweet shop if it meant Kirsty would be my girlfriend. I chuckled. 'I can see where I've gone so wrong. Thank you, young man. I might manage to persuade her to be my girlfriend.'

He smiled and wiggled about in his chair.

'What are you two up to?' Anthony asked.

'Uncle Max wants a girlfriend, and I told him what he has to do,' Beau said.

Anthony ruffled Beau's hair. 'Thanks for helping my brother. He's not good at seeing what's right under his nose.'

Beau studied my face and pointed, 'Look, I can see what it is, he's got a milk moustache.'

Loud laughter filled the air whilst I wiped away the evidence with a napkin. The short time I'd spent with this adorable little boy had reinforced my need to become a father. My brother had found happiness, and I felt proud of the way he'd turned his life around. My father would have been proud too.

*W*hen I returned to work, the staff greeted me with sarcasm mostly, and negative undercurrents flowed through the office. Isabel sat at her desk, and her head rested in her hands. She glanced up when I walked into the room. Her eyes looked strained, and she wore a pinched expression. 'Oh boy, am I glad to see you.' She picked up her phone and spoke into the receiver. 'Can you bring in a pot of tea, please, erm ... Sally?'

'Who's Sally?' I asked.

'My new assistant. The agency sent her yesterday after Amy's abrupt resignation.'

The news shocked me because I'd thought Richard's former personal assistant was keen to stay on at the firm, even after Isabel discovered she'd had an affair with Richard.

A quiet knock paused our conversation. The door opened, and a petite woman shuffled into the office. She placed a tray onto the desk and made a hasty retreat.

'I can't take much more of this. Richard's henchmen are a bunch of chauvinistic pigs. My father said to sack the lot of them, but I can't.'

I knew exactly who she meant. It had taken me years to become resilient to the chauvinistic comments, and I wouldn't sit back and watch my friend suffer the way I did when I first joined the firm.

I shook my head and tutted. 'I know how to handle them.'

Tears dropped onto the paperwork scattered on Isabel's desk. She hiccupped. 'I wondered ... hoped, in fact, that I could promote you to my second-in-command? I know, technically, you're on sabbatical, but your new job will come with a generous pay rise and a bigger office, and you'll still be able to go away on leave once the dust has settled.'

Years ago, I would have snapped up this opportunity, but after spending several weeks out of this environment, I felt unsure whether I wanted to take on a position with extra responsibility. I talked through my reluctance with Isabel, and we agreed my new role as Assistant Managing Director would be on a trial basis, and I had the option to change my mind in the future. The two of us arranged a staff meeting with the HR department, and I got armed and ready to ruffle some feathers.

The news of my promotion didn't sit well with several of the men who'd worked for the firm since Isabel's father was in charge. Whispered name-calling, such as *Prize Pitbull* and *Second in Command Bitch,* susurrated around the room. Hazel from the Human Resources team certainly heard, and she scribbled away on her notepad. I received accusations of favouritism, and two men stormed out of the office. With a calm, steel-like manner, Isabel informed the rest of the employees that jobs would be jeopardised if this sort of archaic behaviour were to continue, and each member of staff would meet up for an appraisal. Isabel sweetened her words by mentioning there were several more opportunities for promotion on offer. The meeting ended on a relatively calm and successful note, and we finished the workday with a few drinks to celebrate my promotion. Again, I made my excuses and left early.

Over the next few weeks, Isabel and I worked long hours to sort through the chaos Richard had left behind. I received the occasional message from Max, and sometimes, I even forgot to reply, but he understood my new job came with extra responsibilities. His time was taken up flying between Portugal and Cyprus because his brother had extended his stay in France, following a scare with Fleur's pregnancy. Most nights, I ate a late supper and tumbled into bed, exhausted from demanding days. I barely had any time to catch up with my friends, who were all caught up in their own lives. After five weeks, my phone alerted me to an incoming WhatsApp message. Henri had sent a group-chat invitation. The following weekend, she had the house to herself because Danny would be in London, and her son planned to stay over at his dad's house, so she'd arranged a girl's night in with Maggie, Isabel, and me.

CHARLOTTE, now with a neat, visible baby bump, agreed to pick us up, and we made our way to Henri's at around 7 pm.

House music filled the air, and Henri danced around the kitchen in her slippers. Heated plates of savoury dishes covered the counters. Harry had sent them from the restaurant.

Maggie, her face flushed with the first glass of wine, giggled and told us about her latest sexual encounters with John. The couple had purchased their first copy of the Kama Sutra that week and she'd left John indoors on the sofa, complaining of a sore back after attempting the *Pretzel Dip*.

'He thought he'd be good at it because he's a baker.' Maggie broke out in fits of giggles, and drops of wine landed on her lap.

Isabel took her phone from her handbag and studied the screen. 'The only pretzel dips I'm familiar with are the kind covered in cinnamon that I buy for the kids. Ah, yes, here it is. Oh my, that certainly looks like a challenge, more so for the men. I don't think I'll be able to look at a pretzel in the same light ever again, and I can see why John may have hurt his back. I have the number of a good chiropractor if you need it.'

Henri stood in the doorway. 'Who needs a chiropractor?'

Tears streamed down Maggie's face, and she took a couple of deep breaths to compose herself. Her laughter became infectious, and Isabel soon joined in the fits of giggles. 'He hurt his back whilst experimenting with a pretzel dip,' Isabel said.

Henri glanced across to me with a bemused look on her face and shrugged. 'What's funny about that? He's a baker after all. Hang on. Tell me in a minute when we're at the dining table. Ladies, dinner is served.'

Henri reached over to top up my half-empty glass of wine, but I put my hand over it to stop her. 'I'll stick to water with dinner. I felt unwell this morning and am still delicate.'

She put the bottle back on the table and poured me a glass of water. 'What's wrong? Did you have too much to drink last night?'

I shook my head. 'No, not at all. I ate some feta cheese the other day that should have been thrown out, and I got sick. I'm okay now and just have the occasional bout of sickness and heartburn.'

Charlotte walked into the dining room and served a plate of lasagne. 'That sounds the same as me when I fell pregnant. You're not, are you, Aunty Kirsty?'

The conversation stopped, and the room went silent.

'Of course not. I'm too old,' I said.

Henri glanced at the other women and back to me. 'No, you're not, young lady. When was your last period, and have you had unprotected sex?'

On my phone, I opened my period tracker app and sat flabbergasted when I realised I was two weeks overdue. In a whisper, I said, 'We didn't have unprotected sex. Oh ... yes, we did. The helicopter.'

'The what?' the women cried out in unison.

'Max and I got carried away in his friends' helicopter. We didn't use protection, but it was only the one time.'

Henri squeezed my hand and passed me a tissue after a stray

tear escaped. 'That's all it takes, darling. I think you could be pregnant. Do your boobs feel sore?'

I nodded.

'You need to do a test,' Henri said.

Charlotte put her plate of food on the table and patted me on the back. 'I have some kits in my bedroom. Let me fetch one, and you can take a test. It even shows how many weeks you are.'

I cast my eyes downwards and counted my fingers. 'I can't be pregnant, but if I was, I'd be five weeks. Isn't that too early to tell?'

Isabel shook her head. 'I knew within days of missing my period that I was pregnant. Are your cycles regular?'

I scrolled through the history on my app. 'Yes, every twenty-eight days. It slipped my mind this time because we've been so busy at work. Why don't I leave it tonight, and I'll do a test in the morning? The food's getting cold.'

'Sod the food. We want to know if you're pregnant. Do you want me to come with you?' Henri said.

'No. Stay here and eat, and I'll let you know. I reckon I'll need an enormous glass of wine when I get back to get over the shock.'

I followed Charlotte to her bedroom, and she handed me a kit. She reached out and hugged me, and a warm sensation spread over me when I felt the hard bump of her body press into mine. 'I'll see you downstairs. I love you, Aunty Kirsty,' she said.

A few minutes later, I walked trance-like into the dining room and slumped onto my chair. Expectant eyes studied me from across the table whilst I sat in silence with my jaw slack.

'Well? Are you pregnant?' Henri asked.

I burst into tears, and the women rushed to comfort me. Henri said, 'Don't worry, sweetie. It'll happen one day when the time's right.'

'Yes, you still have time to find Mr Right and start a family,' Maggie said.

I placed the results face-up on the table. Henri stared at it, covered her mouth, and gasped. 'Oh, my goodness. You're having a baby.'

My mouth went dry, and unable to respond, I nodded.

The women shrieked in delight.

'I'm going to be a mum. What will Max say? He doesn't want children. Do I tell him?'

Isabel retook her seat and poured herself another glass of wine. 'Of course you tell him. It's his baby, too, and he needs to know. Tim said he and Max are coming over next weekend for my parents' wedding anniversary, so you could meet up with him and tell him in person.'

I stood and paced around the room. 'Margot said he doesn't want children. What will I do? I can't raise a child on my own.'

Henri handed me a glass of water. 'Come and sit down. You won't be on your own. We all love you and will do everything we can to help.'

I glanced at Isabel. 'What about work? I don't want to let you down.'

'Don't worry about that. You won't let me down. Anyway, you've got a few months to go before your maternity leave will start and, fingers crossed, the company will be running smoothly under our leadership. First things first, I'll get you checked out by my doctor and then we can make plans. What are you ladies up to next week? Are you free to come along to my parent's anniversary party? I'm sure Kirsty would appreciate the support. You can bring along your other halves as well.'

46

MAX

*T*im dropped us off outside the hotel, and Bert came to help with the suitcases. He greeted Ernest like a long-lost friend, and they stood and chatted whilst Mother and Dee walked arm in arm into the foyer. We'd flown over for the Bantham's golden wedding anniversary, and I hoped Kirsty could find time in her busy schedule to meet up with me. The online messaging between us had dwindled, and she'd not replied to my last message, which I'd sent the previous weekend.

Tim rushed off to help his sister with the evening's celebrations, and I followed the group indoors. Silver and bronze tinsel decorated the foyer, and delicate snowflakes hung from the high ceiling. In the corner, a magnificent tree towered over us at twelve-feet tall, wrapped with flickering lights. Tonight's party was a black-tie event, and Rachel messaged to let me know she'd collected my tuxedo from the dry cleaners and left it in my room.

I sent Kirsty another message and suggested we meet on Sunday. Throughout the day, I checked my phone repeatedly, but the message remained delivered and unread.

Anthony and Fleur arrived shortly before we left for the party, and I nearly lost my balance when a bundle of energy threw arms around my legs. I scooped Beau into the air, and he giggled when I spun him around.

I placed him back on the ground and smiled as he strutted about to show off his tuxedo. Beau wore a dark-blue dicky-bow tie, which matched my brother's, and his blond hair was styled with sticky gel.

Fleur radiated health and looked resplendent in a floor-length silver sequin dress, and the fabric clung to her body and accentuated the tiny bump.

Mother appeared elegant in her deep-green velvet dress, and when Ernest met her gaze, his eyes shone with pride.

After a brief journey, we climbed out of the limousine, and I linked arms with my sister, ready to escort her to the party.

We walked along a flame-lit pathway, shrouded by neatly trimmed bushes, which led into the back garden. A bell-shaped marquee housed the band and a dance floor. Live music filled the air. On the opposite side of the garden stood a bar decorated with fairy lights. Tables and chairs dotted the lawn, and warm air blew over the guests. I waved to Mr and Mrs Bantham, and Mother and Ernest broke away from our group to join the happy couple. My stomach growled at the smell of freshly baked pizza, and I nudged my brother's arm. 'Shall we get some pizza? I'm sure the little man could eat a slice.'

Beau's tiny hand reached up and found mine. 'Yes, please, Uncle Max. I'm starving.'

Tim trotted over to us and whisked Dee away so he could introduce her to distant family members, and his teenage children welcomed Dee warmly.

I saw no sign of Isabel, but her kids strolled past our table and waved. They disappeared inside a smaller marquee set up for the younger generation. We sat around a table next to the pizza van and watched images flash up on a projector screen, which showcased fond family memories that spanned over fifty years. Beau kept glancing towards the tent and fidgeted in his seat. The pizza disappeared off his plate in record time, and he tugged on his mother's dress and pointed towards the tent.

'He wants to join the other children,' I said. 'Let me take him, and I'll ask Isabel's kids if they would keep an eye on him. I'm sure he'll be fine.'

Beau seemed happy to shadow Ethan, Isabel's eighteen-year-old son, who looked the image of his father. When I left the tent, I noticed a group of people walking along the pathway towards Isabel. They seemed familiar, but I couldn't quite place them. The penny dropped—they were Kirsty's friends. I recognised them from her Facebook and Instagram posts but was unaware of their connection with the Bantham's. I stood in the shadows and watched Isabel greet her guests with hugs and smiles. They headed in the bar's direction, and my heart stopped for a moment whilst I stood transfixed. Kirsty, dressed in a midnight-blue evening gown that shimmered in the candlelight, walked arm in arm with a tall, handsome man dressed in a flamboyant baby-blue tuxedo. He whispered something in her ear, and the sound of her laughter echoed around the garden. She stood at the entrance of the marquee, and her eyes scanned the garden before her companion took hold of her arm and guided her inside. My heart raced in my chest, and I hesitated, unsure whether to make my presence known or slip away from the party unnoticed. A lone figure strolled along the pathway; again, I recognised him from Kirsty's photos, and this time, I remembered his name. It was her friend Paul, who ran a detective agency. Isabel had engaged his services to catch out her cheating husband.

Anthony walked over and tapped me on the arm. 'Aren't you going to say hello to Kirsty?'

I gazed at the floor. 'I don't think she'll be happy to see me. She's with another man.'

He laughed. 'Do you mean the bloke in the blue tuxedo? That's Darius. He owns the hairdressers where I get my hair cut. See that man there?' He pointed towards Paul. 'That's his husband. Go on and say hello.'

A sigh of relief escaped, and with long strides, I hurried to the dance floor. For a few moments, I stood statue-still, unable to move until Darius noticed me. His face lit up in recognition, and he pointed in my direction. Kirsty spun around, and our gazes met.

KIRSTY

*H*alfway along the path, Paul announced he'd forgotten to lock the car and turned around to check. My friends knew I was a bundle of nerves at the thought of bumping into Max, and Darius offered me his arm in support. We walked towards a picturesque bell tent decorated with tiny gold lanterns, and my eyes scanned the party for signs of Max, but I couldn't see him anywhere.

Isabel greeted us and whispered that she hadn't seen Max, even though his family had arrived. A heavy sensation washed over me, and I presumed Max hadn't come to the party.

Danny and Henri went off to the bar to buy drinks, and I stood on the dance floor and tapped my foot to the upbeat music. Darius's eyes lit up, and he focused on something behind me. I turned and stared at Max's Adonis-like frame, which filled the entrance. 'Don't stand there gawping like a goldfish,' Darius whispered. 'Say hello.'

Before I could move one foot in front of the other, Max approached and held out his hand. The tempo of the music slowed.

'Would you care to dance?' he said.

I took his hand, and he led me onto the dance floor and pulled my body close to his. His breath tickled my ear when he whispered, 'I've missed you so much.'

His hand caressed my exposed shoulders, and I snuggled my face into his broad chest. We circled on the dance floor for another two songs without speaking. My heart beat faster, and the butterflies in my stomach danced along to the beat of the music whilst Max held me in his arms. The band switched to an upbeat tune, and we broke apart when other guests joined us on the dance floor. Max gestured towards the bar. 'Shall we get a drink?'

I followed him outside and shivered in the cold air. Quickly, Max took off his jacket and draped it over my shoulders. 'I should have dressed more warmly, but I assumed the party would be indoors at this time of the year,' I said.

Max pointed to a table next to a pizza van. 'I sat over there with Anthony earlier, and the overhead heater is enough to keep you warm. Shall we fetch drinks and sit down?'

I rubbed my hands together and glanced at the floor. 'Let's get a drink, but before we sit, I need to tell you something.'

Max frowned and lifted my chin with his hand. 'Look, I know what you're going to say, and I totally understand. You have a new job now so haven't got enough room in your life for me. I just want to spend some time with you whenever you have a spare moment. Even if only to grab a quick coffee. I miss you, Kirsty.'

I shook my head. 'No, you've got it wrong. It's not that. I need to tell you something, but in private.'

Max held my arm. 'Come with me. There's a secret walled garden behind the marquee. Tim and I used to sneak a bottle of vodka out there when we were kids.'

'I can't imagine you being such a rebel.' I laughed.

He sighed. 'There's a lot you don't know about me.'

My mouth went dry, and a lead balloon filled my stomach.

He's right—I know nothing about him. How can I have his baby?

The hosts must have expected guests would wander through the grounds because a smoking fire pit and more seating had been set up in front of the walled garden. Empty beer bottles lay scattered about, and I presumed we'd stumbled across the secret hiding spot where underage drinkers could sample the temptation of alcohol, away from the watchful eyes of parents. We were alone, but how long would it be before other revellers arrived?

'Sit down, Max. I want to talk to you.'

Max studied my face and sat on a nearby bench whilst I paced.

'Look, there's no easy way to say this.' I sighed. 'I'm pregnant.'

His eyes widened, and he sucked in a breath. Max stood and took hold of my hand. 'You mean, we're going to have a baby?'

I nodded. 'Yes. But I expect nothing from you. We hardly know each other, and you don't want children.'

With a grin, Max picked me up and spun me around. 'Oh, my God. I'm so sorry. I shouldn't have done that. You're having a baby. My baby.' He pulled me into his arms, kissed the top of my head, and whispered, 'You're having my baby.'

Not the reaction I'd expected. Unable to contain my emotions, my body shook. Max enveloped me in a hug. Then he took a step back and brushed tears from my face. 'How do you feel about this? Do you want a baby?'

I turned and walked a few steps away. 'Of course, but I'm so scared. Look at me. I'm forty and single.'

Confusion washed over me after Max crouched onto one knee.

'Kirsty Young, we may not have known each other that long, and I'm not sure if you want me in your life, but I love you. I can't help it. I've loved you from the moment we first met, and I can't stop thinking about you. You'll probably think it's too soon but ... will you marry me?'

I crouched on the floor next to him and stroked his face. 'I'm not sure what to say. Do you mean it?' The look on his face told me he meant every word. 'Max Bright, I detested you when we first met, but it didn't take long for me to fall head over heels in love with you, too. I agree it's too soon for you to propose.' I pulled his face towards mine and gave him a tender kiss. 'But my answer is yes.'

EPILOGUE: ONE YEAR LATER

The smell of hairspray filled the air, and Dee finished the final touches after she'd woven delicate pearls into my hair. She held up the mirror so I could study my reflection.

My eyes rested on Dee's face—she had grey circles under her eyes and her face looked pinched and drawn, but as soon as she stroked her belly, her face radiated sunshine.

'Margot won't know what to do with herself with all these grandchildren,' I said.

'I know, poor Ernest is exhausted after travelling between England, Portugal, and Cyprus so they can both be involved in the children's lives,' Dee said.

Henri stood behind me and fastened the tiny buttons attached to the neckline of my ivory dress. I exhaled, and my shoulders relaxed when the zipper glided along with ease. This hadn't been the case when I'd walked up the aisle two months prior as Henri's chief bridesmaid. Fortunately, my sister was a remarkable seamstress and had adjusted my bridesmaid dress to make allowance for my expanded waistline. Not long ago, I'd given birth to my beautiful son, Arthur. He arrived two weeks early, and a mere four weeks before Henri got married. Now my special day had come.

Max wanted us to wed before the baby came, but I didn't want to walk up the aisle whilst pregnant. My ankles had swollen, I suffered from indigestion most of the time, and the heat made me uncomfortable. Also, our little bundle of joy kept me awake for hours on end as he wriggled about inside the womb. At least his shenanigans prepared me well for sleepless nights when he made an appearance.

Arthur Gregory Bright lay fast asleep in his crib under the watchful eye of Elena and Ada.

Max and I lived in England for most of the year and only travelled to Cyprus for a vacation. Tim managed the hotel full time now. We'd chosen to marry in Cyprus because this beautiful country would always hold a special place in our hearts, and our enthusiastic guests flew out to the hotel a few days before the wedding, excited at the prospect of spending time in the sunshine.

Fleur adjusted her top whilst her adorable baby daughter nuzzled at her breast. 'Anthony informs me that Ernest proposed to Margot again. Beau was quite put out when she turned him down because he's determined to be chief pageboy at Granny and Pops' wedding.'

'Why won't Margot marry Ernest?' Henri asked.

'From what I can gather, she enjoys living in sin and says it keeps him on his toes. Although Ernest is optimistic he will make an honest woman of her one day,' I said.

Henri passed me a glass of champagne. 'Come and look outside. The guests are seated, and I can see Max pacing up and down. Shall we make our way downstairs?'

I swallowed a lump in my throat. 'How do I look?' I asked.

Henri took both my hands in hers and smiled. 'You are stunning. And look at your boobs ... mine shrivelled up like prunes when I stopped breastfeeding. Motherhood suits you, and Max is a lucky man.'

I dabbed the corner of my eyes with a tissue. 'I'm so lucky to have friends like you.

'Yes, you are. Come on. Don't ruin your make-up—or mine. Let's go,' Henri said.

꧁꧂

I STILL COULDN'T BELIEVE it ... Mrs Kirsty Bright. Arthur had slept all the way through the ceremony and was still asleep as we walked along the aisle.

'Are you sure we shouldn't wake him up in case he needs a feed?' Max said.

Elena stood in front of the pram. 'Don't you dare. It's your wedding day, and you don't have to worry about Arthur. Just enjoy the reception, and we'll be along in a while. Roberto's waiting for you.'

The guests followed us to the parked coach and climbed aboard. The coach headed to the hotel for the reception. For a few moments, Max and I stood alone on the driveway. 'I'm the happiest man alive. Since I met you, my life has become so balanced. I wish my dad could have been here.' Max pulled me into his arms.

I placed my hand on his chest. 'He is here—in your heart—and in Arthur's heart. Your dad would have been so proud of you.'

Roberto approached us. 'Come on, you two lovebirds. The helicopter's fired up and ready to take you to the reception.'

'Are you sure you don't need to help Elena with the kids before we leave? We have plenty of time, and my wife and I can wait for you in the helicopter.' Max gave me a cheeky smile and winked. 'After all, Arthur could do with a little brother or sister.'

Roberto looked at me, then at Max, and raised his brow. 'What do you mean? What's that got to do with the helicopter?'

Max laughed and slapped him on the back. 'Nothing, old chap. We're ready when you are.'

ACKNOWLEDGMENTS

Once again, I can't thank Harmony Kent—editor, proof reader, and formatter, enough for how much she has supported me through this journey.

Also, to my cover designer, Dan Graham of Aluses Graphics, who is amazing and talented.

A special thanks goes to Michael Abbott and Christina Skinner, who created the initial concept of the design.

Without my family, I would not be able to follow my passion and write. My husband Dean has developed a love of cooking and is now head chef of the family, for which I am grateful. My four beautiful children have encouraged me every step of the way.

Through writing, I have made wonderful connections, from book bloggers (Zoebeesbooks19, you wear the crown) to fellow writers.

To the Wonder Women of Fit for Business and the WOWS – I am so lucky to be surrounded by awesome women.

I'd also like to thank my friends, family, and readers, who have provided me with positive feedback and encouragement.

Now, where's my award …

ABOUT THE AUTHOR

Joanna Cates is married to a patient and kind man and is a mum to four children. She has a vivid imagination and is a born romantic. Although Joanna spent her working life as an accountant, she's always felt far too creative for mere numbers—for which she blames her beloved mother, who introduced Joanna to Catherine Cookson and Stephen King at an early age.

Joanna loves photography, travelling, reading, health & fitness, and socialising with her friends & vodka. Easily distracted, Joanna visualises many of her tall tales while doing the housework.

A Balancing Kind of Love is book 2 in the Love is Crystal Clear Trilogy.

Check out Joanna's website
https://www.joannacates.com/
or Amazon Author page
https://www.amazon.co.uk/Joanna-Cates/e/B08QF9GTFL
And follow her to keep up with her news and latest releases.

Printed in Great Britain
by Amazon